Praise for Nicole Kimberling's *Happy Snak*

"Wonderful, quirky and tremendous fun."

~ *Marjorie Liu, New York Times Bestselling Author*

"This story is just fabulous. It is funny, it is also dramatic and intense at many moments... Gaia is a great heroine as she strikes the right balance between being strong and being vulnerable. The world-building is also very impressive, as this story is as much a wonderful tale as it is a photogenic exploration of the amphibian environment of Ai-Ki Station. When I reach the last page, I'm flummoxed by how much I enjoyed this book. Ms. Kimberling hasn't just told me a fun out-of-this-world story here, she has taken me to a fabulous new world and left me breathless with wonder."

~ *Mrs. Giggles, MrsGiggles.com*

Look for these titles by

Nicole Kimberling

Now Available:

Ghost Star Night

Happy Snak

Nicole Kimberling

A Samhain Publishing, Ltd. publication.

Samhain Publishing, Ltd.
577 Mulberry Street, Suite 1520
Macon, GA 31201
www.samhainpublishing.com

Happy Snak

Print ISBN: 978-1-60504-860-4
Digital ISBN: 978-1-60504-849-9

Editing by Anne Scott
Cover by Kanaxa

First Samhain Publishing, Ltd. electronic publication: December 2009
First Samhain Publishing, Ltd. print publication: September 2010

Dedication

To La Fiamma

Chapter One:
A Clean Sink

In the employee bathroom of the A-Ki Station Happy Snak, Gaia Jones brushed her teeth and pondered a mysterious odor. She took a deep gulp of recirculated air, tasted it and coughed. It wasn't good. The humidifier was turned up too high. And what was that chemical smell? She gagged on the acrid tang. At first, Gaia assumed the smell emanated from her toothpaste. Enhanced with arcane East Indian herbs and state-of-the-art calcium bonders, the toothpaste claimed to harness the powers of magic and science to dramatically increase the longevity of space-faring teeth. The toothpaste label depicted the god Shiva holding a red rocket with the word *A-Ki* stenciled on its side.

A-Ki Station looked nothing like a rocket. It hung, like a massive bowling ball, an interloper between the moons of Mars. The human sector looked tiny; just a circle of boxy towers adhered to a huge inscrutable orb. On Earth, humans were at the top of the intellectual pyramid. Out here humanity clung, wart-like, to the outside of the alien spaceship the size of a small moon.

Gaia spat out a wad of white foam and rinsed her toothbrush, confident that her teeth would endure forever, even if the rest of her was going to die of overwork—maybe today.

Daytime wouldn't begin for another twenty-five minutes, but Gaia liked to open early, to catch the shift-change customers. It was her one advantage over Treat Bonanza. Their labor union prohibited extended hours.

She ran a hand through her short, silky hair. Her face could be beautiful or ghastly depending on the light: high cheekbones, square jaw, full mouth. She wore no jewelry. Gaia shrugged into her yellow and blue Happy Snak smock. She liked the anonymity of a uniform. She liked its wide, deep pockets. The smock resisted flames and grease and repelled overly personal glances. The smock and Gaia resonated perfectly.

Again, Gaia considered the air. Should she get her respirator? Gaia couldn't remember her respirator's current location, or if it was charged. She found her hand-held.

"Find and charge respirator." She tapped the send icon. Then she remembered that her mother system and the hand-held refused to communicate. She sneezed. "Find out why the mother system won't talk to the hand-held. And ask the food court office about the air this morning once they're finally open."

She could call climate control instead, but they charged a fee for answering nonemergency calls. Gaia didn't know how much the fee was, but knew she didn't want to pay it.

Had she become too much of a cheapskate? The manager of Treat Bonanza probably would have called, but he didn't share Gaia's values. He didn't care about serving a few extra customers who just got off the graveyard shift. He had a private shower and toilet. He didn't have to share soap with corps-enlisted women and the maintenance crew. The manager of Treat Bonanza didn't have to personally pay all the bills either. No, she decided, she wasn't a cheapskate, just fiscally responsible. She was, as the many sales brochures she received called her, today's entrepreneurial woman.

Gaia squeezed down the tiny hall that led to the back kitchen of Happy Snak. She surveyed the shining silver tranquility of her completely clean prep sink, which had yet to bear the indignity of greasy deep-fryer baskets. She hit a code on the hand-held and automated processes began all around her.

The hamburger press chirped to life. The hot-holding tray,

laden with inserts of bacon-cheese sauce, mattar paneer and refried beans, blinked on and started warming. The kebab rack began to roll, and the rice cooker began to steam.

Gaia sensed a malfunction. She fixed her gaze on the deep fryer, which was flashing *error* to her via its tiny screen. She punched in a couple of numbers, and then it, too, whirred to life. The day's first problem solved, she looked up through the open doorway to the yellow service counter. The coffee machine gurgled a greeting, its rich aroma valiantly battling the noxious air, which floated in from the grate at the front of the store.

Gaia rounded the service counter and squatted down in front of the storefront grate. She twisted the manual latch open and felt jealous of Treat Bonanza's automated door. All Bonanza's manager had to do was push a button and the whole apparatus rose gracefully up like an opera curtain. Gaia had to muscle hers up ten feet every day. She'd made a halfhearted attempt to save sufficient money for an automated grate after the food-court supervisor commented that Happy Snak's manual model looked cheap. Gaia had promised to update by summertime. That was three years ago.

But before she could heave the heavy grate up, she convulsed in a series of violent sneezes. As soon as the office opened, Gaia told herself, she was going to have some strong words with the food-court supervisor.

Had there been some catastrophic failure of the atmosphere generators? She felt sure that if the food court was contaminated, the station alarms would sound. But then, maybe not. No one else was here yet to notice.

Gaia shoved the grate up. Outside, the food court was dim. A faint blue light illuminated the empty tables and chairs that stood like rows of blue plastic soldiers.

Pressing her hand over her mouth, Gaia stepped out onto the concourse. She half-expected to find a broken chemical line. Instead, in the weak night-light, she saw an alien. She recognized the Kishocha immediately. Kenjan, Consort of the Divine Oziru, Ruler of A-Ki Station.

Kenjan's muzzle swirls were thin, white and symmetrical.

Its cranial tendrils cascaded over its muscular shoulders, but instead of being resilient and bouncy, the tendrils hung limp. It wore a long vest made from small shells, pearls and teeth that had been wired together to form a fabric. The vest stretched down to the alien's mid-calf, shimmering in the eerie light.

Kenjan swayed between two blue chairs. Steam curled up off its black shoulders. A sudden wave of bitter vapors rushed up into Gaia's face. Throwing her arm across her nose and mouth, she staggered back, realizing that the biting stench emanated from the Kishocha.

Kenjan fell to its knees. It clutched at the base of its throat. The two chairs it had been using as support clattered to the tile floor. Then the alien looked directly at Gaia, drew back its arm and weakly flung something small and shiny near her feet. Gaia dodged. The object skittered harmlessly under the front counter.

"Are you all right?" Gaia choked on her words. The Kishocha did not reply or even seem to hear. It just kept clawing at the purple flesh at the base of its throat, and moaning. Gaia knew, from the informational programs all merchants had to watch, that the Kishocha's genital area or "pit" was located at the base of its throat. Was this some kind of bizarre, toxic masturbatory act? The way the Kishocha dug at its most sensitive area did not seem sexy.

Gaia looked up and down the concourse. Empty. Still covering her nose and mouth, Gaia approached.

"What should I do?" Gaia asked. The Kishocha dragged in a sickening, wheezing breath, and croaked out some garbled Kishocha word that she couldn't decipher.

"I don't know what that means," Gaia said.

"Water," Kenjan croaked in English. The alien reached out and gripped her hand. A strange acidic tingling spread across Gaia's palm.

"Okay." Gaia tried to pull her hand away, but the Kishocha held on to her like a lifeline. "We've got to get to my store."

The Kishocha tried to stand, then collapsed to the floor.

"Help me," Kenjan whispered. "I die."

Gaia looked into Kenjan's eyes. Barely visible beneath its swollen black lids was a sliver of violet iris.

"Please, protect me." The alien's speech degenerated into a string of unintelligible Kishocha.

"I'll protect you. Don't worry." Gaia shoved her hands under the Kishocha's armpits. Her hands numbed. That couldn't be good. Clumsily, she dragged the alien back into her tiny store. Her arms shook with the exertion of pulling the alien around the service counter to the big sink in back. Gaia propped Kenjan up against the sink. Her shoulders ached.

She grabbed for the spray nozzle. Her fingers slapped haplessly against it. Her fingers swelled and reddened. She could no longer feel them.

"Please, water." Kenjan lay slumped at her feet. She hit the cold water icon with her elbow and tried to rinse her own hands. It seemed to help a little. Awkwardly, she fumbled the spray nozzle toward Kenjan. Water gushed out over the Kishocha's face and cranial tendrils, jarring the alien back into semiconsciousness. It pulled the nozzle toward its still-bubbling pit. Gaia followed its motions and flushed the oozing area until the water ran clear. The nozzle fell out of her hands and she scraped it back up again. She needed help.

"Kenjan," she said. The alien looked blearily up at her. "Can you hold this? I need to get help." She pressed the nozzle into the alien's flaccid grip, rushed to the service counter and hit the emergency alarm. Immediately, a revolving red light in front of the Happy Snak flashed into life and a siren began to wail. Her emergency screen flickered on. A young embassy man appeared.

"Yes, Ms. Jones? What's the problem?"

"There's a Kishocha dying on my floor," she said. "I think it's Kenjan."

"Remain calm. Help is on the way. In the meantime, do not touch the alien. You're likely to get a severe burn."

Gaia regarded the fat red flippers at the ends of her wrists. "Yeah, I'll watch out for that."

"Please remain calm, Ms. Jones, qualified professionals are

on their way."

She ran back over to Kenjan, who seemed to be unconscious. The spray nozzle lay beside the alien, gushing water down the floor drain. She seized the nozzle and started spraying Kenjan again.

"Hey!" she shouted at Kenjan. "Stay with me. Help is on the way."

Kenjan pulled its eyes open. "Have you protected me?"

"Yeah, I'm protecting you. You're going to be okay."

Kenjan pulled in a shuddering breath. "I feel hot, like the desert."

"*Vasha a migonu*!" A low Kishocha voice barked from behind her. Six Kishocha rushed into her store. Two carried spears. Another four carried a coffinlike box. A pair of human medics followed.

"Oziru am Kenjan Zhota!" The lead Kishocha shoved Gaia aside. She fell backward into the foul water that had pooled on her floor. The Kishocha guards lifted Kenjan and slid the Kishocha into the coffinlike box. The box immediately began to fill with pink fluid.

Gaia tried to regain her feet. "Is Kenjan going to be all right?"

The male medic caught her, forced her back down and slapped a respirator over her face. "They're doing their job, ma'am. Everything will be all right. Keep this on. Maybe you won't have to pay for a new set of lungs."

"Holy Christ, look at her hands." The female medic grimaced. "Get some neutralizer on that." She looked back into Gaia's eyes. "This might sting."

A wild white spray of foam spewed out of the canister. Gaia felt nothing. She stared at the floor where Kenjan had lain. The tiles had blackened and cracked. The theoretically impervious rubber mats had melted. She tried to move her fingers and couldn't. Cold nausea sank into the pit of her stomach.

She said, "I'm going to lose my hands."

Chapter Two: Hands

Gentle bubbling sounds percolated through the cramped grow room of the A-Ki Station Medical Cloning Lab. Of the six tanks, only two contained replacement body parts. One held a heart labeled *M. Miller* and the other held Gaia's new hands. The pair floated gracefully, like two alien starfish, in a small aquarium-like tub in front of her. Gaia liked visiting them, to see how they were coming along. Except for the fact that they had only developed tiny slivers of fingernails, they looked ready to go.

The surgeon said that it was normal to go through a period of mourning for the loss of her old limbs, but that once the surgery was performed, with rehabilitation, she'd have full use of her new hands in a matter of weeks.

She pressed one bandaged arm to the aquarium glass, trying to imagine these new hands on the ends of her wrists. How long until she'd be able to work again? Would the new hands be strong enough to pull Happy Snak out of its downward spiral? Would the deep fryer still recognize and obey her, or would it rebel against a stranger's touch?

The gentle current of the liquid in the tank moved the fingers, which eerily appeared to wave at her.

"Don't worry," she murmured. "We'll be together soon. I'll treat you better than the other ones."

"Good afternoon, Ms. Jones."

Gaia mentally shuddered at the sound of Fitzpatrick, the ambassador's special assistant. He made the hair on the back of her neck stand straight on end. Fitzpatrick smiled to her face, then called her store "Crappy Shack" behind her back. He wore subtle masculine cologne that annoyed her. His hair was too blond and he worked out. Gaia suspected him of chest waxing. His high-powered job did not excuse his manicure or forgive his handsomeness.

Gaia's dislike of Fitzpatrick was outdone by his indifference to her. At most, he thought Gaia was annoying. She knew that Fitzpatrick had never spent more than six seconds thinking about her, which only made her grudge against him more painful. If he had known he was Gaia's enemy, then he would have at least noticed her provocations. As it was he went on with a bland indifference to her hostility that clearly conveyed Gaia's stature in his universe.

That was before the alien encounter. Now Fitzpatrick was paying a great deal of attention to Gaia, and to Happy Snak.

He came to see her every day. And each day he had brought more bad news. Kenjan was dead. The restaurant floor had been destroyed beyond repair. Her pet hamster, Microbe, had escaped and gone on an adventure of his own before being caught by animal control for a charge of two hundred and seventy-five dollars. Inexplicable microgravity failures had disabled the communications array and her insurance payment had been lost. And, most painful of all, Treat Bonanza's sales were up thirty-five percent in the last three weeks while Happy Snak languished. None of this was supposed to happen. In Gaia's fantasy of a bright future in space, she had her hands and always avoided scrutiny from people in authority. She made money. She franchised. Not anymore.

"Hello." Gaia edged away from Fitzpatrick. She tried to get outside the radius of his cologne.

"And how are the new hands doing today? The doctor tells me that you rigorously observe their progress."

"They're doing fine."

"That's really fantastic. Soon you'll be good as new,"

Fitzpatrick said. Gaia refused to be drawn into the exchange of pointless niceties. Her silence became too long, and Fitzpatrick, moved by an innately polite reflex, continued the conversation without her help. "Listen, if you have a moment there are some very important people who'd like to talk to you."

"Which people?" Gaia wasn't going to let Fitzpatrick persecute her with more members of the press corps.

"The Wise and Noble Kishocha Seigata, and the Ever Exalted and Divine Kishocha Oziru."

"Oziru?" Just the name intimidated Gaia.

"Oziru itself."

Gaia hoped her anxiety didn't show. Kishocha Oziru owned Ki Island, which was what the Kishocha called A-Ki Station. Every bit of real estate that the humans leased on A-Ki Station, including Happy Snak's precariously financed nine hundred and fifty-four square feet, belonged to Oziru. Gaia wasn't up to making a good impression on anyone important. Her hair was greasy and matted, and she didn't even have her Happy Snak smock. Her blue hospital-issue jumpsuit was baggy and covered with convenient Velcro closures to allow for easy access to any part of her body. She paused to make sure the seams were fully closed and lined up, so that her clothes didn't look like a badly assembled puzzle. Then there were the *highly* attractive stump-arms.

She said, "I'm not ready to see visitors."

And Fitzpatrick replied, "They're waiting for us in the main conference room. It's just down the hall."

Gaia followed Fitzpatrick down the quiet, carpeted corridor to a door flanked by two human guards. The door slid open with only the slightest sound. Fitzpatrick beckoned her to follow him inside.

Like the rest of the hospital, the walls were peach colored. A long table filled up the room.

At the far end of the table, there were seven aliens. Two sat in tube-steel chairs. The other five held barbed, long-handled spears and stood at attention behind the seated pair.

Oziru dominated the room, even sitting down. While the

guards' tendrils resembled sea anemones in their length and thickness, Oziru's were at least as thick as Gaia's wrist and hung down its back. The tendrils were striped with thin, perfectly even, black and white rings.

Oziru's neck was as thick and muscular as a bull's. Its eyes were violet, like Kenjan's. Delicate white lines curved across its black skin. Thin white stripes spanned the length of Oziru's body, occasionally broken as if they were the interrupted strokes of a paintbrush. Where one stroke broke on the left, its mirror image broke on the right in exactly the same place in exactly the same way. Oziru defined symmetry.

The Kishocha wore an enormous pit guard that looked more like an Egyptian collar than a necklace. Strands of black, white and red pearls hung down from the collar, blanketing Oziru's chest and extending well past its waist. Strands of the same tricolored pearls wound around its forearms. Gaia wondered whether Oziru had matching ankle guards as well, but there was no casual way to glance under the table to find out.

The alien seated next to Oziru was at least half a head shorter and much more slight. Gaia guessed this must be Seigata. Its bowed head made looking at its face difficult. Its cranial tendrils were thinner and shorter, looking almost like tumbling curls of hair. It wore a vestlike garment composed of shells and teeth, wired together with gold.

Gaia had never had the opportunity to view a group of Kishocha from varied castes. Now that she was doing it, the physical similarities and differences between them were very clear. All Kishocha were black with white markings. All had large eyes, and horselike muzzles. All had cranial tendrils. The real difference was in the markings that covered their bodies. While Oziru and the Kishocha seated next to it were perfectly symmetrical, the guards' markings ran askew. One had vertical, zebra-like stripes across its whole face and body. Another had a swirl that looked like an enormous human thumbprint across its chest. Still another had whorls and stripes that alternated in no real order. The only things the guards had in common, apart from their uniform height, were metallic orange eyes.

On the human side of the table Gaia recognized the stately coiffure and severe red lipstick of Emily Blum, the Ambassador and Chief Political Officer of A-Ki Station. The sight of Blum gave Gaia a nasty turn. Blum appeared only when something important and bad happened. Blum brought endless paperwork, fines and lawyers. No regulation-abiding citizen of A-Ki Station should ever have to see her. Even Fitzpatrick was more welcome a sight than Blum. A deep sense of foreboding took root in Gaia's stomach.

Five uniformed security officers stood behind Blum. These were the best-looking security officers she'd ever seen, a striking contrast to the surly guards who slouched around the food court eating sticky rice and slurping Frosticcino. They had no weapons that Gaia could see, not even big flashlights.

All the humans looked shiny. Someone had put the room's humidity up to at least one hundred percent then raised the temperature to an uncomfortable tropical degree to accommodate the Kishocha.

"Divine and Exalted Oziru," Blum said in a pleasant, businesslike tone, "may I present Gaia Jones."

All at once Gaia felt the intense heat of the room. Itchy sweat trickled down her stomach.

"Hello." Oziru spoke in heavily accented English. "You are the owner of Happy Snak." Its voice was so deep Gaia could feel it tickle her inner ear.

"That's me."

"I am Oziru." The Kishocha inclined its head and brought its hands together in a sign of peace. At least Gaia thought it was a peace sign. It had been so long since she'd seen the informationals that she couldn't quite remember. The Kishocha's hands were open, as if miming a book. "And this is Seigata, Kenjan's first sibling."

The Kishocha seated next to Oziru extended a long black hand.

Gaia started forward, her arm extended automatically. "I'm so sorry about your loss."

As she moved, she heard Blum yell out, "Jones!" Then to

her utter annoyance Fitzpatrick seized her by the upper arm and yanked her back. At that same moment, Gaia heard the whoosh of a Kishocha spear cutting the air. The blade slashed across the empty space where she would have been standing.

"*Sho!*" Oziru's voice boomed out across the room. Gaia jumped backward into Fitzpatrick. The guard who'd struck at Gaia dropped instantly to the floor. Oziru murmured a long, string of words at the guard, who resumed its previous stance.

Gaia's heart hammered in shock. She wasn't sure if she was going to faint or just vomit. Fitzpatrick seemed just as scared as she was. She could feel his heart pounding. His grip on her upper arms was painfully tight.

"I was just going to shake—" Gaia stopped as she held up her stumps. "Shake hands."

"Ah, no. This is a spiritual gesture," Oziru replied. "Come, don't cower from me. My guards will not threaten you again. I have enlightened them. Please consider me to be your friend and take a seat."

Fitzpatrick eased his grip on her, and Gaia moved forward. "I'm sorry about getting close to you just now."

"No offense made." Oziru turned to Blum. "I want to speak with Gaia only, and as her current master you may remain, but there will be no interruptions."

"As you wish, of course," Blum said.

With a light hand on Gaia's elbow, Fitzpatrick steered her toward one of the empty chairs at the human end of the table. He sat next to her, but kept silent.

Oziru began. "I have come here to thank you for your kindness to my beloved Kenjan. And Seigata would like also to thank you on behalf of its sibling. Sadly, my consort, Kenjan, has gone to the waters."

"I'm sorry." There was a long pause while Gaia tried to think of something comforting to say. "I hope Kenjan wasn't in too much pain."

From beside her, Gaia thought she heard Blum hiss quietly under her breath.

Oziru appeared to accept her condolence. As its long, thick

cranial tendrils curled and swayed, it placed a long black hand across its throat and its pearls clattered against each other. "It is important that we read the motions with expedience."

"Pardon?" Gaia said.

"The motions of dying." Oziru rose to its full height. Its head nearly brushed the ceiling. "When a Kishocha dies, it secretes the Water of Life. That is what killed your hands and scarred the floor of your dwelling. Its life flows out and carves markings of its final emotions on whatever surface is there. It is important to read these final messages quickly. The words of the gods are changeable and fleeting. Some meanings may fade or be lost."

One of Oziru's cranial tendrils was silently tapping itself against its side, moving like the tail of a mildly annoyed feline.

Oziru walked around the table. When it did, Gaia saw that it was, in fact, wearing ankle guards that matched its gauntlets. The pearl garment that it wore fell past its knees. The Kishocha waved Fitzpatrick aside and crouched down directly in front of Gaia. Even crouched, Oziru's face was almost a foot above hers. The alien was so close that Gaia could smell its sharp fragrance, like roses and battery acid.

"On the official statement, you said that my beloved Kenjan made you its guardian."

Gaia cocked her head. "I don't think so..."

"You said that Kenjan asked you to protect it."

"Yeah, but I just thought Kenjan was delirious or didn't speak English very well."

"My beloved Kenjan was the first Kishocha to master the English tongue. I was taught by Kenjan. So you see, if Kenjan asked you to protect it, then that is really what it intended you to do."

"And so?" Gaia leaned a little closer to Oziru.

"My beloved Kenjan asked you to guard its spirit. My consort gave itself to you. I must know its final thoughts. I ask you to accompany me to read Kenjan's last feelings, so that we both may understand what we are to do."

"Do we have to go now?"

"I have complied with your master's request to wait until you were better healed." Oziru gestured to Blum. "But I can wait no longer. Since you can walk and stand it must be done."

For the first time, Gaia noticed dark circles under Blum's eyes, even through the ambassador's makeup. Fitzpatrick also looked less well rested than usual.

She said, "Well, if we've got to do it, we've got to do it, right? Let's go."

Oziru very slowly closed its eyes and then slowly opened them again. Gaia grasped that this meant something, but had no idea what. The alien said, "I most humbly thank you. My reward to you will be deeper than the great ocean chasm."

Chapter Three: The Motions of Dying

The Embassy Tower's public concourse yawned cavernously empty at three-thirty on a Monday afternoon. Blum and Fitzpatrick led a golf-cart motorcade that hummed along the gray paving-stone-patterned linoleum at a stately clip. Gaia sat next to Oziru in the VIP golf cart.

Oziru's guards were in the car behind them.

Given the confines of the seat and the relative size of Oziru, contact was inevitable. As they drove past the Electrical Authority, one of Oziru's tendrils bumped up against Gaia's calf. It felt soft and cool, even through her hospital jumpsuit. Gaia tried to scoot away.

"Is something wrong?" Oziru asked.

"I'm sorry, but I think your tendril touched me."

"Perhaps it is curious about you."

Gaia felt the blood draining out of her face at the idea of curious tendrils. "But if it touches my skin, I'll be burnt."

"We do not always secrete the Water of Life. You could touch me now and be unharmed," Oziru said.

Gaia felt a tap on her shoulder. She turned and saw one of Oziru's tendrils had crawled around behind her. The pointy end curled almost like a beckoning finger.

Gaia looked back at Oziru.

"You're controlling them, right?" she asked.

"Of course."

"That's a cute trick."

"I learned it from Kenjan." Oziru's cranial tendril dropped away and the alien plunged into silence.

Though Gaia had only known Kenjan for a few minutes, she still felt a certain loss at its death. It'd been the first alien she or any other human had ever seen.

Only a decade before, the airwaves of Earth had thrilled and vibrated to the all-encompassing and completely unintelligible Kishocha transmissions. Communication satellites went down. Radios could receive nothing but endless throbbing chants and searing wails. All contact with the Mars colony was lost.

Panic ensued. Fear reigned. Corn-dog sales hit an all time low. The populace retreated to bomb shelters and church basements. After a few months, the aural assault stopped and the press releases began. The first of these missives confirmed that there was, indeed, alien life. The beings were called Kishocha. They were tall, bipedal, amphibious and hermaphroditic. The Kishocha seemed nonplused by the existence of humans. During a newsflash the world saw the first picture of that alien who would become so familiar: Kenjan.

Standing about six and a half feet tall, Kenjan became an instant idol. Its long, black muzzle was delicately marked with symmetrical white swirls. In place of human hair, Kenjan had luxuriant cranial tendrils. These black- and white-banded tentacles curled and writhed down Kenjan's skull, cascading over the alien's shoulders. Kenjan had glossy black skin, adorned by a white violin-shaped marking which originated at the base of its throat, rolled over the alien's broad chest, narrowed at its waist and ended at Kenjan's featureless crotch. The Kishocha's legs were long and heavily muscled, ending in wide black flippers.

In the newsflash, Kenjan lifted one hand, its six fingers spread to expose exquisite purple-membraned webbing, and waved. This clip played continuously for the next year, accompanied by dubious analyses from scientists, philosophers, rock stars and sports figures.

Sales of popsicles and ice cream cones were steadily rising, but that was to be expected. It was summer, and it was hot. The only difference was that now the popsicles were black and white striped.

The first time Kenjan spoke English, it apologized on behalf of its people for broadcasting their songs so loudly.

"We did not see you living there." Kenjan's low voice rolled out of Gaia's tinny television speaker. "We were talking to someone else. Please excuse." When asked who they were talking to Kenjan replied, "God."

More analysis ensued. Wild debates erupted in churches everywhere. The snack-eating public had a brief love affair with black and white fish sticks. Gaia wondered if, reciprocally, sales of flesh-colored popsicles were soaring on the Kishocha ship.

Then Kenjan was on the television again, speaking almost perfectly comprehensible but distinctly non-native English in a worldwide broadcast.

"I am happy to announce the joyous occasion of construction. It has been decreed that our structures should embrace one another and that we should be allies. The name of our ship is 'Ki' and the name of your buildings is 'A' so our union will be called A-Ki Station. It is exceedingly poetic. Congratulations."

A representative from the newly formed Alien Ambassadorial Corps (who Gaia now knew as Fitzpatrick) came on-screen to present a computer model of the proposed A-Ki Station. From above, the human sector looked a little like a bicycle wheel. Six outer towers ringed the central tower. Skywalks and subways connected the buildings to one another. The outer towers were of identical size and height but varied in color: white, red, blue, green, orange and yellow. The central tower, which would house the embassy, was purple. Gaia imagined it was supposed to represent a rainbow of hope. She wondered if she should get some rainbow-colored rocket pops.

Each tower had a corporate sponsor. Coca-Cola Global owned the red tower.

Even at a diameter of five miles, the human sector took up

less than one percent of the surface of the Kishocha ship. Fitzpatrick flashed off the screen, replaced immediately by a wild-haired old skinny guy who ranted about the possibilities of technological exchange with the Kishocha. He was obviously a physicist. He continued at length about the Kishocha's mastery of the elusive art of creating gravitational fields. The physicist speculated on the Kishocha's willingness to share their technological secrets. Hundreds of scientists would be needed to work on A-Ki Station, he gushed. It was an unprecedented event.

And not just for enthusiastic physicists, Gaia thought. There would have to be maintenance staff and mechanics and diplomats. All those people had one thing in common—they all had to eat. With that thought, her own dream of a future in space had been born.

It had been a beautiful dream and now everything had changed. Everything depended on her.

Gaia looked around at the storefronts of the Embassy Tower's main concourse. The designers had gone high-class here, giving the entire place a Dickensian Village look. Potted trees grew at even intervals. Exclusive shops and government offices rubbed elbows good-naturedly with each other. At Christmastime, this was where Santa hung around with a couple of robotic reindeer, speaking with an English accent and giving out Christmas crackers to the children on the station.

Happy Snak business occasionally brought Gaia up here. She always felt like the entire cast of *Oliver!* might jump out and start singing at any second. Today, apart from a couple of security guards, the concourse was strangely devoid of people.

They turned off the public concourse into Honda Park. This was where the artificial but realistic-looking stream flowed. A wide red bridge arched gracefully across it. Just beneath the surface of the water, koi carp moved like glittering jewels.

"Your water is so pale," Oziru said. "So light."

"Yeah," Gaia said, for lack of any better response. "The fish seem to like it."

They lapsed into silence again and drove quietly onto the

skyway that led to the Coke Tower.

As they entered the skyway, Gaia felt her excitement growing. The Coke Tower main concourse would be packed at this time of day. She could imagine the scene. It would be like a parade. People would cram in on either side to see the aliens, especially the one riding beside her. It would be good publicity. It was too bad she didn't have her Happy Snak smock on.

They emerged from the skyway into utter silence. It looked like an emergency evacuation drill was taking place. Her heart sank. No one would see her big moment.

The main concourse of the Coke Tower was retro-fifties style. The trees were made of silver tinsel. Colored lights at the base of each tree made them slowly change hue throughout the day. The trees were blue-green. Gaia guessed it was around four by now.

There should have been people—lots of them. Oziru gazed curiously at one of the trees.

"They're not real, you know," Gaia said.

"Not real?" Oziru asked.

"They're not alive. Real Earth trees don't look like that."

"They are meant to be trees? Strange."

They drove along red and white linoleum and came to a halt in front of the elevator leading down to the residential-level food court where Happy Snak was located. Gaia hadn't been able to afford the lease in the main concourse. No one but the megacorporates could.

Fitzpatrick walked back to assist Gaia out of the golf cart. As he steadied her, she noticed that she didn't hate his cologne as much as she previously had.

They rode the elevator down thirty-eight floors, and emerged in the old familiar residential food court Coke-38. Its blue chairs were in disarray. This section adhered to no particular style. The ceilings were not lofty. Treat Bonanza's western-style sign and red cowboy-boot logo blinked on and off in the same way she'd always hated. At the far end of the food court, Happy Snak's blue and yellow sign with its jaunty jester logo was dark.

Gaia led Oziru across the deserted food court and down the narrow service hallway to the back door of Happy Snak. Fitzpatrick followed them.

Gaia entered her voice ID. Crammed into the narrow service hallway behind her stood Oziru and Fitzpatrick. Blum, Seigata and their collective minions waited in the desolated food court.

The back door slid open.

Gaia turned to Oziru and gestured inside. "After you."

Oziru made its way through the small door, managing to look stately even though it was forced to stoop. The pearls comprising the fabric of Oziru's robe clicked and scraped across the Happy Snak tiles. Gaia followed Oziru inside. Fitzpatrick remained, lurking in the hallway.

Happy Snak smelled nasty. The rancid odor of old oil and stagnant air gave Gaia a chill. This was the perfume of a dead restaurant, mingled with the cutting acidic scent of a dead Kishocha. Gaia's bandaged arms twitched.

Inside, she could see the real damage. The motions formed deep ruts in the linoleum. They swept from the front gate in long calligraphic strokes only to terminate in a tangle of gouges and broken tile at the base of her sink.

Oziru went to the front gate, crouched down and rubbed its palms slowly against the marks. The alien glanced up at Gaia.

"This is where you began?"

"Yes, I pulled Kenjan from the middle of the corridor to the sink."

"Why to the sink?" If the alien had an expression on its face, Gaia couldn't read it.

"Kenjan asked for water."

Oziru turned its face down toward the motions again, this time pushing its hands forward. As it crawled along the length of the store, it ran its hands through the motions with deep intent. It seemed predatory in a way that disconcerted Gaia. But there was also an unexpected shiver of pleasure in her own discomfort.

During the four years she had run Happy Snak on A-Ki

Station, she had seen the aliens but had never looked into one's eyes or spoken directly with one. At first she'd harbored fantasies of selling them snack foods, but once she'd realized how xenophobic the Kishocha were, she let go of that idea. For Gaia, space had become an escape from banal tedium of life as a divorcee in Seattle.

The Kishocha had been purely tangential to her existence. Happy Snak filled every crevice of her waking thought. She had no friends or even associates. Her only obligation was to her hamster. Her business covered her like a shell allowing her the impermeability of a closed oyster. If any thoughts of loneliness irritated her, she smoothed them over, rolling them within the folds of her mind until they, too, became enshrined in layers of defense.

Watching Oziru crawl across the floor of her dead restaurant with inhuman grace, reading the last wishes of its deceased consort, she realized that she was witnessing something completely new—something that was not in any way derivative. The honor of being the first human to see this belonged to her—and maybe to Fitzpatrick, still observing from the hall.

Oziru leaned forward and licked the furrow in front of it with its long purple and white striped tongue. Gaia watched in rapt fascination while Oziru slid back and forth, inspecting every inch of the markings, tasting them, feeling them.

"This is a holy place." There was a certain finality in Oziru's voice, as if this pronouncement was something she should have been hoping for.

"Well, I like it," Gaia replied.

"And for the last of the motions." Oziru extended its hands toward Gaia's stumps.

"I don't understand."

"Your hands. There are motions on them. I would like to read them." The Kishocha gently indicated her stumps.

"I'm sorry, I can't take the bandages off."

"Are they locked?" Oziru cocked its head at the bandages quizzically. "I think that they unwind from this point." Oziru indicated the taped end.

"No, I mean I can take them off, I'm just not supposed to. Besides, my hands aren't there anymore."

"Have they vanished?" Oziru looked alarmed.

"No, they've just been amputated." Behind her, Fitzpatrick began to whisper into his phone.

"What is that?" Oziru asked.

"They've been cut off."

"Do you still have them?"

"No," Gaia said. "I have some new ones growing in the lab, though."

"You didn't keep the old hands?" Oziru's expression seemed intense, but Gaia didn't know in exactly what way.

"I don't think so... Wait, let me check." Gaia looked to Fitzpatrick, who was still talking on the phone. He motioned her to wait. "Do you need them? I mean, they were really destroyed."

"My Kenjan touched them. I must see them."

Fitzpatrick pocketed his phone and strolled over to where Gaia and Oziru stood.

"The hands are on their way over from the hospital. A courier will bring them on the next tube," Fitzpatrick reassured Oziru, then, to Gaia, "We kept them to examine more closely."

"How long must I wait?" Oziru sighed.

"About half an hour," Fitzpatrick responded.

"Then I will wait." Oziru knelt down beside the motions again. One of its thicker tentacles fell into the furrow of a motion. Oziru rubbed its tentacle back and forth through the rough surface, entirely immersed in its own arcane thoughts. Gaia imagined that she understood its mournful language. She imagined it loved Kenjan in the way that she loved Happy Snak. The silence and the smell of grease grew pervasive.

Gaia leaned against the wall. The humans in the food court got bored. They shifted from foot to foot and passed around sticks of cigarette gum. To them, this drama between her and Oziru had grown stale. They chatted about sports. The

Kishocha guards stood apart from the humans, inert and motionless.

Gaia's energy flagged. The bandaged ends of her arms throbbed. Crabbiness welled up inside her. The Kishocha grew less fascinating and more annoying. The way that the guards in the hall failed to shift uncomfortably during their long wait irked her.

Finally, the courier arrived with the Styrofoam box that contained her frozen hands.

Oziru tore into the box like a child ripping into a Christmas present. It annihilated the carefully sealed biohazard bag and pulled Gaia's dead hands out with unseemly urgency. Her old hands were white and swollen. Red, yellow and purple streaks spider-webbed through the hard flesh. Each hand ended in a stump just below the wrist. She could see a white bone sticking out of the bottom of one of them. Gaia swallowed a jolt of nausea. She felt disoriented by the sight of them. Her hands shouldn't be across the room from her. It made her queasy, but she couldn't make herself look away.

As if they were holy relics, Oziru reverently turned each appendage over. Then, without warning or permission, pressed its purple and white striped tongue against the palm of her former left hand.

Gaia was suddenly, violently ill.

She lunged to the sink and managed to vomit in it, rather than on the floor. She hunched over the sink and supported herself on her elbows. Fitzpatrick slid up behind her and quietly turned the water on. Gaia watched her lunch swirl down the drain.

"Is Gaia Jones healthy?" Oziru asked.

"Not yet. Don't worry though, Ms. Jones will be fine," Fitzpatrick assured Oziru. "Please continue. Don't mind us."

Gaia didn't dare look back; she didn't want to know what Oziru was doing with her old, dead body parts. She also didn't want to continue to watch Fitzpatrick spraying her puke down the drain. She closed her eyes and waited.

It didn't take long. Fitzpatrick tapped her on the shoulder

and whispered, "Oziru wants a word with you."

Gaia's old hands were nowhere in sight. Fitzpatrick withdrew to the hallway.

Oziru sat on the floor next to the motions. "I have reached my conclusion. Kenjan shall be enshrined, and you shall be Kenjan's holy guardian."

Gaia searched her mind for any good response. She found none. Far down the hall she heard Fitzpatrick talking to Blum. Diplomats were never around when you really needed them.

"I'm not sure what you're talking about." Twinges of pain shot up her arms. Vomiting had drained Gaia of her remaining energy.

"Kenjan was a prophet, and here is where that one died so it is only fitting that this place should be enshrined. You will leave your position to tend Kenjan's ghost in my garden. You need never toil in Happy Snak again."

"I like to toil in Happy Snak." Her arms throbbed distractingly. It was bad enough dealing with the embassy's regulations and the health department. Now even the Kishocha thought they could tell her what to do.

"That pleasure will soon be eclipsed by the joy of serving the Kishocha."

"Thank you very much, but I'd rather not."

"You will do as I bid you." Oziru's voice dropped lower. Gaia could feel it throbbing in her chest. Oziru's cranial tendrils lashed sinuously around the Kishocha's feet.

"You are not my boss," Gaia pointed out. "I am an entrepreneur."

A deep silence filled the air. Gaia stared at Oziru, who returned her unwavering gaze. She got the impression that Oziru was not used to being questioned or refused. She knew the Kishocha had a rigidly vertical hierarchy, but she also knew that Oziru must understand that the humans on the station didn't.

Gaia heard footsteps in the hallway, and a rising female voice that could only be Blum's.

Oziru lowered its eyes to the motions. There was something

about the way it looked at the floor that made her feel guilty.

"Look, Oziru," she began. "I'm sorry about snapping at you. I feel sick and my painkillers are wearing off so my arms hurt a lot. I really do want to help you."

The Kishocha did not answer her.

"The reason I don't want to leave Happy Snak is that I need money, understand? Without an income I can't stay on the station."

"As guardian of the shrine, we would never allow you to starve. There would be offerings of food every day," Oziru said, quietly. "You would have my personal favor."

"Starvation isn't my problem. I'm licensed here as a businessperson. If I have no business I'll be sent home."

"I can force your embassy to make you stay. I can stop the air and water and gravity. I can have my way. I am master."

Gaia waited a long time before speaking again. She didn't know if Oziru was telling the truth, but if it really could stop the air and water and gravity, then maybe she should call a diplomat or lawyer. But they seemed scared of Oziru.

"I like running Happy Snak. It makes me feel good," Gaia said. "Happy Snak is my creation. I don't know what I'd do without it."

Oziru rubbed its hand along a furrow in the floor. "You would go on. As we all do when we lose our love and reason. That is our obligation."

Gaia carefully knelt down on the floor next to Oziru.

"Do you miss Kenjan?"

"Kenjan was my beloved consort. No other can ever match the beauty of that one, nor the sweet song," Oziru replied.

"And you want to keep a shrine to that one's memory?"

"I must. Kenjan's ghost must have a shrine to inhabit, or it will wander, hungry. The ghost must be near the sacred waterways, within my hearing. The ghost cannot be here in the human sector away from us. And you must be there to protect Kenjan."

"I can come visit."

"You must be there always."

"Why?"

"Because ghosts are always in danger."

"I don't understand," Gaia said, "but that's okay for right now. Let me ask you this: Why does it have to be me?"

"Because Kenjan has chosen you," Oziru said. "Because only you were there."

"So you want me to guard Kenjan and stay with Kenjan in the shrine, right?"

"Yes."

"And what I want is to have Happy Snak back," Gaia went on.

"That is what you have said."

Treat Bonanza started broadcasting its specials on the commons loudspeaker. She hated Treat Bonanza. She hated that they were right across the concourse, and the fact that they were too corporate to involve themselves in alien religious problems. No one in that store would have helped Kenjan. They probably had some kind of anti-involvement regulation prohibiting it. The next time she opened up a Happy Snak, she would make sure Treat Bonanza wasn't within one hundred yards of the place.

The really great place to open a new Happy Snak would be on the hangar deck, but vendors weren't permitted there. It would be perfect positioning to set up a new store right in the Mutual Interaction Area. It was at the bottom of the Embassy Tower and had a big window in the floor that showed pinkish Kishocha waters running beneath. New arrivals from Earth rushed to it, expecting to see aliens. There were never any there. Wouldn't it be good to have a little stand there so that people could have ice cream to soothe their disappointment?

Gaia smiled and said, "I think I know how we can both be satisfied."

Chapter Four: 30% More

After twelve weeks, both the new snack bar and the Kishocha shrine were finished. Crews worked round the clock to comply with the draconian deadline imposed by Oziru. The Mutual Interaction Area was a thirty-by-thirty-foot space with a Peace Corps office front, the new Happy Snak storefront and an oblong window in the center of the floor through which one could see murky pink water. The air was different, heavy, salty and humid. Dehumidifiers ran constantly, but the Kishocha air curled in through the vents and coated everything with a glaze of moisture.

Tenacious new arrivals had been known to sit by that window for hours, looking down, hoping to catch sight of an alien. No one ever had. Then the construction began.

Already Gaia had seen more Kishocha than even the embassy personnel saw in a year. While the human crew built Happy Snak (which was, to Gaia's delight, thirty percent larger than before) the Kishocha built Kenjan's shrine.

The last room completed was her personal cabin, the area that linked the alien world with the human. Her cabin was not a seamless melding of galactic ideas. The two styles of architecture met in a clash of awkward juxtaposition. Three of Gaia's walls were human-made. They were square and, except for two nondescript sliding doors, blank and white.

One of Gaia's sliding doors opened to reveal a small personal bathroom. She'd put the bathroom on her list of non-negotiables. The other led to the back kitchen of Happy Snak. She wasn't overjoyed to still be living in the backroom of her restaurant, but felt resigned to it.

Gaia's fourth wall curved into her bedroom like an enormous bulging egg. This wall was pearly, smooth and hard. It was the outer shell of the Kishocha shrine. The door in the center of it was made of opaque gray flesh. When open, the Kishocha door was about six feet in diameter. It contracted and dilated like a huge pulsing sphincter. The door was at the end of her bed. She tried not to think about it too much.

To feel settled in, she put up her hamster maze.

Gaia fitted the fist-sized links of clear plastic tubing together and locked them into place. She slid an elbow joint into the three-foot length of tubing and added it to the vertical labyrinth of tubes and egg-shaped chambers. Then she opened a little door near the bottom and waited.

Hot pain twanged up her left arm. Gaia sat back and tightened the straps of her wrist braces. Her new hands still felt soft and strange. Blisters dotted her fingers and palms.

After a few seconds, Microbe, her hamster, emerged from under a pile of curly wood shavings. He hesitated, sniffing nervously at the air around him. His fawn-colored ears twitched articulately around. Feeling a sense of sudden freedom, the hamster jumped into a tube and scampered up. He froze. Seconds ticked by before he continued his exploration. Each time Gaia moved his maze, he had to rediscover every corner.

This time it took Microbe longer than usual. Gaia thought it would take her a while to adjust as well. She eyed the Kishocha door.

The only time an alien had come through was when Gaia had tried to hammer a nail into her weird convex wall. The wall had bled thick pink liquid. Gaia suddenly realized the wall was alive. She'd slapped an elastic bandage over the wound, but a Kishocha worker had come through, given her an evil look and replaced her bandage with what looked like a limpet. Four days later the limpet fell off the wall, desiccated and dead. The wall remained marked with a puckery scar. Shamed, Gaia had found another place to hang her clock.

The current volunteers at the Peace Corps Welcome Center jumped at the chance to help with Happy Snak's construction. They were a husband and wife team named Roy and Cheryl. Roy was a barrel-shaped smiler with a master's degree in anthropology. Cheryl's degree was in post-alien humanities. Her hair was blonde and straight and perfectly matched her curveless body. They were supposed to teach English to aliens, but no aliens signed up for the class. Lacking any Kishocha to teach English to, the couple was deeply bored. Cheryl even offered to pack up the old Happy Snak, as well as Gaia's personal room in the Coke Tower.

As Gaia disgorged the boxes Cheryl had packed, she realized that Cheryl really enjoyed packing peanuts. She used them in every box. Gaia made a game of sifting through the opaque fluff. She ran her hands through it and tried to identify each item before she saw it.

Microbe scuttled softly by in an eye-level tunnel. Gaia went deep. Her fingers brushed against a smooth hard cylinder.

"Mug!" she cried, exhuming her King William ascension souvenir mug. She placed it on her tiny desk, next to her brand-new hand-held—the old, broken one had melted during her alien encounter.

Back into the packing peanuts she plunged, fishing until her fingers touched something cold and metallic.

She frowned. The object was triangular, like a police badge, but with the dangling chains of a necklace. Gaia didn't own any necklaces.

One chain hung from the center of the badge, like a kite string, the other two chains were attached to the upper corners of the badge-shape.

She pulled the object out of the box and still didn't know where it came from. It was a necklace, big, heavy and solid gold. It was the pit guard thrown at her. Cheryl must have found it somewhere and packed it with Gaia's things. As she turned the object over in her hands, her hands began to throb.

Gaia wouldn't have called herself traumatized by Kenjan's

death, but being handless had nearly driven her crazy. She had no idea how profound an impact her appendages had on her psyche. Not only did she speak with them and work with them, she thought with them. She was at her calmest while folding takeout boxes or crimping won tons. With her hands occupied by work, she was free to let her mind wander.

Even delving through packing boxes was enough to trigger a thousand tangents of thought. Though now, every thought ended with Kenjan, Oziru and the Kishocha.

At first she'd focused on the business aspect of her interactions with the aliens. She'd dreamed of the vastness of the untapped Kishocha market and nearly drooled in excitement. Then worrying thoughts of death, pain and nausea would wiggle into her consciousness. A vision of Kenjan's last moments would cloud her thrilling new business venture. She would find herself confused and apprehensive, yet still excited. Not like herself at all.

Microbe had found his way to his second nest chamber and was busily digging and peeing in his bedding. Her hamster had made himself at home and seemed to be settling down to sleep. She dropped Kenjan's necklace into her desk drawer. When she next saw Oziru, she'd return the thing.

Gaia glanced over at her plain black and white clock hanging on her human-made wall by the bathroom. Time to go to work. It was Roy's first day on the job and she didn't want to set a bad example by being late.

Blum arrived like an ill-tempered wind. She flung Happy Snak's gate up, ducked beneath it and knocked aside a yellow plastic chair in her haste. Before Gaia could even say hello, Blum slung her briefcase onto a table, sat down and said, "Has Fitzpatrick arrived yet?"

Gaia had been instructing Roy on the intricacies of the point-of-sale system.

"No, he—" Gaia began.

"He's late, that's what he is," Blum finished. It was one minute before Blum's scheduled arrival time. Her gaze settled on Roy.

"PCVs are not authorized to attend this meeting."

"What's a PCV?" Gaia asked.

"Peace Corps Volunteer," Roy supplied. "Actually, Cheryl and I are both moonlighting at Happy Snak part-time."

Blum raised one slim eyebrow. "And that's relevant because...?"

"I asked him to come to this meeting," Gaia said. "He's going to be in the store dealing with the aliens too. I thought it could be like an orientation."

"I see." Blum slid the top of her briefcase open. "While that's an interesting idea, I'd prefer that you weren't here, Roy. You understand?"

"Of course." Roy rose to leave. As he stepped behind Blum, he rolled his eyes at Gaia.

Fitzpatrick lunged under the half-closed door at thirty seconds past the hour, clearly out of breath. "I'm sorry I'm late."

Blum laid her red-rimmed glare on Fitzpatrick. Gaia had now met Blum on several occasions and had concluded that she suffered from chronic, nagging weariness that propelled her compensatory briskness, impatience and industriousness. Gaia reacted with contrarian laziness. She always felt the urge to slouch and talk in long, meandering sentences to make up for the other woman's fascist aura of efficiency.

"Are you ready to begin, Ms. Jones?" Blum tapped her pen against her briefcase.

"Sure." Gaia lounged back in her chair. "Oh, wait. Would you like something to drink? We've got the cold-drinks station up and running."

"Thank you, no." Blum removed a hand-held from her briefcase.

"I'd like a Frosticcino." Fitzpatrick was immediately skewered by Blum's withering glare. "It's my preferred coffee-like beverage."

Gaia served up two Frosticcinos and handed one to Fitzpatrick.

Fitzpatrick tasted his drink, while expertly avoiding eye contact with his boss. "Delicious."

"If we could get back on task," Blum said. "The ceremony tomorrow is, without question, the most important alien/human interaction since first contact. I want to make sure you understand."

"I think I do." Gaia knew she didn't. To remain calm and to maintain her sanity, she relied on a complete denial of political comprehension. Now Blum meant to shatter her peaceful ignorance. Determined to resist, Gaia deliberately turned her thoughts to the meaningless task of unlikely soft-serve ice cream flavors.

Peaches-n-Lard.

Cran-Liver Surprise.

Taco.

Blum slid the hand-held over to Gaia. "This first volume contains all the basic information regarding protocol. Cover your mouth when you yawn. Don't refuse water, etc., etc. I'm sure you know all this already from your initial orientation."

Gaia hadn't attended the mandatory orientation. She'd given Fitzpatrick coupons for ten free Frosticcinos to sign her off. Fitzpatrick apparently remembered the bribe, because he injected a little extra nervous cheer into his smile. He opened his own briefcase.

"In order to give you a more in-depth look at Kishocha culture, we decided to bring the film Kenjan made for the embassy. Are these full-wall screens?"

"No." Gaia despised restaurants with mammoth screens dominating the walls. She preferred walls to be walls, not interactive shopping networks. In that way, Happy Snak was old fashioned. She did, however, have a few freestanding games. "We can play the film on my Cherry Bomb game."

A few minutes passed while Gaia loaded the film. Blum and Fitzpatrick dragged their chairs over. Gaia hit the start button. The screen went black. Then the words *Kishocha For Humans* appeared, followed by several bars of chiming, gurgling music and footage of a shimmering ocean sunset.

"Wow! Is that their home world?" Gaia asked.

Blum shook her head. "No, it's stock footage of the sun setting off the coast of Fiji. The Kishocha don't use video technology. No pictures exist of their home world."

"Oh." Gaia slumped down in her chair. On-screen, the sunset dissolved, and Gaia found herself staring at the set of *A-Ki Today*, a rather dull talk-and-news show that aired every Tuesday night. The studio set contained a desk, two chairs and a fake window framing a fake spacescape. A very tall, extremely thin Kishocha sat at the desk. Its cranial tendrils were long, like Kenjan's. The tendrils were not striped. They alternated, one pure white and the next pure black. Its face was entirely white, except for an adorable spot over its left eye. It wore no pit covering, which Gaia noticed immediately because the flesh was bright red against its white throat. It wore no clothing and had mismatched eyes—the right was purple and the left gold. The alien's hands were huge.

"Hello to you, friendly humans." The alien spoke remarkably unaccented English. "My name is Wave Walker, and I am a humble servant here to tell you about the race of the Kishocha." The alien paused to lean forward, obviously reading the teleprompter. "This informative monologue will help humans better understand the Kishocha way of living.

"First, an introduction. I am the servant of elegant and lovely Kenjan, who is consort to glorious Oziru, our Imperial Monarch." Wave gestured to a screen, which displayed a picture of Kenjan sitting next to Oziru at the Embassy Club. Both aliens wore garments made entirely of golden chains, pearls and uncut gemstones. Three servants supported Oziru's massive cranial tendrils. "This is Kenjan and this is Oziru. Do you know who is more exalted?" Wave paused, as if waiting for an answer. "You cannot tell? Well, it is easy to tell who is more exalted. See the cranial tendrils? Oziru's are beautifully huge. This means that Oziru is of divinity.

"'But Wave,' you say, 'what is divinity caste?' Don't worry. I'll tell you everything. The Kishocha have many, many castes, but there are six main levels, the same as the number of fingers on your hand." Wave held out its massive webbed hand to emphasize its six digits. Off-camera a voice whispered, "Humans only have five fingers, Wave."

Wave cowered. "I'm sorry, my master. I forgot the humans are bereft of a finger."

"It's all right. Just keep going," the voice said.

Gaia paused the film and looked at Blum. "Why didn't they edit that out?"

"Kenjan liked the raw quality," Blum said.

"Is that Kenjan talking behind the camera?"

Blum nodded curtly.

Fitzpatrick said, "Let's press on."

Wave pulled its hand back, concealing its fingers beneath the desk.

"The six levels of Kishocha are like this: divinity, structure, priest, soldier, servant and cleaner. Divinity is the highest rank. The divine have a very hard job. They sing the prayers that move the currents of the sea and the currents of the wind. They dance the sacred motions that invoke gravitation. They are closest to the god, and most holy, and most important. On A-Ki Station there is only one divine Kishocha, and that is Oziru. Remember that we must all bow down in supplication to Oziru. Without Oziru, we would be lost and sick with no hope and die. Let's all say, 'Thank you, Oziru! We love you!' Okay, go!" Wave held its hand up to its ear, as though waiting for a response from the imaginary audience.

"Thank you, Oziru. We love you," Fitzpatrick whispered.

Wave continued.

"Next beneath divinity caste is structure caste. This sphere we live in, that you humans call a ship, is really just another kind of Kishocha! There are five big Kishocha called structures whose loving embrace creates Ki Island. We must thank, love and care for the structures, because without them we would float naked in the void without water or shelter.

"You humans may not live inside the structures, as we do, but the name of the structure upon whose back the buildings that make up your human space station ride is Protective

Cradle Everlasting. Please sometimes say thank you to Protective Cradle Everlasting for allowing your buildings to live, like barnacles, upon its back."

Gaia stopped the show. "I am completely lost."

"The Kishocha orb is made from five interlocking biological entities called structures," Fitzpatrick said. "They call it Ki Island."

"I got the words okay. But what do they mean? Are the walls alive? Are they...you know, watching me?"

"We don't think so," Blum said. "Not any more than your hand or lung is watching you. From what we can surmise, the structures are sentient beings but not intelligent. They respond to injuries and stress, but aren't able to speak except to Oziru."

Gaia glanced askance. No wonder that Kishocha had been so pissed off when she'd hammered a nail into the wall.

Fitzpatrick went on. "We think these structures are simply massive, shelled organisms. They are huge creatures the size of whole continents. It has been suggested that the structures are themselves colonies of smaller organisms that act synchronously like sentient coral might behave."

"Sentient coral?" Gaia felt a helpful surge of extra blood rushing to her brain as she struggled to comprehend.

"We do not, however, know anything for certain," Fitzpatrick said.

"Does that clear it up?" Blum asked.

"Um... yeah." Gaia pushed play again.

Wave scratched its muzzle. "After the structures, come the priests. My master, beautiful Kenjan, is a priest who also holds the rank of divine consort. Every day, my master sings songs and makes love to the eminent Oziru. Please, my master, show yourself to the disconnected-eye camera device so that the humans can see true beauty."

"If I go, no one will be here to hold the camera," Kenjan's voice responded.

"The human there can hold the disconnected-eye." Wave pointed off-screen. While arrangements were being made, Gaia mechanically rose and refilled Fitzpatrick's Frosticcino. Finally,

Kenjan appeared on-screen.

The alien glided forward and lowered itself into the upholstered chair next to Wave's desk. As Kenjan approached, Wave lay across the desk in a supplicant bow.

Kenjan wore no adornments on its cranial tendrils. They tumbled freely over Kenjan's shoulders and over a broad collar of gold and green stones that began at the alien's throat, covered its shoulders and spilled down its chest. Kenjan also wore a wide, low belt hung with white silk panels. The effect was like seeing some ancient, animal-muzzled god reclining on a cheap, overstuffed beige chair.

As Kenjan spoke, Gaia began to notice a marked difference in Wave's and Kenjan's demeanors. Kenjan's speech and movements were languorous and sensual. But that made sense; it was Kenjan's job to be sensual.

"You may rise, Wave."

Wave's head popped back up. "How lovely you look today. Say, are you wearing the clothes of the human designer called Nidal Habibi?"

"Yes, how sensitive of you to notice."

"So, my master, what is the priest caste?"

"The priest caste is the law-making class of the Kishocha." Kenjan's voice was low and smooth. "We hear the laws from the god and relate them to our subjects."

"Who is the most important priest on Ki Island?" Wave asked ingenuously. "Besides you, oh most beloved one."

"I am merely the consort, Wave. My job is to make Oziru happy. The ruling priest is Seigata, my noble sibling, purest of heart and hearing. Seigata also is the personal priest to Oziru and myself. Everything we touch is blessed by Seigata."

"Except the profane human things."

"Why point out facts which are better ignored, Wave?"

Wave looked embarrassed and coughed, then perked back up. "We happen to have a picture of Seigata. Secretly obtained! How exciting..." Wave gestured to the tiny screen that was used for news clips from Mars or Earth. The human cameraman had enough sense to zoom in close.

Through a thick tangle of deep green vines, they saw Seigata kneeling on a smooth blue floor next to a small pool. The high priest was speaking and dipping objects into the water. Some objects resembled dishes, others, jewelry or clothes. A tiny yellow bird flapped by, startling Seigata.

Gaia frowned. "They have birds inside the orb?"

Fitzpatrick leaned forward, obviously excited by the prospect of the internal biosphere of the orb. "We suspect they have much more than that. We know there's a lot of water flowing through there, and Kenjan told us that there is quite a bit of vegetation, although it wasn't very specific. Kenjan could verge on caginess."

"I wouldn't call it cagey," Blum said. "More like extremely arrogant. Talking about the Kishocha part of the station bored it, and so Kenjan never did. I don't think the alien was deliberately trying to withhold information. After we persisted in our questions, Kenjan did go through the trouble to make this program. Kenjan said it was to answer all of our silly, dull questions at once."

"Yes, so it could get back to asking silly, dull questions of its own, like where do human babies come from. I spent hours answering that question," Fitzpatrick murmured. "Kenjan promised to let me know more about the life cycle of the Kishocha in return, but managed to avoid ever making good on the promise."

Again Blum moved in to modify Fitzpatrick's rancor. "Kenjan understood that we were fascinated by the Kishocha, it just didn't care. Without cynicism I can say that humans inhabit A-Ki Station purely because Kenjan was amused and intrigued by us."

"We were like Kenjan's sea monkeys," Fitzpatrick said, and Gaia finally thought she understood the situation. Their sponsor, Kenjan, was gone and without that one special alien, A-Ki Station's fate had become precarious. But that didn't make sense, did it? How could the Kishocha care so little about the entire human race?

"But I thought we were exchanging things with them."

"Such as?" Blum tapped the tabletop.

"Top-secret stuff?"

Fitzpatrick emitted a noise that was too much like a laugh to pass for a cough. "I'm afraid not. When Kenjan died, we weren't certain whether we'd be allowed to stay here or not. Luckily, they wanted you. Before that, we thought we might have to dismantle the whole station."

"So please refrain from shirking your responsibilities," Blum said. "We hope, someday, to convince the Kishocha to share the technology for their gravitational field generators with us."

"We were making headway before Kenjan's convenient death," Fitzpatrick remarked.

"Convenient?"

"Not for us." Fitzpatrick rattled the ice in his Frosticcino. "But it's beneficial for many high-ranking Kishocha. Kenjan was not all that popular with them."

"But none of that concerns us," Blum said. "Right now we need to find another high-ranking ally among the Kishocha or our station is finished."

Gaia's response was a noncommittal "hmmm". They resumed watching Kenjan's program. Wave interviewed Kenjan about the remaining three classes of Kishocha. The soldier class was pretty self-explanatory. They defended the Kishocha from enemies of the god and also policed the Kishocha population. Wave outlined the three major laws, which the soldiers enforced: Love the god, obey your superiors, and honor the water. Blum noted that these were the three precepts that Gaia should pay most attention to. In addition, there were myriad rules of etiquette that she couldn't be expected to learn overnight. But if she could manage not to blaspheme against the Kishocha god, talk back to any important Kishocha, or dump bleach in the Kishocha waters, human/Kishocha relations would probably be okay.

The servant class, which included artisans as well as laborers, seemed to occupy the largest segment of Kishocha society. Wave cheerfully admitted being at the very bottom of the servant class, and thus being obliged to give respect to virtually everyone.

"I am very good at bowing. Wouldn't you say, beautiful Kenjan?"

"It is only one of your abundant talents," Kenjan replied.

Gaia scowled. "How could Wave be really low if it serves someone really important?"

"Well," Fitzpatrick answered, "close association does not confer genuine status, even among human cultures."

"I guess." Gaia slumped down in her chair. She felt sorry for Wave, who had to bow to everyone, and mildly irritated by Kenjan's condescending attitude.

The last Kishocha class was comprised of cleaners, who apparently mostly handled sewage. The cleaners also disposed of the dead.

"Cleaners are not very smart," Wave said, "so you must not be cruel to them just because you can. If you are angry with your master, that is not a reason to kick or torture a cleaner. We need the waters of Ki Island to be even more pure than the Kishocha Ocean. The cleaners prevent—" Wave stopped, perplexed. "My master, what is the human word for *shakkiam*?"

Kenjan pulled a slim electronic dictionary out of the desk drawer. It perused the screen for a few seconds, and then said, "Toxicity."

"Toxicity," Wave repeated. "Toxicity, toxicity, toxicity. The word for *shakkiam* is toxicity."

"Or it could be poison," Kenjan said. "But toxicity sounds more poetic, I think."

"Definitely. So you can see that the cleaners, although they are stupid and small, are very important. Be kind to your cleaners. Do not try to feed them rocks or explode them. Do not throw them at targets for a bull's-eye game. Would you like Oziru to throw you like that? No? Then pet your cleaners and leave them alone. They need to do their job." Wave's stern expression softened a little. "But you were not going to do any of these things, were you? That is because you are good humans. Now go outside to play."

Wave paused briefly, glancing from side to side, apparently through with its speech but uncertain how to conclude. The cameraman was also at a loss. Finally he said, “Do you want me to cut now?”

Kenjan cocked its head. “No, but you may extinguish the camera.” The visual ended abruptly. There were no credits.

“So,” Fitzpatrick said. “How did you like it?”

“That was really weird,” Gaia said.

“But you understood the basic information?” Blum barely waited for Gaia to nod her response before continuing. “Insofar as we can tell, the position you’re going to hold is part of the priestly caste. Unfortunately, I can’t tell you much more about your duties. All Oziru would tell me was that you would make sure the ghost was fed.”

“Seigata told me that too, but what am I supposed to feed it? Fries?”

Fitzpatrick cut in again. “Apparently, that’s just a figure of speech. The Kishocha will bring offerings to the ghost. All you have to do is make sure no one, including you, gets possessed.”

“Right.” Blum pressed relentlessly on. “The Kishocha fear that the ghost may try to escape from the shrine by possessing the life of another.”

“You don’t think that the ghost is real, do you?” Gaia asked.

“No,” Blum said.

“Just checking.” Gaia slurped her drink. “Do I have to be there all the time?”

“No, there’s a special period when offerings to the dead are made. It’s from about ten p.m. until around one a.m. You should probably try and be present in the shrine during this time.” Fitzpatrick withdrew a slim case from his inner pocket. “It’s a time based on the Kishocha rising stars, so it varies throughout the year. I had this programmed for you. It’s a Kishocha clock.”

“It says *Made in Malaysia*.” Gaia pointed at the label.

“It’s not a real Kishocha clock,” Fitzpatrick said. “But I didn’t think you wanted a six-foot pillar of water that you couldn't read."

Blum rapped her knuckles sharply on the table. She clearly felt the conversation was going astray.

"I'm sorry, but I have to be at another meeting in ten minutes, so let's try to move along." Blum rubbed her eyes.

"You look pretty tired. Maybe you should just bag the meeting and take a nap," Gaia suggested.

Blum gave her a tight, hard smile. "That would be nice, wouldn't it? But then who would keep this whole place from collapsing around us?"

Gaia was about to answer when she realized the question was rhetorical.

Blum continued, "You have no idea how much bureaucracy is involved in keeping this station running, Ms. Jones. The amount of paperwork is absolutely voluminous, not to mention the meetings with the Kishocha, which can take all night and accomplish absolutely nothing. All I want from you is your solemn vow that you won't become a source of pain to me."

"How do you mean?"

Fitzpatrick cleared his throat. "I think CPO Blum is asking you to take this job seriously. You'll be subsidized by the embassy for your time, so please make sure that you're actually there, on time, to accept the offerings."

"That's really all?" Gaia asked.

"Were you hoping for something more exotic?" Fitzpatrick asked.

"No, I just don't know why someone else can't do this."

"The deceased asked specifically for you to be its guardian," Blum said. "The thing you have to understand about the Kishocha is that Oziru really is all-powerful in their society. Kenjan was Oziru's lover and also some kind of visionary. So if Kenjan asked for you, then Kenjan gets you. The Kishocha don't understand free will. They believe in absolute obedience. They wouldn't understand if we said that you just had other plans. You've been a good sport so far, and we do appreciate it, but I simply must demand that you take this duty seriously. I don't think it's melodramatic to say that every human on this station could be affected by your actions." Blum regarded Gaia with deep weariness.

Gaia had so many questions. What if she got tired of this job? What if she wanted to take a vacation or go home? She considered demanding answers, but suddenly knew she didn't really want to know. For the time being she'd continue to be cooperative. Maybe later an escape plan would present itself. When she needed it... If she needed it.

"Could you at least tell me about the summoning ceremony?"

"Mr. Fitzpatrick has been looking into that, and so you may address your questions to him. I need to be going. Have a good day, and good luck tomorrow night. We're counting on you." Blum collected her things, shook Gaia's hand, and left.

After she was gone Gaia turned back to Fitzpatrick.

"Another round?" She shook her cup and rattled her ice at him. He accepted her offer, visibly more relaxed now that Blum had gone.

He straightened his tie, seeming to come to some inner decision. "You know, I feel like you and I got off on the wrong foot."

"That's probably because you called my store Crappy Shack," Gaia said.

Fitzpatrick's eyes opened in amused surprise. "What?"

"You heard me."

"You hold a grudge because of that?"

"I also don't like your cologne." Gaia couldn't believe how petty the words coming out of her mouth sounded, but there it was, the truth.

"I'll try to find a different brand." A smile tugged at the edges of Fitzpatrick's mouth.

Now that she'd stated her reasons for hating Fitzpatrick, she felt stupid. It did sound petty, but then badmouthing her store was equally petty.

"I'm really, truly sorry. I know you and I haven't been on the best of terms, and I do sincerely apologize for offending you. I think I'm just more used to dealing with corporations than I am with entrepreneurs. I didn't realize you had put so much of your heart into Happy Snak."

Gaia thought of deflecting both Fitzpatrick's sentiment and his apology, but she realized that he was sincere. More than that, he was that most rare of creatures—a man who really knew how to apologize. Professional necessity or not, she was impressed.

"It's okay, I'm not mad about it anymore."

"I'm sorry, but I couldn't find any meaningful information on the ghost invocation ceremony or your duties as a guardian. Seigata did mention that you needn't worry about being possessed by the ghost because unlike Kishocha souls, which are made from water, human souls are made from fire. Everything else it told me was either oblique or vague to the point of meaninglessness."

"What do you mean?" Gaia called from the cold-drinks dispenser.

"For example, I asked what you were to do with the food offerings. They said that the ghost would eat them. I said, 'Yes, but what will Gaia have to do after the ghost has "eaten" them,' thinking that after a while all the dead fish could really be a problem."

"I was just wondering what I did with them myself." Gaia handed Fitzpatrick his refreshed drink.

"Seigata looked really appalled and replied that you shouldn't be handling any kind of secretions, especially not that of a *kaijamfutan*. That's the term for wandering ghost, incidentally." Fitzpatrick took a sip of his drink. "How are your Kishocha language skills coming along?"

"I've been taking the refresher course for the last few weeks. I can say, 'What would you like to drink with that?' And I get along pretty well with the simple stuff. I understand more than I can speak."

"That's always the way, isn't it?" Fitzpatrick said. "I did find out some things about your swearing-in ceremony. You're getting a tattoo."

"Of what?"

"I don't know. I apologize. It's supposed to be a way to mark humans who are allowed in Kishocha waters. Until now the Kishocha never actually marked anyone. Make sure to come see a doctor if you have any pain."

"This doesn't make me feel better about the ceremony. I'm wondering which part of my body you've consented to have molested this time, you know?"

"The Kishocha didn't mention. Are you very frightened?" Fitzpatrick's expression became so unexpectedly gentle that Gaia almost nodded. But then she remembered who she was talking to.

"I'd describe my emotional state as more angry than fearful."

Fitzpatrick shrugged. "In my experience I've found those two feelings to be rather closely entwined. Much like attraction and irritation." He leaned back.

"I'm not that complex," Gaia said flatly.

"Before your act of heroism I would have agreed with you and yet here you are, making diplomatic advances that we've been working on for years in just a few minutes. Right now you are the most important person on A-Ki Station—maybe even in the entire human race. To say you are not complex is patently wrong."

Gaia felt herself blush. Was this—could Fitzpatrick actually be—complimenting her? There had to be a catch. And yet she felt a rush of pride. She was going to be allowed in Kishocha waters.

She said, "Are you trying to get me in bed?"

"I am merely attempting to put your current importance and power into perspective." Fitzpatrick retrieved Wave's video and slid it back inside his briefcase. He glanced around.

"Blum didn't want me to focus on that. She believes that you don't truly understand what you are doing and that it's better for you not to." Fitzpatrick spoke quietly and quickly, his eyes locked on hers. "I do not agree with her position. I think it's crucial that you understand that all of our hope is with you now."

All at once, heady egotism collided with tooth-grinding anxiety. She could, if she wanted to, have Treat Bonanza thrown off the station entirely. But this delirious joy entwined itself tightly with the very basic knowledge that if she made a mistake now, and the aliens left, taking their miraculous technology with them, she would be the biggest fuckup in recorded human history.

Gaia's hands felt sweaty. She needed to avoid thinking about uncertainties. She needed to focus on an easily graspable and easily controlled subject. "Do you think they'd like Coke or Pepsi more?"

"Excuse me?"

"I was thinking of switching the soft-drinks distributor, and I'd like to choose the brand they seem to like. Have you noticed that they like one or the other?"

"You know, I think I did try to give the liaison a cola once."

Gaia sat up straight in her chair, totally attentive. "And?"

"They didn't like either."

"They don't like cola at all?"

Fitzpatrick laughed, but Gaia wasn't sure why. "They said it tasted like poison."

A slow realization dawned on her. "These guys really are alien."

Chapter Five:
Purifying

When Gaia entered the Kishocha shrine to meet with Seigata, it was the first time a human had stepped into the alien realm. She approached the Kishocha door and it dilated open. She walked through a domed chamber about twice the size of Happy Snak. Light emanated from a ring of luminous spots near the center of the ceiling. The walls were made from shiny, pink shell-like material. The walls flowed seamlessly into the floor.

The floor of the chamber was comprised of three concentric levels. First was the walkway where she stood. It was about ten feet wide. Next was a twenty-foot drop to a circular trench surrounding a small, star-shaped island. The island was raised slightly above the level of the outer walkway. The gulf around the island reminded Gaia a little of a zoo exhibit—the kind that keeps predatory animals separated from zoo patrons. Gaia edged out toward the drop to see the island a little better. The Kishocha had erected a little hut of black and red scallop shells on the island. The hut had a doorway and a round window, but no furniture that Gaia could see. Inside the shadowed recesses lay a heap of unidentifiable parcels. Offerings, maybe?

And what were the offerings anyway? Could they be blood sacrifices? Gaia didn't see anything that looked like an altar. Apart from the hut on the island, the shrine was empty. Seigata had yet to arrive.

Gaia wished it were Oziru she was going to meet. She felt

like Oziru might like her.

About a quarter of the way around the room, another iris-like door dilated open.

Seigata moved with absolute restraint. Each of the alien's steps was a deliberate action. Seigata held its hands up to its black and white chest, keeping its fingers folded into an elaborate geometrical pose. Six attendants followed, each carrying some ritual object.

Seigata approached with agonizing slowness. When it came within six feet of her, it stopped and finally looked up.

"You may approach, Gaia Jones," it said. Gaia walked close to the wall, worried about accidentally falling in the trench. One of the attendants set something that looked like a yellow dog bed on the floor. Another attendant carried a huge spiraling shell. It decanted some pinkish fluid into the dog bed. Seigata lowered itself gracefully into the moist, spongy seat and motioned her to sit.

She sat cross-legged on the floor, near enough to hear Seigata but not obnoxiously so. From this vantage Gaia could admire Seigata's amazing person. Its long tumbling cranial tendrils were ringed at the base by thick gold wraps, giving the effect of an elaborate crown. Dangling strings of cut jewels hung down the sides of its face. Seigata wore golden rings on all its fingers and silver on the talon-like tips of its webbed toes. The Kishocha wore the same robe she'd noticed in the medical conference room, a garment made of teeth and blue cowry shells.

"How are you today, Gaia Jones?" it asked. One of its attendants set a small, low table between them. It placed two half-shells filled with pearlescent white fluid and small transparent lumps on the table.

"I'm fine, thanks," Gaia said, "and you?"

"I am feeling well, but sick sorrow lingers in my heart." Seigata gestured to the shells. "I thought we might do pearl drinking to begin our acquaintance. Do you agree?"

"Okay."

Seigata handed her a half-shell, then raised its own to its

muzzle and slurped the whole mass down. Gaia lifted her own shell. The stench was overpowering. It smelled like the worst part of a rotten fish. Gaia tried not to breathe. She knew she somehow had to get this hideous-smelling item down her throat. As she opened her mouth she caught slight whiffs of armpit and fart. She gagged. Then, in a burst of bravery, slid the gooey mass into her mouth and forced herself to swallow.

Her stomach considered the pearls. It rolled them around for one indecisive moment before arriving at the conclusion that they should be rejected immediately. Gaia's mouth began to water.

"Excuse me." She swallowed a couple of times to buy herself a little time. "I haven't brought you anything."

"That is excusable," Seigata said.

"Oh no! I'll be right back." Gaia bolted from the shrine, arriving at her own private toilet at the critical moment. She heaved, projecting the Kishocha "pearls" in the basic direction of the bowl. Pearlescent chunks spattered against the stainless steel. Gaia flushed. She whipped around, rinsed her mouth and dashed to the cold-drinks dispenser. She got a Coke and took a long, desperate gulp. Her stomach resisted briefly, and then agreed that Coke was good. Gaia got a box of Clammi! brand clam juice and made her way back into the shrine. Would she be puking every time she met with the Kishocha? What would they think about that?

If Seigata thought her actions strange, the alien didn't let on. It accepted, but didn't attempt to drink, her box of Clammi! Rather, it handed the Clammi! to a servant who rang a small gong. Another servant entered the room, took the Clammi! and held it reverently.

"And now, Gaia Jones, to the tasks of the day." Seigata held up a hand and a servant approached, carrying what looked like a large, flexible sheet of red plastic. It was folded elaborately, like an origami starfish, but one deft tug unfolded the entire thing. Chunky geometric letters covered one side.

"This is the proclamation and oath of the Guardian of the Shrine of Kaijamfutan of Ki Island under the Divine Guidance of

Exalted Oziru. Please repeat after me: Now that the contemptible ghost has come to dwell, humiliated, on Ki Island—"

Gaia dully repeated this. She wasn't religious, but it seemed mean to speak ill of the defenseless dead. Seigata continued.

"There must be a protector for its cursed spirit, for even a contaminated spirit is given mercy by the Exalted Oziru." Seigata paused. Gaia echoed this part with more gusto.

"I will be the protector of the *kaijamfutan* who was called Kenjan in life. I will give to it the prayers of succor. I will give to it the food. I will be strong against its deceitful corruptions, and hear none of its mournful pleadings until the end of my days."

Gaia repeated everything until the last part.

"But what if I have to go home, to Earth?" Gaia asked.

"Then you take the ghost with you."

"I have to take the little house?" Gaia gestured across to the shell grotto.

"No, just the ghost that dwells within. It is not so difficult. Many guardians wander with ghosts, swimming and begging. In this way they see the whole of the ocean. Not many of us do." Seigata lowered its hand, and the servant withdrew with the oath. "Will you complete the oath, please?"

A nasty feeling churned through her stomach. She was reluctant to make a commitment. She didn't believe in ghosts. What less substantial promise could she make? To her, this oath should have had the emotional impact of the disclaimer on a bottle of aspirin. *By opening this bottle of pain killers you release Mega Analgesic Corp. and all its subsidiaries of all liability for accidental decapitation via faulty bottle cap, etc.* And yet, she balked. Fitzpatrick had her psyched out.

But, if something really bad happened, she could always go back to Earth and hide. A Mongolian yurt wasn't that bad.

She took a breath. "I will be strong against its deceitful corruptions, and hear none of its mournful pleadings until the end of my days."

"Excellent." Seigata's voice soothed her. The alien raised its hand again and another servant came forward, carrying an oyster the size of a large dinner plate. As the servant drew near, the shell opened. Nestled inside the grayish folds of wet oyster flesh were two bracelets: one red, one black. They were oblong and wide, like cuffs, but the material they were made of was thin as paper. Once they were close, Gaia could see tiny, subtle fractal shapes beneath the shiny shell surface. Seigata picked them up.

"Allow me to confer upon you the symbol of your rank. Please hold out your hands."

Gaia nodded. Tattooing seemed imminent, and she was ready.

She removed her wrist braces and gingerly presented her hands. She worried that her hands would flop listlessly at the ends of her wrists but they held firm. The surgical scars were still quite red.

"These marks of honor will cover your battle scars."

"Great." Though the scars had a certain Frankenstein-monster chic, she wasn't attached to them.

Seigata slid the bracelets over her arms, bringing them to rest just above her wrists. They felt fairly tight, but strangely velvety inside. They tingled. Worry gnawed at Gaia's composure. The tingling got worse. Seigata rubbed its thumbs over the flexible surface of the bracelets, whispering.

"To be Kenjan's guardian is most important of all. Kenjan was a heretic in life and vengeful in death. Possession is always a danger and those lowest Kishocha, the workers and servants, are weakest against ghosts. You have a great burden to carry, but you must never weaken. Remember that responsibility can sting, but nothing is greater than serving society. Be unafraid." Seigata squeezed the bracelets and a horrible burning sting spread from under them.

Gaia tried to pull back, but Seigata held her fast. As she watched, the bands began to visibly drain of color, until both were a flaccid gray. It only took seconds. Afterward, Seigata peeled the bracelets back to reveal two wide bracelet-shaped tattoos. There was no blood, just a vague, lingering ache.

Gaia suppressed her anger at the pain. She began to get the uneasy feeling that she'd signed a contract without bothering to read the fine print. All her interactions with the Kishocha had been very physically taxing. She'd learned some things about the aliens.

Never touch a hurt Kishocha.

Never eat anything they give you.

Trust your nose when it tells you that their food will kill you. It will.

Never let them put anything on you.

Always ask questions.

Always, always, always ask questions.

Gaia decided to put this last revelation into practice immediately.

"Will these hurt forever?" Gaia asked.

Seigata laughed. "No, only for a few minutes."

"If you're a Kishocha."

"No, a marking was tested on another human before we tried to give it to you. The man said it was fine, and no death occurred."

"That's good I suppose." Gaia fought to restrain her sarcasm. Getting angry right now wouldn't do any good, so she just listened carefully as the alien spoke.

Seigata explained that the grotto on the island was the ghost's sanctified residence.

Gaia figured that part out already. The ghost's house was very small, but then again, it wasn't like anything substantial was going to be living there. Seigata presented her with a fleshy roll of papery things. These were the prayers that she must learn. Gaia didn't read Kishocha and said so. Seigata replied that they'd been translated into American Clan Human writing, and added that the ghost spoke English so it would understand.

"My time is precious, now, for there is much to do. So I will call the waters and be gone."

Seigata rose. Gaia followed the alien to the mysterious

second door. A thrill of excitement and trepidation ran through her. She'd never seen the Kishocha part of the station. Now Seigata seemed to be leading her to it. Then she remembered the fine print and hung back a little. Who knew what was on the other side of that door? It could sting, burn or nauseate her. Seigata beckoned her forward.

"These are the sacred waters of Ki Island," it said.

The corridor beyond looked pretty much just like the chamber she stood in. Blank, pearly walls but where the floor would be a lazy pink river flowed.

"Now I will call forth the waters." Seigata sang a long, low series of notes. All along the inside of the trench, tunnels gasped open. Pink water rushed into the empty trough. Now and then confused fish or crustaceans tumbled through. When the water equalized, a thick band of water ringed the ghost's island.

"It is now ready for the coming of the ghost, and you are ready to receive it. You should take this night to meditate on the meaning of your position and to purify yourself for the Summoning." Seigata walked Gaia back to her bedroom. The door closed, and Gaia was back in the human realm. She rubbed her hands over the new tattoos to try and relieve the tingling. Once she returned to her bedroom, she wrote Fitzpatrick a message.

From now on, I want ten thousand dollars for every time an alien physically alters me.

Sincerely,

Gaia

Five minutes later, Fitzpatrick responded:

As you wish.

F.

Chapter Six: The Summoning

Though comparatively large, Gaia's new living quarters were too small to comfortably contain a full ambassadorial entourage. She felt silly. She sat on the end of her bed waiting for Oziru to call her to the Summoning. Blum occupied Gaia's only chair. Fitzpatrick paced the room. Four secretaries lounged uncomfortably against her bathroom wall. Roy and Cheryl, her new employees, sat cross-legged on her throw rug and played cards. Once she went in, they were to escort Blum and minions out, and lock up Happy Snak. Gaia suspected they just wanted to see more Kishocha up close. Roy held his camera in his lap.

"I can wait alone," Gaia said.

"It would be best if we saw you off," Fitzpatrick said. "Aren't you uncomfortable having this door in your bedroom?"

"It's a little creepy sometimes."

"Maybe we should build you a small foyer so that you have some privacy." Fitzpatrick gingerly touched the Kishocha door. "I don't like that they can have access to you at any time."

"We have to follow the requisite course until Gaia establishes a relationship with Oziru, then we can negotiate for better living arrangements. She already lives far above her Kishocha caste," Blum said.

"Still, the mental strain will begin to wear." Fitzpatrick unwrapped a stick of cigarette gum. "Don't you think, Gaia?"

"The mental strain is beginning to wear right now."

"Would you like some gum?" He offered his pack—a blue Gitanes-brand box with a gypsy on the label. Gaia declined. She hardly ever chewed cigarette gum.

The door dilated open. Fitzpatrick stepped back. Roy held his camera at the ready.

Oziru leaned into the doorway. It briefly acknowledged Blum and then held out its hand to Gaia. She took it automatically.

"It is time."

Gaia fought the urge to run, suddenly fearful of what would happen to her. Belatedly she wondered if she should have dressed up for the ceremony. "Should I change?"

"We like you as you are." Oziru started into the shrine. Gaia held back, suddenly needing to confirm arrangements for her absence.

"Roy and Cheryl will let you all out," she told the assorted diplomatic personnel.

"I think I might stay here until you get back," Fitzpatrick said.

Oziru countermanded him instantly. "You are not needed now. Return to your dwelling. Gaia Jones will call for you if necessary. If I suspect you of lingering to spy I will call down my wrath upon you."

"Of course." Fitzpatrick inclined his head. "I meant no offense."

It was a good effort, but Oziru was too powerful for Fitzpatrick to defy. Gaia gave him a weak grin and stepped into the shrine. By the time she looked back, the door had closed.

The shrine was more humid than before. Light still emanated from the domed ceiling. The pink moat was calm. The walls glistened with a sheen of condensation, as did the floor. Even though the walkway was ten feet wide, Gaia worried about falling in the moat. Oziru kept hold of her upper arm. Should she be reassured or worried by that?

As they walked around the edge of the room, Seigata and its attendants came into view. Seigata wore a long shell robe and stood beside the coffinlike box Kenjan had been put inside.

Seigata's six attendants knelt along the wall. The top of the box was translucent. Dark shadows moved through the pink liquid within. Gaia recoiled. Was there something inside the coffin with the body?

Kenjan was alive when it had gone into that box. A grim, sick feeling moved through Gaia. Had Kenjan just been shut in there to die? Why would Oziru do that to someone it loved?

Maybe that had been a different box.

"I hope that you will feel at peace here on our island in the void," Oziru said. "I am grateful for your commitment to the well-being of the ghost. Ghosts cannot swim the waters alone."

"It's no problem." Gaia shrugged out of Oziru's grip. Oziru didn't try to keep hold of her, but it was clear to Gaia that Oziru had chosen to release her.

"The Summoning might be difficult for you. If you feel frightened, you may cling to me."

"Thank you." And if Gaia felt frightened of Oziru, whom should she cling to then?

Oziru stopped about six feet from the box and ordered Seigata to begin. Seigata discarded its long robe. Gaia saw delicate markings over the alien's chest and limbs. She smelled its thick caustic scent. An attendant crawled forward and gathered Seigata's robe up before slinking back. Seigata gave a sign, and its attendants began a polyphonic chant. One rang a bell at nonsensical intervals. The chanting echoed up through the dome, amplifying exponentially. Gaia heard nothing else.

Seigata walked to the water's edge and leapt into the air. Seigata piked its body, twisted and plunged under the water. Moments later the alien burst up from a different spot, twisted and dived back down.

Water crashed. Waves overflowed the moat, sloshing up over Gaia's feet.

Seigata continued, churning the waters to a frenzy with its acrobatics. A wave surged into Gaia's shins. She teetered and grabbed for Oziru's arm. She missed and stumbled. Gaia struggled to regain her footing. She found her feet just as Seigata shot back into the air again. It arched over the entire ghost island, then it drew up its knees and plunged into the water, cannonball-style. The resulting wave slammed into Gaia and Oziru. Gaia flailed. Oziru glanced to her curiously as she struggled to remain upright.

A few seconds later, she steadied herself. Seigata rode a ripple over to them. Its nostril slits gasped open and the membranes pulled back from its eyes. The alien looked directly at her and she thought its expression was that of a physician staring down an infectious disease. She stepped slightly behind Oziru.

An attendant approached with Seigata's robe and held it while the alien redressed. Seigata said, "This chamber has been purified."

"Then take the ghost to its home," Oziru intoned.

Seigata made a sign, and its attendants encircled the box. Two attendants carried it to the edge of the moat, opened the end and dumped Kenjan's body unceremoniously into the water. Kenjan's limp form slid out in a thick sheath of mucousy membrane. The attendants left the shrine, taking the box with them. Kenjan's body sank. Were they just going to leave it there to rot?

Seigata moved to the edge of the water, singing a piercing chant. Two more attendants followed, each carrying a half-clamshell of black fluid. They crawled along the floor writing double rows of squiggly letters. The shrine was big. This could take a while.

Gaia wanted to ask if that was all the violent water there would be, but sensed this was a non-talking moment. She was glad the room was warm, since she was drenched. Water dribbled down her back. Oziru watched the surface of the water intently, as if it was restraining its every urge.

Gaia, too, watched the water looking for the shadowy motion she'd seen inside Kenjan's coffin. She hoped it had only been her imagination, but felt deep unease at the idea that there was something alien under the water. Something other than Kenjan's corpse. Something that would be living right on the other side of her bedroom door.

Once the circle of writing was closed, Oziru turned its attention to Gaia.

"May I have your hand?"

Gaia balked. "Will it hurt?"

"Only a little," Oziru said. "It is necessary. The ghost must be bound by blood."

Gaia extended her arm. She focused on the next pain and suffering payment. Maybe she could buy a new fryer.

An attendant handed Oziru a needle. Oziru pricked her finger and caught the droplet in a small vial of yellow liquid. Gaia's blood sank to the bottom.

"Stay back against the wall." Holding the vial, Oziru walked to the line of calligraphy. It turned to Seigata. "Approach Kenjan's servant."

Seigata gave a sign, and two attendants rose and exited the Kishocha door. They returned immediately, leading Wave Walker, from the informational film.

In person, Wave stood close to six feet tall. Its cranial tendrils hung limp and partially obscured its face. Dazed and groggy, Wave staggered between the two attending Kishocha. Its body was white and thin, with enormous hands and feet.

The attendants pushed Wave to the floor at Oziru's feet. Seigata withdrew to join the attendants' chant.

Oziru sang a series of three deafening notes, then said, "Oziru am Kenjan, I call you to reside here. I bind you to your protector, Happy Snak's Gaia Jones, and I give you your servant Wave Walker to accompany you. Come to receive your binding."

Oziru then knelt beside Wave. Gaia watched the expression on Oziru's face as it contemplated the servant—the curled lip, the narrowed eyes. Was that regret? Disgust? She couldn't be sure. Oziru lifted a knife, pushed the tip into Wave's wrist and dragged the blade across Wave's skin. Not deeply, but decisively. Black blood streamed out, dripping on the floor. Wave's only reaction was to stare. Wave looked drugged. A rivulet of alien's blood wound along the floor until it dripped into the moat.

Gaia didn't want to see this or know it had happened. She felt powerless to interfere and yet she could not be a mute witness.

"Please stop," she said. Oziru stopped cutting. Its gaze was terrible. Gaia couldn't believe the alien had heard her above the chanting.

"It must be done." Oziru bent to its work. The Kishocha cut a new furrow on Wave's arm, paused and started a third.

A hand burst up from the water, seized Oziru's knife and hurled it away. Kenjan pulled itself up on the edge of the moat. Gaia leapt back against the wall, gasping with the new and sudden knowledge that Kenjan was still alive—had been alive for weeks inside that coffin. Kenjan was no ghost; at least not by human standards.

For a moment Oziru and Kenjan simply looked into each other's eyes. Wave groaned weakly. No one seemed to notice or care. Oziru gently pushed Wave's arm aside and said, "My beloved, you have become a ghost. I bind you to this place and to your guardian until the currents cease to move the sea."

Kenjan opened its mouth, but didn't speak. It took in Wave and the ring of writing on the floor and finally Gaia. Then the Kishocha exploded with rage. It howled and thrashed and screamed out strings of unintelligible syllables. She thought she caught a few words, like "traitor" and "hate", but she couldn't be sure.

Keeping her back to the wall, Gaia sidled toward her bedroom door. This night had turned out so differently than she'd planned. She had expected a ceremony wherein a non-living ghost-concept would, in theory, be brought into Happy Snak. Gaia didn't believe in ghosts but had been comfortable with a ghost-concept as a religious metaphor. A ghost-concept was intangible. It did not howl.

"Silence!" Oziru's voice throbbed like a thunderclap. Gaia froze. The attendants stopped chanting. Kenjan stopped shouting.

Wave still mumbled to itself.

"Kenjan." Oziru's voice was barely audible now. "This

human is your guardian now. Take her blood and accept your mortality." Oziru held out the vial. Kenjan downed it like a shot of whiskey and hurled the vial at Seigata.

Seigata calmly sidestepped. The vial shattered against the wall.

"Kenjan—" Oziru began.

"I deny this companion." Kenjan jabbed a finger at Wave. "I will not take its flesh." Kenjan's muzzle contorted in a paroxysm of fury, but the alien said nothing more, just dived beneath the water and vanished.

Oziru sat like a statue. Two attendants dragged Wave back from the water's edge. One of them bent and wrapped the Kishocha's injured arm with a fleshy-looking bandage.

"Is it over?" Gaia asked.

"Be quiet!" Seigata said.

"No, she may speak." Oziru stood. "It is over. The ghost does not want this servant, and I cannot bear to look at it for it belonged to Kenjan. You may have it. It is called Wave."

Oziru left without another word. Seigata and the attendants trailed after it. The Kishocha door twisted shut. Gaia eyed the pool of water where the not-at-all-dead Kenjan lurked. Then she turned her attention to Wave.

She prodded the alien's uninjured arm with her toe. Wave didn't respond. In fact, the Kishocha seemed incapable of responding. Its pupils pulsed. Its jaw hung slack.

"Wave?" she said. Wave's muzzle twitched and it groaned out a word, "*Pofuham.*"

Gaia tried to look *pofuham* up in her electronic dictionary, but found no entry for that or for any other word Wave said. The alien was too strung out to communicate, even in its own language. The best Gaia could do was to wrap some bandages around its cuts and hope it sobered up.

Gaia shoved her hands under Wave's armpits and dragged the alien toward the human side door. The shell floor was still wet from the ceremony and she slid a couple of times. She set Wave down, and discovered that she couldn't open the door. Though clearly biomechanical and voice activated, Gaia couldn't figure out how to make it obey her.

She spent the next ten minutes prying, pulling and pounding at the door and surrounding wall. She looked up the Kishocha word for open in her dictionary. The door didn't respond to "open".

Gaia tried the entry that lead to the Kishocha side. Same story. Wave groaned. Gaia went back to the alien. Blood oozed out from its cuts. Gaia pulled off her Happy Snak smock and wrapped it around the alien's arm.

Her bra was held together by a safety pin but who, apart from Kenjan, was there to see it? She decided to call Fitzpatrick. But she found her phone had gone dead. Water had seeped into the cracked housing.

"Shit!" Gaia threw the phone down. It skittered into the water. "Goddamn it!"

Suddenly, the remains of the phone came flying out of the water, whizzed past her head and slammed into the wall behind her back.

Kenjan's head emerged from the pink water. Its tendrils twined over each other. Gaia trembled. She crossed her arms over her chest.

"I thought you were supposed to be dead." Gaia's voice shook.

"*Migiu*," Kenjan said. The door to her bedroom twisted open immediately.

"Thanks." She turned back to Kenjan, but the alien had gone.

Wave's skin felt clammier. Gaia hurried to drag Wave into her own bedroom.

"*Migiu*," she said to the door. Nothing happened. She looked up *migiu*. The dictionary read, *to dilate*. Inspired, Gaia looked up the word for contract, and said, "*Hidero*." The door twisted closed. Gaia sank down to her bed.

She had managed to get through a door with only minimal help. It was a small triumph, but she clung to it.

Gaia got her first-aid kit and mechanically plastered bandages around Wave's arm.

The Kishocha groaned, but didn't seem to see her. Gaia wrapped Wave in a couple of thermal blankets. As she stood, looking at the damaged, delirious alien, her legs suddenly buckled. She landed on her knees a few inches from Wave. Her hands shook. She was cold and wet.

What was she supposed to do now? The only thing she could think to do was wait. Maybe when Wave woke up, the alien could tell her what it needed.

A slight scratching sound made her jump nearly to the ceiling. She whirled and saw Microbe industriously digging at a piece of cardboard she'd put in his labyrinth specifically for him to industriously dig at. At least that plan had worked out.

Gaia watched Microbe working. She knew she wouldn't sleep. She reached under her bed and withdrew a stack of five hundred unfolded takeout boxes. One by one, she folded them all.

Chapter Seven:
Wave

Gaia's eyes itched. Somewhere between takeout box number two hundred fifty and three hundred, they'd dried out. Crooked stacks of folded boxes leaned over her bed like disintegrating columns of the Parthenon. Some toppled over. Gaia lost the ability to stack neatly at box number four hundred sixty-three. It was only five a.m. She'd have thought that folding them all would take longer. Wave had yet to regain consciousness.

Gaia rubbed her bare wrists. The medics had instructed her to wear her braces for another two weeks, but she'd tried to wean herself early. The fresh tendons and muscles were still weak and shaky. Sometimes she was struck by the irrational fear that her new hands would simply fall off.

Gaia was less upset than she had been a few hours before, but not because the situation had improved. Sleep deprivation had diminished her capacity to feel any strong emotion. A soothing bleak inevitability had settled over Gaia, narrowing her range of feeling, like the cool clouds compressed the sky over Seattle. She had a furious Kishocha living just outside her bedroom and another bleeding on her floor. But getting excited about either problem seemed pointless now. Gaia employed this method of mental limpness more often that she would have admitted to anyone.

She decided to order supplies. She wandered out of her bedroom to the food lockers in her store's back kitchen.

She slid open a refrigerated food locker and fell into the easy habit of dictating.

"Recording supply list—as of October ten, we have only one case of Clammi!, definitely need to stock up...also need a gallon of Orange number 17." Gaia closed food locker twelve and slid open the door to number thirteen.

"Order two more cases of churro mix... Need ketchup packets... Wet-naps are okay... There are fucking mushrooms growing in the bottom of this locker, goddammit!" Gaia crouched down to get a closer look at the fungi. The mushrooms were slender and long, with tiny blue caps. Gaia raised the hand-held to her lips again. "Get some industrial-strength fungicide."

The dull clatter of falling takeout boxes caught Gaia's attention. She rushed back to her bedroom. Wave was sitting up. The black spot over its eye gleamed like fresh paint.

Wave stared at her as though she was a completely unexpected thing. Wave asked, in English, if it was dead. Gaia replied that it was not.

Though still groggy, Wave brightened. "Do you speak English well?"

"Sure," Gaia replied.

"How lucky English is the only human language I know. My name is Wave Walker—like Jesus Christ, you know?"

"No."

"Jesus Christ walked on waves. I can do that too. My flippers are as big as your prophet's flippers were!" Wave held up its feet, spreading out the toes until the membranes between them pulled taut. As it shifted around to display its feet, the Kishocha winced, suddenly perceiving its injuries. It stared quizzically at the bandages. "Here is the source of my pain."

"How are you feeling?"

"Dry and not very well. And much surprise at living. How do you feel?"

"I'm okay. I'm Gaia Jones."

"You certainly are. I am happy to meet your radiant person. All of us Kishocha have heard of your bravery. We know that

Gaia Jones rules Happy Snak and has been chosen to be the guardian of the *kaijamfutan.*"

"I'm happy to meet you too." Gaia wondered if Wave was still too groggy to explain what was going on. All indicators showed Kenjan to be vibrantly alive, and yet no one at the ceremony seemed to find its resurrection surprising. "Do you remember anything from yesterday?"

"I remember little, except strange dreams of crashing water."

"Kenjan isn't dead," Gaia stated flatly.

Wave's face grew serious. "The esteemed Kenjan is a ghost now. It pains us all. I am only a servant, and I am so sad, but that does not change the ghost into alive again." Wave stared sadly at its bandaged arm. "Gaia Jones?"

"Just Gaia is fine."

"I am so sorry. Forgive me. I am ignorant and to blame. Please correct me whenever I am wrong." Wave flattened itself across the floor. Gaia recoiled from Wave's subservient display.

"It's okay. What were you going to say?"

"Why am I alive?" Wave cocked its head sideways.

For a moment, Gaia thought Wave was asking a philosophical question, which she had no idea how to even begin to answer. Then she realized that Wave was asking about yesterday's aborted sacrifice.

"So I guess you were going to be..." Gaia hesitated, searching for a nonconfrontational synonym for "killed".

"...a companion in death for the beautiful Kenjan's ghost," Wave supplied.

"Yes, and so Oziru was, well, cutting your arm."

"In order to lure the hungry ghost with flesh." Wave didn't seem displeased, which disturbed her.

"And Kenjan came bursting up out of the water and knocked the knife out of Oziru's hand. And then Kenjan screamed something I didn't understand and then Oziru said, 'Accept your place.' And Kenjan got really pissed off and dived under the water. Then Oziru told me to take you, and I brought you in here." Gaia took a breath. "So you see, Kenjan is definitely not a ghost. That one is right behind that door somewhere."

"The ghost rejected my company?"

"I don't think Kenjan is a ghost," Gaia said. Wave frowned.

"With all due respect, I must say the noble Gaia should stop insisting that the delightful Oziru am Kenjan is not a ghost. Your words make it harder for we who are bereaved. I personally attended Kenjan while it died. The breath stopped, the blood stopped. Then—"

"Yes?"

"The glorious Oziru lay over the capsule and wept tears of acid. When the breath of Kenjan stopped, Oziru howled with desolation, and before Seigata could intervene, the powerful but grief-stricken Oziru commanded Kenjan's spirit to return."

"So?" Gaia leaned closer to Wave.

"So, the gorgeous Kenjan arose as a *kaijamfutan* and is haunting Ki Island." Wave ended its story with one long sad look at the door.

"But Kenjan's breathing again, right?"

"Yes." Wave's shoulders drooped even lower. "Such was the power of lightning."

Gaia puzzled over this statement but didn't pursue it, tenaciously hanging on to the subject of Kenjan's bodily functions. "And Kenjan still eats right?"

"Even ghosts eat."

"That isn't what humans call a ghost," Gaia said, triumphantly.

"Really? What is it called?"

"It isn't called anything. You're still considered to be alive."

"Even after a human has been dead? It's still thought to be alive?"

"Yes."

"How many once-dead humans are there?"

"Not many, but there are a few. My brother's heart stopped once for about thirty seconds."

"Have you ever been dead?"

"Not to my knowledge." Gaia gazed at Wave. What was she supposed to do with this alien—correction: these aliens? Because now she had two, and that got her thinking. "Can I ask you a question now?"

"Certainly."

"What am I supposed to protect the so-called ghost from?"

"Criticism and exorcism." Wave adopted the same informative television presenter pose that it had in the video Fitzpatrick had shown her. "While alive, the ghost had many detractors and they may come to criticize it after death. Some of those same people, especially Scholar True Current, may call for exorcism, which is usually done with a holy spear or blackening poison and so you can see how it could be quite dangerous for the ghost."

Gaia wondered how it could have slipped everyone's mind to mention to her that fending off spear-wielding scholars might be part of her duties as a guardian. "Do you think that's likely to happen? The exorcism, I mean?"

Wave let go with a snuffly laugh. "No one would dare exorcise this ghost unless it started to act as though it was alive. Oziru would not allow them to live. But there will certainly be criticism."

"Is that also done with a holy spear?"

"No. Rocks, mostly. But a critic must have a fine throwing arm to get its opinion all the way across the moat, and scholars are not known for that, so the ghost should be all right."

And that was...good news?

"Powerful Gaia Jones?" Wave said. "May I please entreat you for some water?"

When Gaia brought water, Wave didn't drink. Instead it poured the liquid over its bandages and asked for more. Gaia accommodated Wave's repeated requests until, after a few minutes the thermal blankets were sopping wet. Then Wave asked if it could lie back down and sleep more.

Gaia resumed inventory of both her meat products and her general situation. Was there any way to get out of this? She'd been handed responsibility for two specific lives in the most complete possible way, and indirectly gained control of all human beings on A-Ki Station.

She couldn't believe that she'd let this stupid situation get so out of control. Why hadn't she asked more questions at the outset?

She didn't really care about Kenjan. How could she? She just cared about the new restaurant location she'd gotten saving the alien. Wave, on the other hand, elicited a sting of guilt. Gaia could already feel herself beginning to like the Kishocha.

If she understood this situation correctly, Wave had become her slave. She couldn't even think of such a relationship for more than a few seconds before a shudder of distaste rushed over her. Slavery was wrong. Treating living people like they were dead was wrong. Deliberately pouring water on your own bed was wrong. There was not much right about the Kishocha today.

But she knew that if she went through the motions of her duties as Kenjan's guardian and as Wave's owner, she'd grow used to them.

It would be prudent to evade attachment now.

If she left, where would Wave be? Would Fitzpatrick take responsibility for the alien's life? Would Wave then just become a pawn of the embassy? Or, worse, a trophy?

Gaia rested her forehead in her palms. She felt as though her brain had suddenly grown too heavy for her neck to support. The past few weeks had slid by without impediment, because Gaia had never stopped to think about anything. That kind of mental limpness worked for her when she was in the throes of crisis and confusion, but it was a hell of a way to live every day. She had to stop and decide, without rationalization or ambassadorial threats, whether she was going to keep going down this road or flee.

But she was so tired. It was six-thirty. In an hour Cheryl would be coming to help her with the set-up. In an executive decision, Gaia decided that she wasn't up to work today. She needed rest and quiet more than she needed help inventorying her wet-naps. She and Wave both needed a little time. After entering an apologetic message into the storefront display, Gaia turned all her communication devices to sleep mode then returned to her room, tiptoed around Wave and climbed onto her box-strewn bed.

Still, she did not sleep. Why had she let the Kishocha tattoo, cut, scrape and bruise her? Why did these things seem not only inevitable, but also correct? Why wasn't she angry?

Gaia didn't know if loneliness or curiosity drove her. Maybe it was just convenience. For the price of only a few hours of discomfort, she had gained connection and importance. The power came cheap, and yet Gaia felt so weak. She did not want to meet her new obligations, but knew she could never respect herself if she ran away. She just had to keep going.

So thinking, she passed out.

While she slept, Gaia's voice messages multiplied. By the time she woke, in the early afternoon, she had nearly half an hour of them. Both Blum and Fitzpatrick wanted to know how the Summoning had gone. Then a message from Roy who wanted every last detail of the ceremony, and a lone message from Cheryl asking if she was supposed to come to work today. Cheryl also remarked on Gaia's locked door and inquired if she was okay. Last, Gaia's mother excitedly reported seeing her on the WOW! Media Blast channel and commented that she looked pale and seemed mean.

Gaia drummed her fingers against her hand-held, sourly trying to deduce which messages she could ignore.

"Are you troubled, my master?" Wave asked.

Gaia jumped and knocked over another stack of boxes. Wave was awake and looking more refreshed than before.

"Please, just call me Gaia."

"Of course, I am deeply regretful to have caused need to correct me again." Once more Wave lay flat out on the floor.

"Please stop doing that too. Humans just don't prostrate themselves before others. Well, Americans don't, at least."

Wave shot bolt upright. "Is this pose correct?"

"Good enough." Gaia slouched forward, compensating for Wave's now excellent posture. "Look, Wave, I want to talk to you."

"And what a coincidence. I love to talk!" Wave folded its white hands and leaned far forward so that its muzzle was lower than Gaia's nose. Gaia decided to ignore this submissive posture. She could explain about groveling and related annoying topics later. "Can I ask what's troubling you now?"

"I've got a lot of messages to answer and—" Gaia broke off, looking at Wave. "I just can't figure out what I'm supposed to do with you."

"Anything you want. I am your servant."

"That's just so wrong."

"No, I am a good servant."

"That's not what I meant," Gaia said. "Anyway, what can you do? I mean, what do you usually do?"

"I am the Grand Experiment." Wave dropped its voice theatrically.

"And that is...?"

"I am the proof of Kenjan's wisdom. I was the lowly servant chosen by the exalted Kenjan to learn."

"Learn what?"

"Everything!" Wave opened its arms expansively. "I know many various things. The exalted Oziru am Kenjan taught me stories and philosophy and mathematics and English language. And I learned. And, as a result, that one's wisdom was proven. Even the wise Righteous Sea had to admit that I could learn."

"So you can learn." Gaia tried not to sound nonplused by this proclamation. She knew the point eluded her, but didn't feel up to pursuing it to its murky and dubious end.

"Yes! I can learn. I can learn to do anything for I am intelligent." Wave sang out this last part. "Any task I can comprehend. Tell me what to do and I will learn to do it. I am flexibility."

"Do you want to work for me?"

"I not only want to, Gaia Jones, but I must. For I am a good servant, and you are my new master."

"If you don't want to work for me, I'm sure I can get the embassy to get you a stipend," Gaia said.

Wave blinked at her in confusion.

"Money to help you live," Gaia clarified.

"Um... Money pieces...?" Wave looked even more perplexed. The alien cradled its bandaged arm.

"You don't have to be my servant."

"But"—Wave sagged—"why do you not want me? You are the master of a food-making place, is that right? I can make food. I told you I could learn."

"I do want you, but only if you actually want to work for me."

"What else would I do? Please, explain my duties and allow me to serve."

"Are you sure you're up to it?" Gaia asked. "I mean, you're hurt and...things."

Wave looked down at its hands. "Work and learning is sometimes a strong distraction from sorrow."

The Kishocha didn't really understand the concept of paid employment, Gaia realized. Kishocha castes being as rigid as they were, aliens were simply born into a profession. So she spent the rest of the day explaining what she expected of her new employee, beginning with using a human timepiece (Gaia's ex-husband's watch) and ending with the Kishocha's wages.

"I don't understand," Wave said apologetically. "You give me money pieces, but then what will I trade my money pieces for?"

"Whatever you want."

"I see." Wave's gaze wandered over the room. "So after this, where will I be allowed to sleep?"

"Where do you sleep now?"

"I used to sleep in Oziru am Kenjan's forechamber on an eel-skin sponge nest, but not anymore."

"So you don't have anywhere to stay?"

"I thought I would sleep on a floor, like I did just now." Wave gestured to the spot where she'd dragged the Kishocha's unconscious body the previous evening.

Gaia rejected the notion entirely. "You can't just lay on the floor in my bedroom."

"Can I lie under a table?"

"No."

Wave looked hurt. "Do I have to sleep in the shrine? It's spooky in there."

"We'll think of something." Gaia wondered where she could get a sponge nest, then realized she didn't even know what an eel-skin sponge nest was. Luckily the very same was delivered to Happy Snak in the early evening by Oziru's servants. The sponge nest was, literally, a nest. It was approximately six feet in diameter, with a red eel-skin exterior and an inner lining of soft yellow sponges. Along with the nest, the servants brought two green bowls and a transparent orb. The orb was about the size of Gaia's head and filled with squirming creatures that closely resembled baby snakes.

Wave once again fell to the floor, gushing effusive thanks to Oziru's servants. About halfway through Wave's speech, Gaia realized that the alien was thanking Oziru on her behalf. The items were for her, not Wave, in spite of the fact that she'd have no use for a sponge nest of any kind. It was then that Gaia began to get a feeling of the true separation of the Kishocha castes. She realized that Wave's status in the hierarchy was somewhere near Microbe's or a dog's. Oziru was, in effect, saying, "Here's Kenjan's ex-pet Wave, and here's its bed and bowl."

This was not a working environment Gaia felt comfortable promoting.

As soon as the other Kishocha left, Gaia turned to Wave. "Well, where are you going to put your stuff?" she inquired innocently, as though she had no ulterior motive.

"Oh, these are not mine. These are yours, to do with as you see fit."

"Mine? I thought they were yours. Isn't this the bed you used to sleep on?" Gaia scratched her head in mock confusion. "I don't really have any use for them. I guess I'll throw them in the garbage."

Wave's eyes widened, and the Kishocha's mouth dropped open. Wave looked so sad that Gaia was nearly deflected from her lesson in personal possessions.

"...garbage?" Wave whispered.

"Unless you want to buy them from me."

"Trade them for my money pieces?"

"Exactly."

"I don't have any money pieces yet," Wave said.

"But you will. So do you want me to save them until the end of the week when you have some money?"

Wave nodded.

"The question is: Where are you going to put it all?" Gaia suppressed a rush of guilt. This was a little cruel. "I happen to have a little supply room that you could rent from me for one dollar per month. Would you like to see it?"

"If you deem it proper and wise, then I don't need to see it."

"You're not even curious?"

"Slightly," Wave admitted, "but not because I question your judgment."

"Of course not." Gaia led Wave back through the kitchen. The supply room was adjacent to her bedroom and measured eight by ten feet. Because it was meant for storage it had a plain tiled floor with a drain in the center. One wall was Kishocha-made, so it emanated a constant heat, which would be advantageous to Wave. Gaia could tell the sponge nest was an inherently damp furnishing. The sponge nest took up about half the room and left a little space where Wave could keep its baby-snake orb.

Gaia gave Wave the room key, which prompted another long discussion about personal space and privacy. Wave asked if it had to keep the door closed, even when it was lonely, and Gaia assured the alien that solitude wasn't mandatory.

"The idea is that you have your own room, and I have mine, and we don't go into the other person's room without asking."

Wave experienced an epiphany. "Is it like we are playing

democracy?"

"What?"

"We're playing like we're equals. I love the game democracy. The lovely Kenjan and I used to play it all the time. The noble Oziru played one time, but that one did not like it at all. The noble Oziru stopped playing when the lovely Kenjan licked seductive Oziru's pit without begging permission. Then the game was over, and I had to go sit in the clam beds."

"Why?"

"It was the ineffable will of great Kenjan."

Gaia left the subject alone. They agreed on a price of one dollar for the bed, bowl and orb set. Once Wave's possessions were situated, Gaia gave Wave a hand-held which contained the A-Ki Station Food Service Workers Training Informational Interactive Seminar. She hoped the seminar would keep Wave quiet and busy for the rest of the evening. Then she started returning her messages.

Chapter Eight: The Unspeakable Hum of Machinery

By the time Gaia finished returning her calls, ghost-feeding time was nearly upon her. In anticipation of more thunderous splashing from Kenjan, Gaia kicked off her shoes and cuffed her pants.

She commanded the strange pucker of a door to dilate. Still and silent, the shrine seemed a completely serene place, its pink waters calm and glassy. Kenjan was nowhere in sight, neither under the water nor inside the shell grotto. Through the clear water, she could see submerged cave entrances on the island. Kenjan, she supposed, lurked in one of these. Gaia bent and gingerly touched the water's surface. Minuscule ripples rose around her fingers, only to expire in the water's impassive smoothness. Gaia watched these waves disperse, their warped, broken reflections reassembling into still wholeness. Silence pressed in around her.

Beneath the water, Gaia glimpsed a frond of black and white striped sea-grasses waving in the torpid current. Kishocha plants had colonized the walls with amazing speed. Already thin grasses and tiny, vibrant polyps had anchored themselves sporadically along the wall.

Gaia crouched above the water in mesmerized relief. Kenjan was hiding from her. Good. If the alien hid from her, there was nothing she could do—nothing she had to be responsible for. Her attention turned to the aquatic plants shimmering beneath the surface. She'd thought they were quite far away, but actually the ringed fronds were very close, just larger than she'd thought. She peered harder down into the water, then leapt backward, involuntarily shrieking in alarm. From just a foot beneath the surface, Kenjan's purple eyes glinted up at her. The black and white fronds were Kenjan's cranial tendrils. Kenjan leaned against the mottled wall, drifting amongst the gnarled protrusions of sponges and crustaceans. Gaia's heart thudded. The alien had been there the whole time. She'd just been unable to see it.

Camouflage really worked.

Gaia crept back to the water's edge. Kenjan remained motionless and staring. Then slowly it raised one long black hand. Kenjan's fingers broke the surface, beckoning her closer. She retreated. Kenjan's hand waved at her again, then curled its fingers into the "okay" sign. She took a steadying breath. She was going to have to meet Kenjan sometime, it might as well be now. She crouched down by the water's edge.

Kenjan rose up until its head broke the surface. "You must be my guardian." Kenjan's accent was less pronounced than Wave's. "Can you tell me your name again, please?"

Gaia relaxed a little. The alien didn't seem angry or bloodthirsty. It wasn't steaming. "Gaia Jones. I'm the owner of Happy Snak."

"What is Happy Snak?"

"I sell food and beverages."

"I see!" A glimmer of comprehension lit Kenjan's violet eyes. "You are a cooking person."

"Yes."

"And I chose you to be my guardian? I wonder why?" Kenjan cocked its head to one side, regarding her.

"I think it's because I was the only person available."

"Perhaps, but you behaved quite heroically nonetheless. My beloved Oziru provided me with a visual log of your actions. I do not remember much from the day of my death—only the feeling of dying."

"It was probably traumatic."

"It was." Kenjan floated slightly away. "But exciting. I

always wondered what it would be like to die."

"Yeah? And?" Gaia watched the gently lapping water. She wondered if all Kishocha were this candid or if Kenjan could be considered quirky.

"When death comes for you, you will know the secret."

Definitely on the quirky axis, Gaia thought. Aloud, she said, "If you don't mind me asking, do you know how you died?"

"I provoked the god by blasphemy and I was struck down."

"How were you struck down?"

"You were there, you should remember." Kenjan scowled. "My punishment had been foretold, but my arrogance was so great that I could not hear any warning. But then, that is the nature of the true heretic, yes? Even now, I feel I was right."

This was not the answer she had expected. More than that, it was not the answer she needed in order to understand how to keep Kenjan healthy and well, as was now her duty. She decided to try another tactic.

"To me you looked like you were having an allergic reaction. It looked like the pictures of Kishocha being allergic to bleach on that First Aid Media disc I got."

"Except that I was not doused with bleach."

"There are a lot of things the Kishocha can't tolerate, and you were in the human sector," Gaia continued reasonably.

"Gaia Jones, did it never enter your mind that to be rendered poisoned by things which have no effect on others is to be punished by the god?"

"I always look for an explanation that excludes gods."

The Kishocha rolled around in the water. Pinkish ripples sloshed over Gaia's feet. "I suppose you would say that being struck by lightning is just a mistake."

"Yes, I would."

"Then you don't think it's sacrilegious to carry a message to my beloved?"

"Not sacrilegious, but as far as I understand your situation, if you keep trying to act like you're alive they're going to exorcise you. What's that mean? Kill you for real?"

"You would look at it that way. After being exorcised, I wouldn't be able to talk anymore, and my body would rot and be eaten by cleaners. That's what humans call dead, yes? To be rotten and rejoin the structure?"

"Yeah, pretty much." Gaia wrung out her sodden cuffs. "Though I'm not sure about returning to the structure."

"When Kishocha rot, it rejoins the structure as filth through the mouths of the cleaners. Then maybe its soul is reborn. That's the reason I know for certain I was obscene. I was not allowed to be reborn at that time. Truthfully, I don't know if I'll ever be reborn."

"What if you're not?"

"Then I'll never love my Oziru again. Not even as a cleaner, eating my beloved's shit."

"Thank you for putting that image into my head."

"That's the lot of the heretic. I knew my fate would be crushing, but the pull of my obscenity was too strong." Kenjan smoothed its cranial tendrils down. "But enough of myself. Tell me of you, who I will now swim beside forever."

Gaia would have preferred to avoid ruminating over the fact that she had entered into what the Kishocha believed to be a lifelong pact. Still, this was going better than expected. No angry raving, and Kenjan's manner remained elegant and its speech considerate. Kenjan paused thoughtfully while it contemplated her.

"Since we will be having a long relationship. We should begin with courting questions. Tell me about your pog state."

Gaia blinked. "...pog state?"

"When you were smaller. Did you have pog siblings, or were you alone in the birthing pool. I'm sorry, I meant to say did you have any company in your mother's vaginal area?"

Gaia wished she had thought ahead enough to record this conversation. Fitzpatrick, she suspected, would have been interested. "I have one brother. He's a lot younger than me. What about you?"

"I have several siblings," Kenjan said. "But the only one on Ki Island is Seigata."

“I met Seigata a couple of times.”

“And what opinion did you form of that one?”

“We didn’t really connect.” She didn’t think that mentioning the way Seigata radiated contempt would facilitate effective interaction at this juncture.

“No, you would not. Seigata believes that humans are beneath us in holiness.”

So Kenjan already knew about the contempt. No point in beating around the bush, then. “Do you also think humans are beneath Kishocha?”

“A hard question.” Kenjan languorously pushed off the wall and swam a little, moving and turning in the water. “I think that humans are children of a different god than Kishocha. And the gods can fight about which of them is most holy in their heavenly abode. The thought should not concern you and me.”

Gaia glanced at the Kishocha-side door. She supposed she should open it soon and let the other Kishocha bring their offerings.

“We should not ask these theological questions of each other. For myself, I do not care where humans stand in the hierarchy of holiness. I only care about knowing my guardian.” Kenjan floated close. “Are you beloved consort to anyone?”

“Not anymore.”

“Then you are left alone, bereft by death like my Oziru.” Kenjan cast its eyes down. “I am so sorry.”

“I’m not a widow, I’m just divorced.”

“I do not know the word.”

“My beloved isn’t dead,” Gaia explained. “He just isn’t my beloved anymore.”

“You cast the beloved aside?” Kenjan’s eyes widened. “How strange.”

“We both decided we didn’t have much of a future together.”

“Like soldiers meeting in a tryst before battle.” Kenjan’s low, smooth voice rumbled across the water. Its cranial tendrils caressed the water’s surface. “The moment is ephemeral as clouds passing over the moon. Then the meeting is over and you are left with sticky memories."

"Something like that." Gaia nodded her agreement, although she recalled being left with a lot more angry memories than sticky ones. Sometimes getting to know another person intimately wasn't a good thing. Some people's secret inner beauty is massively overwhelmed by secret inner ugliness.

"This situation must be very strange for you."

"Unbelievably strange." Gaia glanced at the Kishocha door. "But, in a way, not that different. I'm supposed to make sure you get food, right? It's just the same as my other job, really. You must be hungry."

"I admit that I am."

"Then we should get this show on the road. How does it work? Do I go open up that door now, and people bring you food?"

"That is what might happen." Kenjan sighed heavily. "Or there might be no one there, and I may go hungry. But in that case, I will implore you for chicken satay."

"How do you know I've got chicken satay?" She stood, crossed to the door and opened it. As Kenjan had feared, the dim hallway and lazy pink canal were empty.

"I've smelled the delicious sauce. It is so wrong of me to eat bird, but I adore it. The Kishocha believe that to eat a bird is to consume the spirit and to gain the wonderful and terrible power of flight. So only Oziru may eat flying things."

"But you've eaten chicken."

"I have. It was wrong of me," Kenjan conceded. "But I had to know if I could fly." Gaia noted that although Kenjan tried to project the appearance of guilt, it seemed satisfied with its wrongdoing.

"Did it work?" She doubted that it did, but then again, these were aliens.

"No." Kenjan sighed dramatically. "But I heard that some humans fly by psychic power. I heard it on the television machine."

"You heard wrong. Humans don't fly. And they especially

don't fly by psychic power. The only way humans fly is by using flying machines like airplanes and hang gliders and stratolifts and things like that."

"I investigated these objects," Kenjan said. "At first I thought that humans could control gravity, but they only manipulate the currents in the great ocean of air. Human machines are glorious, and yet they hum unspeakably."

"So, you're into flying machines, huh?" Gaia asked. Kenjan was, and began recounting in detail the history of its love affair with the mechanisms of human flight. Of these, the helicopter was Kenjan's favorite because it resembled an insect.

Occasionally, Gaia glanced at the door. No Kishocha darkened the threshold. She started to feel bad. It was like throwing a party and having no one arrive.

After an hour, Gaia's attention began to flag. Sensing her weariness, Kenjan wound its commentary on military-attack helicopters to a close.

"You seem very tired now," Kenjan asked. "Have I filled you with boredom?"

"No, it's just past the time I usually go to bed." Her gaze drifted toward the empty door. She wondered if the shrine's hours of operation were rigidly set in Kishocha scripture or if she was allowed to close early, for lack of business.

"Then perhaps, my beloved guardian, it is time to close the door and sleep. I expected to see no one tonight. It is too soon. Just a double order of chicken satay with extra toast and cucumbers will satisfy me."

"The cucumbers haven't been delivered yet," Gaia said. "But I have some dill pickles. Do you want one of those?"

Kenjan slid back into the water, leaning its head back to submerge its cranial tendrils, which had gone dormant as they dried. "Whatever would please you most, my dear protector. I will simply await your return and listen in anticipation to the hum of snack-making machinery."

Chapter Nine: Feeding People

Every employee's first day on the job is rough, but Wave's was rockier than most. The day started off with a volley of sirens and flashing lights set off by a short gravity failure. Gaia was startled awake by the noise only to find herself floating six inches above her bed. A couple of seconds later the gravity returned and she plopped back down onto her sheets, stunned.

A rude awakening indeed.

Ruder still to find compostable cutlery, straws and other light objects that hadn't been tied down strewn around the Happy Snak dining room. Gaia and Wave started early, first straightening up, then addressing the mundane details of food service.

Wave's first real problem was the Second Skin Plasticized Hygiene Dip, which conformed beautifully to Gaia's hands and peeled off easily, but adhered to Wave's more porous skin like glue and had to be removed by a reproachful Kishocha doctor. After rubber gloves were located for Wave, the alien's orientation resumed. An inherently fast learner, Wave mastered the cold-drinks machine in no time.

Gaia let the alien investigate the food-storage lockers, reading the boxes and getting acquainted with the words, while she continued counting inventory. After only five minutes, Wave had a question.

"What is this liquid?" Wave held up a jug. "The label says

Orange number 17."

"It's orange dye."

"Is it to drink?"

"No, it colors the food. I use it in the sweet and sour sauce to make it more interesting."

"Is it orange fruit flavor?" Wave asked.

"It doesn't have any flavor," Gaia replied.

"But it smells delightful!" Wave unscrewed the top and took a huge whiff of the dye. Gaia walked over and sniffed the jug.

"I don't smell anything." Gaia frowned at the bottle.

"Please, wise and noble Gaia, may I please drink some orange?" Wave clutched the plastic jug.

"I guess..." Gaia poured a tiny bit into a plastic cup. She handed it to Wave who greedily gulped down the contents. Wave's eyes slowly closed, its muzzle wrinkled, its cranial tendrils quivered. Then the Kishocha opened its left eye, followed by its right. Wave's lips were stained vibrant red-orange.

"Beautiful taste, color of golden sun! Flavor of all heavenly delight!" Wave blurted excitedly. "More orange please, I beg you. Oh, orange... Orange! Even the name is delightful."

Gaia cautiously poured Wave a little more orange dye. Again Wave threw it back like a shot of whiskey. The Kishocha's cranial tendrils stiffened until they resembled rubber snakes, then dangled, gently vibrating. Gaia worried that she might have poisoned Wave, but the alien didn't keel over.

"Oh mighty orange, hear my love!" Wave cried, then began to sing in Kishocha. Quietly, Gaia put the orange dye away in her room. When Wave finished singing twenty minutes later, Gaia was stocking ketchup packets and individually wrapped midget dills. "Gaia, where is the orange?"

"I'm cutting you off."

"Excuse me?"

"I don't think you should drink too much orange in one day." Gaia crammed the last midget dill into its dispenser.

"No?" Wave asked.

"No." Gaia pressed a note of grim firmness into her voice.

"Will I get some tomorrow?" Wave clutched its empty orange cup.

"Maybe after the store's closed."

"Then I will cheerfully begin my duties, knowing that orange awaits me."

Gaia waited until she heard Wave flop across the dining room before she removed the hand-held.

"Order a couple more gallons of Orange number 17," she whispered, then pushed the send icon. It was almost time for Roy and Cheryl to arrive. She wondered how they would react to Happy Snak's newest employee.

Roy couldn't stop grinning. He sat to Gaia's left. Wave slouched shyly to her right, and Cheryl faced Gaia across the slick yellow expanse of tabletop. Bright, cheerful "sun-lite brand" lighting fixtures suffused the dining room of Happy Snak with a warm morning glow. Beneath their feet, white and yellow floor tiles gleamed in unscuffed glory. Everything was new. The butter-yellow paint still emanated a slight wet smell. Above the counter, three new menu-board screens displayed her carefully planned list of available snacks. In the old Happy Snak, she'd settled for a handwritten sign. Now full-color moving pictures and dazzling graphics blazed over her front-counter area like a perpetual fireworks display. Near the front doors, Gaia's narrow bank of video games flashed exciting silent images. Gaia had turned the sound off for the employee meeting.

She'd realized the necessity of an orientation, now that she had employees, but hadn't fully planned for the disruptive quality of an alien. Neither Roy nor Cheryl listened as she described the override mechanism for the register. They sat, enraptured with the novelty of Wave.

Roy took a breath, beaming, and blurted out, "You are just so cool!" Cheryl rolled her eyes.

Wave slouched harder. "I am sure I am not. I am the average temperature."

"You're so great! I love you," Roy burbled.

"Calm down, Roy. I think you're scaring it," Cheryl said. Then, suddenly realizing that Wave spoke English, she added hastily, "Not that you can't speak for yourself, right?"

Wave scrunched down harder, its chin only inches from the yellow tabletop. The Kishocha's long cranial tendrils curled in front of its eyes and muzzle. "I am shy."

"Oh God," Roy gasped. "It's adorable."

Gaia looked down at her tattoos, embarrassed by Roy's unabashed awe and adulation. Whenever she felt any truly strong attraction she couldn't look at the object of her admiration. She'd once had the opportunity to meet one of her favorite game designers, the woman responsible for Wreck Diver and Subconscious. When it had come time to say hello, Gaia had suddenly turned away, pretending that she hadn't been waiting at all. Naked veneration undid her.

She'd just have to bag the employee meeting. No one was going to learn any error codes today.

"Listen," Gaia said. "Maybe we should go over register codes another time."

"Huh?" Roy didn't look at her. His enraptured gaze locked on Wave. The alien. The Kishocha. Gaia's failed strategy for the meeting had been to treat Wave as just another member of the crew.

"Yeah." Cheryl's expression was especially perky. "Let's just get to know each other today. I'm sure there are a lot of challenges ahead and we have to get a ground-floor understanding of each other first."

"What?" Gaia looked at Cheryl's tightly laced fingers. Wave peeled a cranial tendril away from its eyes.

"I'm sure we've all got different cultural values, and a little conflict is inevitable. But the more we know about one another, the more we can respect each other's individual and cultural diversity," Cheryl said. Gaia hadn't realized Cheryl was capable of speaking embassy-dialect English.

"I can't believe you're an alien," Roy mumbled in hushed awe. "From another, entirely different planet."

"I am from another galaxy," Wave said.

"It just gets better." Roy grabbed his head as though trying to prevent his skull from popping open from mind-blowing delight. Cheryl smiled so hard Gaia thought her face would crack.

"So," Gaia said, "what's your home world like?"

"Wet." Wave's voice was barely audible.

"What else?" Roy clutched the edge of the table.

"Purple." Wave's voice hadn't gained any strength.

"Is the sky purple?" Roy asked.

"The sky is blue," Wave said. "It contains oxygen."

"So, what part of it is purple?"

"Excuse me, but are you going to eat me, Roy?" Wave asked.

Roy dissolved into little giggles. Cheryl looked horrified.

"Roy isn't going to eat you, Wave, don't worry!" Cheryl's knuckles whitened. "What made you think that?"

Wave said, "Roy stares and snuffles like a predatory thing."

Gaia and Cheryl turned their attention to Roy. If there were a less predatory man on or off Earth, Gaia would have liked to meet him. Cheryl snorted in quiet laughter, also contemplating Roy's predatory qualities.

"Roy isn't going to eat you," Gaia said.

"How can you be sure?" Wave peeled a couple more cranial tendrils off its muzzle.

"For one thing, Roy's a vegan." Cheryl's hands had relaxed. She rifled through her pockets, eventually producing a pack of cigarette gum.

"That means he doesn't eat meat, or anything that came from an animal," Gaia clarified.

Wave suddenly bolted upright, apparently alarmed by this. "You eat clams, right, Roy?"

Roy tried to compose himself, failed and managed a weak and giggly, "No."

"Are you being punished?"

Roy shook his head and then it was Wave's turn to lean

forward. Gaia took this to be a good sign. She noted Wave's cranial tendrils, easily the most expressive part of the Kishocha. The very tips of Wave's tendrils curled and uncurled very slowly in a way that Gaia interpreted as a combination of wariness and curiosity.

"You must be very powerful spiritually," Wave said. "To resist the lure of clam every day."

A smile twitched at the edge of Roy's mouth, but he suppressed it. "It's hard sometimes, but I make it, with Cheryl by my side."

A thought seemed to strike Cheryl. "Are you single, Wave?"

"No, there were many in my birthing pool."

Cheryl tried again. "What I meant was, is there someone you're in love with?"

"I'm not sure the Kishocha pair off like we do," Roy said.

"Never without permission!" Wave said. "I am not a sneaky."

Gaia stepped in. "I think Cheryl was just asking because she and Roy are married, and she wondered if you were married."

"Married?" Wave tilted its head quizzically.

"Like Kenjan and Oziru," Gaia said.

Wave's cranial tendrils stood straight out from its head.

"Cheryl is like Oziru?" Wave slid away from Cheryl, lowering its head again. "Forgive me, I did not understand your superiority."

"No, Cheryl isn't like Oziru," Gaia said. "However, like Oziru and Kenjan, Roy and Cheryl are in love and live together. They live next door in the back of the Peace Corps office."

"And to show frenzied devotion, you and Roy do the sex often?" Wave asked.

"Not as often as you would think." Cheryl snorted.

"Hey!" Roy sat up straight. "I had to brush up on my Kishocha."

"Whatever, baby," Cheryl said. Gaia decided that she absolutely didn't want to know how often Roy and Cheryl had sex, and took evasive conversational action.

"Wave, is there anyone who needs to know where you are?" Gaia felt a little embarrassed at not wondering, until now, if Wave had friends who were worrying after it.

"No. The ghost knows that I am here to help take care of it. And I am not permanently paired with any person, except with the ghost. I wish I could tell the ghost about my new and exciting position at Happy Snak. Kenjan always said that I was most adaptable to learning things, and look! Now I am learning how to override the cash register." Wave turned to Gaia. "Code key F2, void key, 32543, code key F3."

Gaia burst out laughing. "That's great, I can't believe you remembered that."

"Not only that," Wave announced smugly. "Frymaster override: clear, clear, reset. Sanitization unit override: manager 123 clear. Kwickthaw override: Pull out the plug and plug it back in again. I am the master of the machines. I know their secret-code ways. All machines must do as I say and bow before me. Worthless, asymmetrical things, they will have none of my clams!" Wave drew itself up to its full height and crossed its arms.

Roy emitted a soft snicker. "I just love this guy."

During the week before grand opening, Roy managed to get over being starstruck by Wave. As the two learned the intricacies of Happy Snak, they formed an amicable relationship. Cheryl started off a little stiff and formal toward Wave, but eventually she also relaxed. Gaia was glad. She just wanted the grand-opening party to go smoothly.

The day of the opening, the four of them finished preparations early enough to get a head start on drinks. Gaia guiltlessly broke into one of the cases of beer Blum's office had sent over. Cheryl twisted the top off her beer with one hand, deftly unwrapping a stick of Nico-Nico cigarette gum with her other. Gaia slid a cup of Orange on Ice to Wave, who declined the beer on the grounds that it smelled like pee.

Cheryl took a long appraising look at her husband, much

like the one Gaia herself had given Roy when he arrived earlier that day. He was shirtless, which Gaia was pretty sure was a violation of health department regulations. Roy also sported an enormous shell choker and a boa-like swag of fresh, moist kelp. Where had he gotten it?

"Roy," Cheryl said, "do you feel like a tool? Because, baby, you look like a tool."

Gaia internally flinched at her scathing tone, but Roy only laughed. "I may look like a tool to you, but you'll be the one feeling underdressed once the welcome party gets under way. Isn't that right, Wave?"

Wave looked startled at being abruptly yanked into the conversation. Then the alien smiled hugely, showing all of its teeth, now stained bright orange.

"I'm sorry. I do not know what tool Cheryl thinks you look like, Roy, so I cannot say."

Cheryl snorted. Roy smiled indulgently at Wave.

"Okay, so here's the plan," Gaia said. "Everything's on the house tonight. The opening ceremony starts at six, but we have to make absolutely sure that these freeloaders are out of here by ten o'clock so I can go feed Kenjan, okay?"

Roy and Cheryl nodded their agreement.

Wave asked, "What's on the house?"

"Complimentary," Gaia clarified. "Do you know what that means?"

Wave nodded seriously. "We tell all the people that they are so beautiful—even if they are ugly."

Cheryl choked back a laugh. Roy clapped her on the back.

"Not quite," Gaia said. "It means that everything is free today."

"We don't ask for money pieces?" Wave looked appalled. "But the handbook says that we must always take the money pieces before presenting the product to our honored guests."

"Yes, normally that's true," Gaia said. "But tonight we are giving everyone samples."

"Samples?"

“Like presents,” Roy said.

“But the handbook says that we can’t give anything away, not even an empty cup which costs us ten money pieces to buy. It constitutes loss.”

“You truly are an excellent example of a budding capitalist,” Cheryl remarked, with some disdain.

“Thank you, but the capitalism game is easy, so I can’t be too inflated.” Wave dismissed Cheryl’s backhanded compliment with a shrug.

Gaia chose to ignore the other woman’s lack of love for free enterprise. She had her hands full with the aliens. “See, Wave, most people who are coming tonight, especially the Kishocha, haven’t ever tried our product, so we give them a taste for free. They like it and want more, but we won’t give them more unless they have money, and then we have business, and then I can take the money and give some of it to you for your pay, and you can buy orange. Do you understand?”

“We are luring them with our treasures?”

“Something like that,” Gaia said.

Wave looked down into its orange glass. “But the Kishocha guests won’t ever be able to come back because they don’t have any money pieces.”

“Maybe not money like ours, but they’ve got to have something,” Gaia asserted.

Cheryl said, “I hate to break it to you, but they don’t have anything. They’re a cashless society.”

“Are you sure?” Gaia looked for confirmation to the alien, who nodded and slurped more orange. Irritation ground through her stomach. This was a major glitch in her plan to dominate the Kishocha market. “Well, that’s a problem.”

“Only if you want to attract them as customers.” Roy spoke as if this would be the last thing on any right-thinking person’s mind.

Gaia had to nip this anti-business sentiment in the bud. “Why wouldn’t I want to attract them as customers? They’re a vast untapped market. I own a snack bar. What’s wrong with that?”

"Nothing. Nothing at all." Roy backpedaled, seeming to realize he'd insulted her pride. "All I'm asking is do you even have anything that the aliens would want? So far they haven't wanted to trade anything with anyone. Not technology, not personal histories, nothing."

Gaia allowed herself a smug, victorious smile. "I've got orange. They'll want that."

Wave perked up at the mention of the dye. "Speaking of orange, may I have another orange?"

"Are you sure you want to do that? You're getting pretty wired." Cheryl asked.

"I am super okay to working at the party." Wave gave Cheryl the thumbs-up. "Please, another orange."

"I'll get it." Roy departed to freshen Wave's drink. Cheryl watched him go, silently shaking her head. Gaia wondered about the two of them. Certainly the strain of living on the space station with absolutely nothing to do would wear on their relationship. Any relationship really. There was always a give and take between everyone. Even the humans and the Kishocha.

Or maybe not. Fitzpatrick had called humans "Kenjan's sea monkeys".

Well, maybe she had the opportunity to take their relationship beyond that of pet and curious owner. And even though it might be solely based on trading goods, was that so bad? Commerce had worked for human cultures for centuries. She might as well at least try it with the Kishocha. "Your people must have something to trade, Wave. What about shells?"

The Kishocha seemed aghast, but then its expression cleared. "Shells are sacred things. They cannot be worn by any but priests."

"But then what are those things I saw around the necks of the Kishocha who built the shrine?" Gaia asked.

"What things?" Wave inserted its long tongue into its paper cup to capture the last drops of orange that remained.

"Those little gray round things on a string. Some Kishocha would have a couple, others had fifty of them."

"Those are not shells." Wave snuffled into its cup. "Those are gambling pieces. Say, do you think Kishocha could trade gambling pieces for orange?"

"That's what I was thinking."

"So that you can have fun gambling with us?"

"No, I just think they're neat looking and exotic, and humans might want to wear them as jewelry," Gaia said.

"Gambling pieces are not precious," Wave warned.

"Well," Cheryl said, "maybe not to you, but there's nothing like them on Earth. So on Earth they're valuable."

"The law of supply and demand! Scarcity equals expense, yes?" Wave leaned forward, expecting praise.

"You play this capitalism game well," Gaia said.

"I play 'working' well too," Wave said. "Cheryl plays it better than me though. You must love to work, Cheryl."

"Not usually. You know, when I joined the Peace Corps, I thought I was through working in restaurants. I promised myself I'd never come home smelling like a french fry again." She made the remark in the same dry, dismissive tone she used on Roy.

"It's not like I'm forcing you," Gaia said. The comment irked her. Making fries and other fatty, salty snacks was Gaia's vocation—her passion, even. And she wasn't married to Cheryl. She didn't have to put up with her challenging personality.

"No, that came out wrong," Cheryl backpedaled, "I'm saying that you just never know where your life's going to go. I mean, my husband's wearing fucking kelp, and I'm actually really glad to be working at Happy Snak."

Roy returned with Wave's drink. He and Cheryl exchanged a warm smile that undermined Gaia's initial assessment of their relationship. Clearly, they liked each other.

"Certainly," Wave said. "One day I am cleaning fungus from the beautiful Kenjan's flippers and playing democracy and begging for clams and apologizing for Kenjan's heresy and then I think I'm dead, but then I'm drinking orange and being in the real democracy. There are no clams here."

Gaia and Cheryl only blinked. Happily, Roy kept the

conversational ball in play with an eloquent, "What are you talking about?"

Wave sighed heavily. "Because the human sector is dry, clams do not grow here, and I miss them. I am not ungrateful, but when we are in a democracy, I can say that I miss clams. I really do."

"I think Roy was talking about the heresy part," Cheryl said.

"Oh," Wave brightened. "Such happy days! Since I was Kenjan's servant, it was my duty to carry Kenjan's excuses and apologies and rationalizations to the divine Oziru and the noble Seigata. Kenjan was always committing heresy. Every day Kenjan had to apologize. The divine Oziru was always soft to Kenjan because Kenjan was so beautiful, but eventually the god endured enough impudence and struck lovely Kenjan dead."

"How did God do that?" Cheryl folded another piece of cigarette gum into her mouth. Roy looked slightly pained at her action.

"By killing Kenjan, of course." Wave stared down into its glass again. "At first I was so worried that the god would strike me dead too. But then I remembered that a faithful servant follows its master into the burning dry desert, so I'm okay."

Roy's watch alarm chose that moment to beep.

"It's five thirty," he said. "Blum will be here any second."

As if she'd been waiting for her name to be mentioned, Blum appeared, rapping authoritatively on the gate. Even in a cocktail dress and heels, Blum managed to look stiff and businesslike. Several minions cringed behind her, awaiting her commands.

"I hope everyone is ready," Blum said. "It's showtime."

Chapter Ten: Grand Opening

Fitzpatrick arrived one minute after Blum.

"I'm so sorry I'm late." Like Roy, Fitzpatrick wore a faux pit guard, but his was eighteen karat gold.

Gaia could not help but comment. "Nice necklace."

"I've taken the liberty of acquiring one for you." Fitzpatrick drew the jewelry out of his pocket. It was made of four strands of blue plastic beads. The brooch that hung down from it was a large white plastic triangle embossed with a smiling Mickey Mouse head.

"You've got to be joking," Gaia said.

"I thought you liked animals. Don't you have a pet rat?"

"Hamster."

"Some rodent, anyway." Fitzpatrick waved the difference aside. "I hope you're not too sickened by them. They're the best I could do in twenty minutes. I brought two more for the PCVs but I see they came prepared."

Gaia glanced back to see Cheryl fastening a shell choker. It matched Roy's. Wave watched Cheryl with obvious envy.

"Actually, I do need one more," Gaia said. Fitzpatrick tossed her another necklace, which sported Donald Duck's grinning visage.

Gaia caught Wave as the alien was slinking to the cold-drinks station. "Here you go, Wave. I'm sorry it's so goddamn ugly."

As Wave took the necklace, its cranial tendrils stiffened.

"For me to wear?"

Gaia shrugged. "I guess this is a formal occasion."

"But servants aren't allowed," Wave said.

"You're playing democracy now."

"But to wear it in front of the divine Oziru and the blessed Seigata... It's heresy."

"Not if I tell you to. And for the record, I'm telling you to."

Wave bounced with repressed mania. "Then I must follow you even to the dry and scorching desert." Wave ran its fingers over the bas-relief Donald Duck. "So beautiful! I am in heaven!"

"Good."

"Ms. Jones," Fitzpatrick called. "Can you please assist me?"

As Gaia turned, she pulled out her hand-held.

"Look into getting a box of these cheap pendants." Gaia watched as Wave fondled Donald Duck's beak. "And order some clams."

The grand opening was not a party Gaia would have chosen to attend, but the embassy was footing the bill. It was loud—and not in the controlled, lunch-rush way Gaia enjoyed. The dining room was choked with people in formalwear, looking inappropriate among yellow plastic chairs.

The diplomatic team chatted with the corporates, who ushered along choice scientists, as well as their spouses and lab assistants. Gaia overheard hushed conjecture about the recent string of gravity fluctuations. Reporters trolled the fringe. Space Corps uniforms were divided into two groups. Fancy dress uniforms laughed with the corporates while lowly gray uniforms patrolled the periphery. Eager for free booze and a chance to mingle above their station, the maintenance crew and dock techs snaked through the crowd, heading inexorably toward the front counter.

In its capacity as Kenjan's silent servant, Wave had already met some of the people at the party. Now Wave had risen to superstardom. Reporters questioned the Kishocha. Corporates reintroduced themselves. Wave lasted ten minutes before it got scared and asked to go hide in its room. The guests reluctantly let Wave retreat, but only in anticipation of Oziru's arrival.

As Wave slunk away, three servant-class Kishocha came through Gaia's bedroom door. Each carried a massive spiraling horn. They rounded the front counter without preamble. They didn't acknowledge the humans around them, not even when one spilled shiraz on its feet. The humans quieted at the sight of them. Most had never been so close to an alien.

Gaia moved away. She'd already been too close.

With no visible sign between them, the Kishocha blew into their horns. Tooth-chatteringly deep notes blasted out, displacing all other sound in the room.

A column of Kishocha soldiers marched through the kitchen and into the dining room.

The crowd shrank back from them. Blum and Fitzpatrick stepped forward. Gaia wound through the back of the crowd to find her place between them.

Gaia stood facing a guard whose neck was wound with a dozen strings of gambling pieces. The silver-gray beads were intricately carved. Some depicted animal or plant forms. Others were carved into latticed shapes. The guard noticed Gaia's interest. For a moment, their eyes met before Gaia looked shyly away.

The low reverberation of horns continued as Oziru entered. Two servants walked before the alien. The first poured water out of jug-sized conch shells, and the second laid fronds of kelp. Oziru followed, wearing its robe of red and black pearls. Seigata walked behind Oziru, carrying an oblong box. Water sloshed over the lip as Seigata walked.

When Oziru reached Blum, the horn players stopped.

"Welcome, Oziru," Blum said.

"I come to bestow my blessing on this place." Oziru reached into the box and removed six fist-sized shells. The Kishocha laid these out in a line at Gaia's feet. The alien dangled one of its tendrils in the box. Oziru closed its eyes. Reddish slime oozed out from the tendril and floated over the top of the water like oil. Then Oziru upended the entire box of water. It sloshed forward across the shells and across Gaia's dress shoes.

"Awake," Oziru commanded.

From each of the shells, thin tentacles emerged. The creatures were like a cross between snails and sea anemones. Some tendrils reached as far as a foot. The snails began to crawl, each taking a separate, random path across the floor or up the wall. There was a puddle in the middle of the floor now. Gaia watched the slimy path of her new inhabitants warily, wondering what the health department was going to say about them. Nothing good.

"May your house grow as these cleaners grow." Oziru shook her hand.

Polite applause followed, though Gaia thought that if it was possible for people to clap in a confused manner, the assembled collection of suits and cocktail dresses was doing it. For Gaia, being confused by the Kishocha was normal.

Blum spoke next, and at length. A consummate professional, she didn't seem to notice or care when one of the snails climbed over her shoe and devoured her ornamental buckle.

Gaia was so astounded by watching this that she missed the cue for her own speech. Fitzpatrick nudged her forward. Never one for the limelight, Gaia self-consciously mumbled her way through six minutes of thank-yous and gave up the floor to the Corporate Alliance rep.

Oziru departed at the conclusion of the formalities. The alien left as it had come, in a blast of sound and excitement. Once the horns stopped and the horn players withdrew, the humans were silent for a couple of uncertain moments before they erupted into a roar of excited conversation.

Gaia didn't know how to approach conversation. She was unused to functioning outside the structured environment of business interaction. Luckily, everyone else did most of the talking, phrasing most of their conversation Q & A style.

Q: How do you feel about being chosen to be the guardian to a Kishocha spirit?

A: It's all right.

Q: Does your new position conflict with your own faith?

A: No, I'm an atheist.

Q: How do you feel about the Kishocha?

A: They're all right.

Gaia glanced at Fitzpatrick and sensed she was letting down the embassy. Fitzpatrick was actually chuckling down his sleeve. He pushed his way into the little clot of media people and drew her away.

"Why are you laughing at me?" Gaia demanded.

"You're funny." Completely in his element, Fitzpatrick sauntered from clot to clot of people eliciting smiles and laughter wherever he went. Gaia reminded herself that this was one reason she disliked him, but she couldn't help wishing she had that kind of easy grace. Or that she could bring herself to drift along beside him, riding the wake of his superior social skills. But she could not.

Blum was also totally at ease, although her minions followed her like obedient ducklings as she moved among the guests.

Gaia decided to slink away. She could mingle no longer. She didn't think anyone would notice if she left for a few minutes. They all knew each other, and though she was the guest of honor, she seemed superfluous. Cheryl kept the hot foods coming. Roy kept the cold drinks flowing.

Gaia slipped into the back and sat on her bed. Even with the door closed she could still hear the noise. She decided to go farther. Placing her hand on the warm shrine door, she whispered, "Dilate."

Heavy, salty air rushed over her. Inside the shrine, strange weak light radiated from the water. Phosphorescent algae? The light that usually emanated from the ceiling had apparently turned off. She wondered how that was controlled. She hadn't seen a timer or control panel anywhere, but then the whole place was biomechanical. If there was a control panel, chances were she wouldn't recognize it. She still hadn't figured out the location of the voice activation switch for the door.

Kenjan was nowhere in sight. She stepped into the silence of the shrine.

"Contract."

Gaia sat down, leaned against the wall and rubbed her eyes. When she opened them again, Kenjan's head was just emerging from the water. The alien's black and white ringed cranial tendrils shook themselves free of the water like independent entities. Kenjan's skin shimmered, dripping streams of algae-saturated water. It stared into the darkness. Gaia could see its irises adjusting and its nostrils dilating as it sniffed the air. She waited until Kenjan turned toward her.

She said, "It's just me. Gaia."

Kenjan pulled itself up on the narrow lip of its moat. The alien glowed like an apparition.

"You are not supposed to come to me except for feedings, you know."

"Yeah, whatever." Gaia waved the remark aside as though she could dissipate thousands of years of tradition with a single gesture.

"Come closer, please, my guardian."

Gaia scooted nearer to the alien. She could see Kenjan's nostrils flare as it took in deep draughts of air. It opened its mouth.

"Oziru held your hand," Kenjan breathed. "Let me touch it."

"No."

"Why not?" Kenjan demanded.

"Because the last time I touched you my hands dissolved." A note of reproach colored Gaia's voice.

"I will not hurt you again." Kenjan raised both hands with its fingers twisted into an arcane sign. "I swear never to eat more of you. Neither body nor spirit will I ingest of you. Now may I touch your hand?"

With great reluctance, she extended her palm. Kenjan wrapped its long black fingers around her wrist and moved its muzzle across her sensitive skin, inhaling deep draughts of scent, mouthing the empty air. After a moment, Kenjan closed its eyes, head bowed into Gaia's palm. Its cranial tendrils hung limp and desolate.

"My last words to Oziru were so angry. Why didn't I tell Oziru that it was my only true love?"

"You were probably still shocked from being declared dead."

"I shouldn't have called Oziru a traitor." Kenjan released Gaia's hand. "Oziru cannot resurrect me and you should not indulge me. I insulted my beloved and now that one's feeling for me is killed."

Gaia patted Kenjan's shoulder. After her divorce, she'd been lonely too. But it wasn't the same, was it? Oziru and Kenjan had not chosen to part. Fate and society had separated them. No, their situation was nothing like choosing to get divorced.

Kenjan slid down to lie prone on the narrow ledge of floor between the water and the apparently impassible calligraphy line. "When my beloved walked through the shrine tonight it did not even look at me. I feel like my body is hurt inside, like I am dying again. I have never been so full of sorrow."

At a loss for any meaningful consolation, Gaia said, "Would you like to hold my hand again?"

Kenjan reached for her, once more pulling the scent of Oziru into its muzzle, saying, "I am humiliated to be so pathetic."

Gaia said, "It's all right. Take all the time you need."

Chapter Eleven: Free Samples

During the subsequent weeks, business at Happy Snak boomed. For the first time in the company's history, people waited outside the gate to get in. They were not desperate for a cola. They waited for Wave, A-Ki Station's hottest new celebrity. At first Gaia let it happen. Every manner of person could be found in Happy Snak asking Wave to pose for a picture. Wave loved to talk and could be drawn into long conversations. The worst offenders were a team of physicists from Boeing Spacelabs who seemed to have developed a unified questioning strategy.

The scientists so lacked subtlety that they openly recorded Wave's every word, asking the alien to speak loudly and clearly so its voice could be heard above the cold-drinks dispenser. Then they'd begin a series of inquiries.

Scientist: What do your people's gravitational generators look like?

Wave: Oh, beautiful. You would kiss one if you were allowed.

Scientist: Do they somehow house a singularity?

Wave: No, there are lots of them.

Scientist: But how do they work?

Wave: They are far too important to work!

Scientist: What are they made of?

Wave: The same as everything else, only more holy.

And so on until Gaia called Wave back to its duties. The most amazing thing to her was that people would come in, demand Wave's attention and not buy anything. At times upwards of twenty people loafed in the dining room and only one or two had any intention of purchasing a snack. She could not believe their deadbeat mentality. At least Roy and Cheryl made a pretense of working while interacting with the alien. These people were just loitering.

She was planning to charge a refundable cover charge when she heard Wave tell a stalwart young lady from Boeing that their conversation was over. She had not purchased any snacks and therefore was undeserving of the attention of a Happy Snak employee. The Boeing woman stood, somewhat stunned, then walked to the counter and ordered a burrito.

When Gaia questioned Wave about its sudden economic enlightenment, the alien responded that it had heard her complaining to Fitzpatrick and decided to take action. Since then the steady stream of information seekers and tourists had been dutifully buying snacks, effectively paying admission for the alien show.

Together, they settled into a routine. Every morning Gaia woke up before seven o'clock and started prepping for the coming day. Wave usually emerged as soon as the alien heard Gaia moving around. Wave was clearly not a morning person and worked in a zombie-like fashion, stocking cold-drink cups and starting the coffee machine. They had learned early that Wave couldn't handle frozen products. Its skin was very delicate and sensitive to dry cold. Wave had the tongue-on-the-frozen-pole syndrome over its entire body.

About the same time they discovered the freezing problem, Wave contracted an unsightly skin condition that caused it to peel like a molting snake. The Kishocha physician inspected Wave for two seconds and then berated Gaia loudly in broken English. Why had she kept Wave from swimming? Did she hope to kill Wave through bloody red cracking? Eventually they'd established that Kishocha needed to be immersed in their water for a few hours every day in order to keep their skin healthy. Since then Gaia had released Wave for a couple of hours to swim.

So every day, after Wave finished making coffee, the alien departed for Kishocha waters. Then Roy and Cheryl arrived around ten, looking groggy. Gaia would have finished the coffee by then so Roy and Cheryl would argue over whose turn it was to make more.

Cheryl and Roy bickered constantly. It was their way of showing affection. They argued about every detail, from how much salt to put on the fries to the best way to make toast. Initially, Gaia had been going to show them the operations manual, which would settle all these burning questions, but soon she realized that clear-cut instructions would spoil their fun. And since they were working out of boredom, for next to nothing, a good time was crucial.

At ten thirty every morning, Happy Snak opened its doors.

Gaia threaded souvlaki onto skewers. Roy and Cheryl called orders back and forth above the constant dull roar of the exhaust hood. Gaia was comfortable in the noise. The din of people talking, paper crumpling, machines beeping, whirring and buzzing, and thin strains of barely recognizable Muzak blended to form a kind of white noise that allowed her to concentrate. At night there was Wave's constant stream of talk and a comfortable din of conversation that made speaking completely unnecessary. Increasingly, she thought of Kenjan.

The business outlook at Kenjan's shrine was less optimistic. During the week following Kenjan's summoning only one Kishocha visited: Wave. Daily, the alien wordlessly deposited chicken satay with extra toast and pickles in a blue and yellow checked paper boat. Wave always kept its eyes averted.

Somehow Gaia had to attract the Kishocha to Kenjan's shrine. She knew from Wave that Kenjan had followers. Where were they? Did they even know that it had died? Was the alien so disgraced that its disciples were gone forever?

That Sunday's food went uneaten, except by cleaners who seemed to regard the main course as toxic. Although they ate the paper boat, lemon and pickle, they left the Cajun clam strips in a little soggy heap. Monday's chicken satay didn't attract Kenjan's attention, but had been more interesting to the cleaners, who ate everything, including the bamboo skewers.

She needed to get the followers in here, and not just for Kenjan's continuing existence. If the Kishocha were to become her customers she first needed to attract them to the shrine. As far as she knew, the aliens had no mass media so advertising was out. She'd have to go on word of mouth.

Gaia thought the lack of shrine traffic might also be related to the pair of Kishocha guards who arrived in Kenjan's shrine the day after the grand opening. She didn't know what had prompted their deployment. Kenjan hadn't spoken to her since the guards arrived.

One of the guards was the much-beaded soldier from the grand opening. This pleased Gaia and formed a nugget of an idea. She decided this guard would be her first customer.

It was Tuesday night, nine fifty-nine p.m.

Gaia prepared to launch her word-of-mouth marketing scheme. She decided to treat the taciturn guards to some free samples.

She glanced to Wave as it punched buttons on the cold-drinks dispenser and handed a corps woman her fizzy drink.

"Thank you and please have a nice night," Wave droned, carefully forming each word, as though the phrase was a mantra that had lost all meaning.

Ten o'clock.

A series of chimes burst from overhead, and a sultry woman's voice broke out over the carnage of the Happy Snak dining room.

"It is now ten p.m., and Happy Snak is closed for the night. We hope you've enjoyed your visit. Happy Snak will be open again at ten-thirty a.m. for all your snack food needs. Have a pleasant evening."

The last few stragglers stood, stretched and lumbered out. Mechanically, Gaia bid them good night.

She walked back through the kitchen to her room and opened the shrine door.

As usual, the guards flanked the door to the Kishocha waters. The guard on the left wore the impressive array of shell and bead necklaces heaped around its neck like leis on a Hawaiian tourist. The one on the right wore a single, but exquisite bead on a string. Both held spears.

Each guard sported short cranial tendrils and broad, nearly symmetrical facial markings. The guards didn't look at her, not even when she stood directly in front of them and began to speak in the Kishocha she'd been practicing with Wave all week. "Good work today. You two have done so well that I thought I'd treat you to a little snack. Wave?"

"Yes, Gaia?" Wave lurked by her bedroom door.

"Could you bring a couple of glasses of orange for our stalwart guards?"

Wave softly padded over to her.

"Gaia, they won't ever have any money pieces," Wave said quietly, in English. "There is no point in giving them a sample."

"I know. I just thought that they might like a snack. They've been standing, doing nothing, for hours. And we can work something out with the money if they should happen to want more."

"They are guarding. No treats on guarding duty. Are you sick or possessed?"

"Wave," Gaia said through gritted teeth, "I think it's important to get these guards to like us, and I think giving them a little treat right now would be a good start. Maybe they'll like us so well they won't spy on us all the time."

"You are so brilliant," the alien said, "and so evil. It is so wrong to tempt the mighty warrior caste and bring them low with desire for beautiful orange. To ensnare the noble warriors, who are so clean and pure, it is certainly an outrage to the correct order. It is sneaky, like begging clams from noble children when you already have a clam of your own hidden behind your back."

Gaia wondered how much of Wave's life was devoted to the singular pursuit of clams. Wave wore a bizarre expression, somewhere between mad scientist and ecstatic martyr. The alien surreptitiously glanced at the two warriors. Its cranial tendrils lay flat against its head. "I will get the orange."

If the guards had heard Wave, they gave no evidence of it.

Gaia looked for Kenjan, but the alien wasn't in sight. It was probably underwater again. She stepped between the guards and commanded the Kishocha-side door to dilate.

Outside, the tunnel was half-flooded. It was made of smooth shell and dimly illuminated every few yards by glowing bands. A small promontory directly outside the door had a couple of curved steps leading down into the water, but no other walking surface was evident. Gaia supposed the Kishocha just swam everywhere.

Gaia stepped back.

"Tell me," she inquired of the much-beaded guard, "what are your names?"

"I am Fucha, servant of Oziru's house, and this is Kooli, who serves the holy Seigata," replied the guard with the necklaces of gambling pieces. Both the guards' names seemed to have multi-tonal elements that Gaia didn't think she would be able to say correctly and while she was happy to fudge some Kishocha words, she didn't want to mispronounce anyone's name.

Wave seemed to grasp her conundrum. It sidled up beside Gaia with two paper espresso cups and a half-full jug of orange. "The names mean Stinging Jelly and Little Shark."

"Do you mind if I call you Stinger? That would be your English name." Gaia told the guard from Oziru's house.

Nonplused, the Kishocha replied, "You may address me in any way you see fit." Stinger was taller than the other guard and more sinewy. Its nails, long and black, glinted. Stinger's copious beads clicked together gently as the alien spoke.

"I also will respond to any name of your choosing," Seigata's guard said colorlessly. "But please inform me of the name in advance, or I may not understand that your exalted personage is speaking to me and thus inadvertently disobey your orders."

Gaia had never experienced arrogant subservience before.

The guard seemed resigned to following her orders, no matter how stupid they might be. Gaia immediately warmed to the Kishocha for it.

"Wonderful, I'll call you Sharkey then."

Sharkey had broad shoulders and thicker limbs. Guards, Gaia noted, seemed to have more body fat than the servant class. Gaia could picture Sharkey stalking the Hawaii shoreline looking for unsuspecting swimmers to bite. Sharkey was even colored like a shark, its back a deep gray and its stomach white. Sharkey's teeth gleamed and the two broad markings on its muzzle were nearly symmetrical, except for a slight downturn on its right side that made the alien appear to smirk.

Or maybe the alien really was smirking. Gaia still hadn't fully deciphered Kishocha body language yet.

She took the two tiny espresso cups from Wave and handed one each to Stinger and Sharkey. No more than a couple thimblefuls of orange sloshed in the bottoms of the cups. Wave was being stingy. Gaia gave her employee a silent approving nod. "Why don't you get a cup of your own, Wave, and a cola for me. Then we'll have a toast."

Wave zipped out and returned with three super-slam cups. One was two-thirds full of cola, one was empty, and the other full of ice. So entertained was Gaia by watching Wave dump at least a pint of orange into its cup that she failed to notice the slight shuffle of Kishocha feet. Gradually, though, the shuffling grew too loud for her to ignore.

Five Kishocha lurked on the narrow promontory just outside the door. As Gaia watched, an entirely black Kishocha pulled itself up out of the waterway, greeted the others then gazed furtively inside.

"Wave, why aren't they coming?" she murmured.

Wave glanced up from its orange cup and shrugged dismissively. "I do not know."

"They're coming to give the offerings, right?" Gaia asked.

"Maybe. The glorious Kenjan had many disciples, but also many enemies. Now, here I have dispensed your cola. Let us do a toast."

"I wish they'd just come in." Gaia watched the huddled, nervous-looking Kishocha gathered at the shrine's entryway. "Enter freely!"

The Kishocha stepped back. Three of them dived into the waterway.

"They are probably too afraid to come inside. I was afraid of humans before I walked among you." Wave methodically dropped piece after piece of ice into Gaia's cola.

"Really?"

"Yes, you smell scary," Wave said.

"Do we humans smell scary?" Gaia asked Stinger and Sharkey.

"Yes, Your Excellency," Stinger replied.

"This place smells of death," Sharkey added.

"Is that true, Wave?"

"Oh certainly, Happy Snak smells terrifying, especially the bits-o-bakun smell," Wave said. "This is the smell of terror and nightmares."

Trying to suppress a chuckle, Gaia emitted a snort.

"After our toast, Wave, go invite them inside to do whatever it is they do. And that's enough ice, thanks."

"The Happy Snak manual says that the ice should displace thirty percent of the beverage-cup volume." Wave added one more ice cube. "Any fewer ice cubes could cause loss to the company in the form of over-poured beverages."

"You are some kind of dream aren't you?"

Wave handed over Gaia's drink and stood at attention. It was time for the toast.

"To our brave guards!" Gaia raised her cup. After a second, Wave raised its, and the guards followed suit. She drank, and, in a kind of domino effect, the Kishocha all drank, ending with Sharkey.

Wave smiled hugely, revealing a full set of jagged teeth stained vivid orange. Stinger stared fixedly into the bottom of its cup. Sharkey looked utterly placid for a few moments, then abruptly crumpled its cup, hurled it to the ground and stabbed it repeatedly with its long spear.

Gaia jumped back, vaguely registering two more distant splashes as the remaining Kishocha loitering at the door dived back into the waterway.

"What the hell are you doing?" she demanded.

"Profanely delicious," Sharkey said. "I will lose my purity if I succumb to the orange. I have rejected the orange for the good of your mighty self and all on Ki Island."

Stinger was lost in blissful intoxication. The Kishocha's cranial tendrils stiffened and shuddered, just like Wave's. Stinger was, in fact, staring at Wave's huge cup of orange in blank incomprehension, like a man who'd just seen someone give a dog a million dollars and didn't understand how it could happen.

"I'm glad you liked it." Gaia eyed Sharkey's spear. "Do you think those Kishocha are going to come back tonight?"

The three Kishocha stared at her blankly. Sharkey asked, "Which of us are you addressing?"

"Any of you. Just speak up if you know the answer."

"No," Wave said. "Soldier Sharkey has managed to intimidate its lessers with a show of unnecessary force. They will not come back tonight."

"Are you speaking impudently to me, Wave?" Sharkey's voice lowered.

"I am speaking to Gaia Jones," Wave retorted. "She is your better."

Sharkey leaned toward Wave in a manner Gaia found menacing. Wave held its ground.

"I will also speak." Stinger stepped forward, flourishing its spear dramatically. The beads around its neck clattered. Wave's nerve broke. The alien bolted back to Gaia's bedroom. She heard Wave's door slide shut. Sharkey regarded Stinger with smoldering irritation. Stinger continued: "I, too, think that the disciples of Kenjan have dispersed and will not return tonight, Honorable Guardian. But we should not fear, for they will return again at another tide. We should instead concern ourselves with immediate questions." Stinger bowed its head then glanced coyly up at her. “Do you think I could beg from you one more taste of orange?”

“No,” Gaia said. Stinger’s muzzle sank. “But I’ll trade you another orange for one of those beads.” Gaia pointed at the array of white, silver and black beads around Stinger’s neck. Stinger considered her offer. Then it unthreaded a black and silver swirled bead, knelt and offered it to Gaia.

“Your will is done,” Stinger said.

As Gaia’s hands closed around the bead, she broke out into a slow smile. A milestone had been reached, an intergalactic barrier broken. She had just made her first Kishocha sale. Nothing could stop her now.

Chapter Twelve: Sacrificial Clams

"Nova Grill-a-Dog Spike! Catch customers' attention with this ultra-retro-style rotating hot dog rack! Cast aluminum model comes with bun steamer and nostalgic light-up sign."

Gaia tapped the "next" icon. She rolled Stinger's bead around her palm and waited impatiently for the next page to load.

"Remote kiosks. New items. Xiao Industries Remote Concession." A blue and yellow hot dog cart appeared on Gaia's screen.

The announcer continued, "Capture sales in nontraditional venues. Sidewalks, lobbies, docks, anywhere! Independent power and water supply. American-standard refrigeration. Fully electronic point of sale system with programmable reader board. Durable, lightweight. Comes in three colors or customize with your own corporate identity. Awning sold separately."

Gaia hit the detail key. Xiao Industries' logo appeared, borne forth out of nothingness by a swell of hopeful music. In addition to the features mentioned in the previous catalog entry, the new kiosk was suitable for use poolside with closed and insulated electrical circuits. It was a go-anywhere do-anything little piece of potential earning power. Gaia listened intently then heard the list price.

Expensive was too weak a word to describe the price.

Gaia had a vision. The kiosk gleamed Happy Snak blue and

yellow. Happy Snak's harlequin logo grinned down from the exorbitantly priced awning. Emblazoned beneath its wide white smile were the words *Mini-Snak*.

She had to have it.

The question was how to get the money. Gaia tossed Stinger's bead into the air and caught it, then eyed its weird carvings. This little item was definitely worth a kiosk. She only had to find the right buyer. Who on the station was desperate for Kishocha trinkets? Roy and Cheryl were—but they had no money.

How much would those Boeing scientists pay to have their very own piece of Kishocha material to investigate? Gaia looked up the price of the kiosk again, wrote it down and added twenty percent. Then she texted a message to the Boeing research department. She expressed her interest in selling Stinger's bead and the price she'd be interested in selling it for. She expected to have the money by the end of the day.

Everything was working out—well, nearly everything. One obstacle to complete happiness remained: her depressed ghost.

Well, that wasn't the only obstacle. She would also love a swell, rich boyfriend to order around. But fulfillment of that desire bordered on complete fantasy, so she focused on the more attainable goal of cheering up Kenjan.

She'd noticed that Sharkey and Stinger didn't arrive at the shrine until later in the day. Gaia figured she could get Kenjan to talk to her again if the guards were absent.

"Dilate," she told the door. The door complied. She was early, and no guards were visible. Gaia listened, then called, "Kenjan?"

No response.

Nothing new there. Being treated as though it was dead had to have dealt a catastrophic blow to Kenjan's confidence. No wonder Kenjan stayed hidden underwater. The few Kishocha who'd braved the shrine a few days ago hadn't reappeared yet. Gaia wondered if they ever would.

She spied the Kishocha in its shell grotto. The alien's muzzle was illuminated by the faint glow of its hand-held. When it became clear that Kenjan was aware of her presence but choosing to ignore her, Gaia decided that now was the time for action. She took off her Happy Snak smock, pants and shoes. She would talk to Kenjan, whether Kenjan liked it or not. She'd swim across.

She crouched and peered down at the pink water, which reddened as it deepened. Sliding into the warm water, Gaia carefully avoided touching any of the plants or other creatures that had taken tenuous root along the wall. She didn't have any urge to die of some intergalactic poison. Gaia paddled along gently. In spite of her concern over Kenjan, she felt giddy. It had been a long time since she'd gone swimming. She used to swim all the time. She'd even gone diving in the submerged sub-basements of the buildings of A-Ki Station a couple of times, but it gave her the creeps to navigate among the cables and girders. Interestingly, she was more buoyant in the Kishocha water than in Earth seawater.

A few strokes brought Gaia to Kenjan's island. She pulled herself up by a couple of shell handles that she'd seen Kenjan use. The surface of the island was rough, but not unpleasantly so. She approached the grotto and knocked.

Through the latticework, Gaia could see Kenjan staring at her in shock.

"Why are you here?" it finally asked.

"I decided to come see you. Can I come in?"

Kenjan stared at her again, as though she'd asked the alien to move Jupiter a little more to the left. "No, you are not allowed here."

"I don't mean to be rude."

"I will possess your spirit and escape to go be with my beloved. I cannot help it. You must save yourself."

"You couldn't possess me, even if you tried," Gaia answered.

Kenjan snaked a hand out through the latticework and seized Gaia's arm. A thrill of fear zinged through Gaia's body. Then its expression changed from hope to disappointment. Kenjan let her go, its apparent possession attempt a total failure. “You are correct.”

“What would you have done with my body?”

“Walk to the bed of my Oziru,” Kenjan murmured. “Lie down upon the moss, sing and weep, and beg for my love back.”

Gaia scratched her forearm. Water dripped from her sodden underwear. She shifted back and forth. “I came to ask why you haven’t been talking to me lately.”

“Am I required?”

“No, but Wave is really worried about you.”

“Sweet Wave,” Kenjan said. “So loyal.”

“So what’s wrong?” Gaia asked.

Kenjan threw up its hands in apparent frustration. “I am dead. What could be right about it?”

“I know that. But I thought we were starting to get to know one another. We might as well.”

Kenjan regarded her evenly. “Do you understand how wrong you are in every conceivable way?”

“Uh—” Gaia began. Kenjan cut her off.

“You are standing where you are forbidden to be, speaking to one who is anathema, wearing less clothes than humans are required to wear. Moreover, you are two hours before the time of offering!”

“I wanted to talk to you before the guards got here.”

“You are behaving incorrectly,” Kenjan said.

“Like you behaved so correctly when you were alive. You said you were a heretic, and Wave told me about how it was always having to apologize for you. You’ve got nerve bitching me out for not doing things right.”

“Insubordinate creature,” Kenjan growled.

“Mopey bastard,” Gaia shot back.

“Unforgivable rudeness to your superior.” Kenjan’s cranial tendrils lashed.

“My superior?” Gaia’s eyes widened incredulously. “You are such a hypocrite!”

Kenjan stood and then hesitated. All anger drained from the alien’s face. It slunk out of the grotto, sat down at the water's edge and pulled its knees up against its chest.

"Go away, rotten tormenting guardian." Kenjan spoke halfheartedly. "I am not a hypocrite."

Gaia sat next to Kenjan. Her butt was better equipped than her waterlogged feet to deal with the rough crust of the island. "I'm sorry I called you that. Look, I didn't come here to get into a fight. I just wanted to talk. I want to get to know you since we're going to be together a long time."

"For eternity," Kenjan said miserably.

"Right, and I want us to be, you know, friends."

"I have no friends but Oziru."

"With that attitude you'll never get any." Gaia felt somewhat hypocritical herself, lecturing Kenjan on friends when she was a virtual shut-in, but the alien didn't need to know that. And at least it was talking to her. "What's Oziru like?"

"Oziru is a secret sea-cave no one has ever entered. Warm water flows there, heated by the molten fires of the earth. But the journey is darkness and heavy pressure and cold for so long that one gives up hope of finding heat. One fears death. Then, one turn and another, and there is heat and fiery light and blind fish. One is never cold nor hungry nor alone. But then separation comes, and one is once more utterly naked, unprotected and unloved in the cold sea."

"You were cold and hungry before you met Oziru?"

"No, it was only a metaphor for the starvation of my heart," Kenjan said. "I was told you also use metaphors in language."

"We do, but with aliens it's hard to tell what's a metaphor sometimes. But maybe we'll grow to understand each other."

"Maybe... I did not realize before that you are also a heretic."

"I'm not a heretic," Gaia said. "I'm just human."

Kenjan thrummed, the corners of its mouth curled up in that Kishocha smile-emulation expression. "Being human is enough."

Gaia inspected her toes. Her toenails had been neglected for a long time. She wondered if she should paint them some color, but then couldn't figure out what color would be best.

"I'm sorry you're lonely," she said.

Kenjan shrugged. "I'm sure it will pass, once the heat of Oziru's love has become a dim memory for me."

Gaia renewed her intensive toenail scrutiny. Maybe green was the color—or black, like Kishocha nails. She shifted, trying to get comfortable on the rough surface of Kenjan's island.

"Like I said, we don't know each other very well," she said. "But I'm here to talk if you want."

Kenjan regarded her for a long, slow moment. "You must truly go now, or the guards will discover you. I will call my followers to care for me."

"Okay." Gaia followed Kenjan into the water and was glad when it helped her out on the other side. Drippy and chilled, she watched the alien descend beneath her, spiraling down until the Kishocha's body became an indistinct form in the red depths.

How interesting to go down there. Leaning back over the water, Gaia turned her head so that her ear was beneath the surface. Ethereal notes, like whale song, vibrated through her eardrum. Was this Kenjan's voice? Gaia grinned. Somehow she'd imagined Kishocha didn't communicate underwater. This was just one more secret she knew about Kishocha.

Would she share it with Fitzpatrick?

She thought she very well might. Gaia rushed into her bedroom, found the necessary items and dialed. Fitzpatrick's face appeared a moment later. He sat in his office, desk scrupulously clean, tie straight and stylish.

"Ms. Jones. To what do I owe this honor?"

"I just wanted you to hear something. Don't disconnect until I tell you to."

"What fool would disconnect a call from a woman in a wet green brassiere? Is that a condom?"

Gaia nodded, tearing the foil packet open with her teeth. "You're going to need some protection where you're going."

"Oh my," was the last thing Fitzpatrick said before she stretched the latex over the body of her hand-held. She'd heard about this trick from other divers who worked with film companies. She knotted the end of the condom, padded back into the shrine and dunked both her ear and her hand-held below the surface.

Kenjan still sang. Long complex trills that sounded both savage and operatic. She could have listened for hours, but it was too close to the time of offering to risk being caught.

When she returned to her room and peeled the condom off her hand-held Fitzpatrick was not alone on her screen. Half a dozen aides and embassy personnel had gathered around the desk, listening. Rapt. Gaia snatched up her discarded Happy Snak smock and grinned sheepishly at the assembled suits.

She said, “So what did you think?”

Fitzpatrick’s mouth curled up into a warm, sensuous smile. All he said was “Beautiful.”

When Gaia re-entered the shrine at the appropriate hour, it bustled with activity though Kenjan remained inside the shell grotto.

Kishocha gathered at the entrance. At Wave’s urging, they trickled into the shrine. One held a basket of clams.

“Most excellent Gaia,” Sharkey said from behind her. She hadn’t noticed the guard’s approach and made a mental note that the guard could be much stealthier than she’d imagined a creature with big flipper feet could be.

“I would never give you any order or imply that I know more than your excellent person, but perhaps now would be a good time to summon the *kaijamfutan* so that it can eat.” Sharkey averted its eyes.

“Well, that is my job, isn’t it?”

“Yes, Great Guardian, it is. How wise you are to notice that,” Sharkey said. “I am in awe of your endless and deep soul.”

Gaia became aware at that moment that the Kishocha in general, and Sharkey in particular, understood and fully utilized sarcasm. She felt a little disappointed, but also freed. She walked to the edge of the water. “Hey, Kenjan, there are some people here to see you!"

Slowly, Kenjan stood and walked out of the hut. The assembled Kishocha fell to their knees. Kenjan slipped into the water and swam across to where Gaia stood.

"Did you just summon me?" Kenjan's voice was soft and languid.

"Your friends are here." Gaia crouched down closer to Kenjan. Inadvertently, she placed her hand inside the calligraphy line.

Kenjan whispered, "You should use the real prayer to summon me, for the sake of those giving the offering."

"Right, thanks." Gaia winked.

"Gaia Jones!"

The sound of Wave bellowing her name startled Gaia out of her glee. She spun around to see Wave standing near the Kishocha entrance to the shrine.

"Gaia Jones! Respectfully, please come over here at once if it is not too inconvenient, my master," Wave shouted, gesticulating wildly.

"Now, that was really a mouthful," Gaia commented nervously to Kenjan.

"Please, my master!" Wave's tone had grown increasingly desperate. "Respectfully, step away from the honored ghost at once and come here immediately if it pleases you!"

Gaia walked back toward Wave, who'd reached a state of near panic. The dozen or so Kishocha standing near Wave pulled away from her as though she was contagious.

"You crossed the line," the alien whispered in dismay.

"It's all right," Gaia tried to reassure the assembled Kishocha. The aliens looked actually repulsed. Gaia knew she'd screwed up.

"You'll be possessed! Contaminated and devoured," Wave said. "You must be exorcised immediately."

"I'll go to get the blessed Seigata," Stinger said.

"We should simply destroy the possessed." Sharkey leveled its spear at her throat. Gaia froze, looking down the razor-sharp blade. The soldier kept its eyes fixed on hers. "The ghost is very powerful."

"Don't!" Wave threw itself between Sharkey and Gaia.

"Cease!" Kenjan's voice thundered through the tiny room, echoing off the walls. Gaia's ears rang. She knew the Kishocha had a powerful vocal range, but had no idea that they could be so oppressively loud outside of the water. "Stand down, soldiers."

Reflexively, Sharkey whipped its spear down and started to kneel. Then the guard reconsidered, and stood again.

"We take no orders from ghosts," Sharkey said defiantly. Stinger looked more unsure and lingered in a semi-crouch.

Wave leapt forward. "You must take orders from Gaia Jones though."

"This human is possessed," Sharkey retorted.

"Are you a priest to say so?" Wave demanded.

"The servant has a point." Stinger rose sheepishly up beside Sharkey.

"This servant is above itself." Sharkey reached out, ripping the necklace from Wave's throat. "Who are you to wear this?"

"I gave that to Wave," Gaia hissed. She'd stopped being afraid around the time her ears had stopped ringing. Now she was just angry. "You have no right to try and exorcise me. Humans are immune to ghosts. They can't hurt us. Seigata said so. That's why I'm the guardian, not you."

Silence fell as all present contemplated this incredible information.

"May I have permission to speak, oh my beloved guardian." Kenjan's voice rolled casually across the water.

"Sure." Gaia's voice trembled with anger. She was relieved to find Kenjan so calm.

"It's true that humans cannot be touched or possessed by ghosts. You see, their souls are made from fire, not from saltwater," Kenjan said. "If a ghost were to try to take a human, the souls would consume each other."

"Fire?" Wave looked, wide-eyed in awe, at Gaia. "So

powerful!"

"Fire is profane," Sharkey said.

"But powerful," Stinger commented.

"Seigata will hear of this," Sharkey said. "I hope your exalted personage has not been lying about the composition of your soul." Sharkey and Stinger withdrew and took up their former places on either side of the door to the Kishocha waterway.

Gaia felt all her blood rush to her head. Her veins throbbed at maximum capacity. "Don't think you two are going to just stand there after what you've done."

Stinger and Sharkey glanced at each other, then at Wave.

"What do you mean, Gaia?" Wave asked.

"I mean you." Gaia jabbed a finger at Sharkey. "You just had a spear at my fucking throat, and you—" Gaia turned her accusing finger on Stinger. "You didn't even try and intervene. Just get the hell out, both of you."

"But it's their job to guard, Gaia." Wave flattened itself on the floor before her. "Please be understanding!"

"Oh?" She turned to Stinger and Sharkey. "Who are they guarding? Me?"

"Yes, Exalted Guardian," Sharkey said.

"Without question, Exalted Guardian," Stinger chimed in.

"Then I guess you'll be going back to Oziru and saying you've really fucked up," Gaia said.

"Oh no!" Wave dropped down to its knees. "Please, Gaia, don't."

"For God's sake, Wave, will you stop begging." Gaia shook with anger.

"I'm sorry." Wave mashed its face into the floor.

"Stop it." Gaia seized Wave's arm and yanked up. "Get up off the damn floor."

Wave remained limp.

"My beloved guardian," Kenjan said. Gaia let go of Wave and turned. Kenjan was lying half-in and half-out of the water. "Please be kind and gentle to your servants. If you are fierce I may never eat. The ones bearing offerings have all fled from your wrath." Kenjan gestured to the space where the rest of the Kishocha used to be. All that remained was one small basket of clams.

Gaia's anger suddenly went flaccid. Kenjan was dependent on her for its very existence, as was Wave, and she suspected that Stinger and Sharkey might also face grave consequences if she rejected them. Gaia surveyed the four Kishocha and felt grudgingly sorry. She had the sudden sense that she was the foreigner here, and somehow she must try to bend, even though she didn't really understand why or in what direction.

Gaia wasn't used to bending for anyone. She had her own business, partly because she wanted to be the master of her own destiny and partly because she couldn't work for other people. Somehow she always ended up being fired or leaving in a flurry of bad grace and mutual dislike.

But she owed it to Wave and Kenjan to be better than that this time.

She didn't know what her responsibility was to Stinger and Sharkey, but the idea was beginning to creep in that sending them back to say that they'd failed would cause some great harm to befall them. Would they be killed? While part of her mind felt gratified by that, since Sharkey had been perfectly willing to kill her, another part felt horrified and disgusted.

Gaia was not a deep thinker; she relied on action. She needed an action to keep her on track. She needed to feed someone. Luckily, there was someone waiting to be fed. She retrieved the basket and carried it to Kenjan.

"Keep one, for yourself."

Gaia said, "I hate clams."

"Then keep one for Wave."

Gaia reached into the basket and took one rough, barnacle-covered clam.

Kenjan nudged the basket back toward her. "And one each for Stinger and Sharkey. They are good and faithful guards."

"They're homicidal."

"They simply have no education."

Taking Kenjan at its word, Gaia picked up two more clams. The basket then contained only three.

Kenjan rolled over onto its back. Its cranial tendrils spreading out from its face like stripy hair. It twirled a tentacle around its finger. “You can feed me three meat tacos with no cheese.”

Chapter Thirteen: The Infinite Pain of Love

The case said *Live Fish.* Gaia unfastened the locks carefully, making sure the shipping container was right-side-up and the expiration date far in the future. She'd once received a case of supposedly live salmon that had been packed for three years. It was the vilest thing that she'd ever seen, even in a professional kitchen where vile things were fairly routine.

Roy crossed his arms.

"It's really amazing the things we humans will do to make sure we have every conceivable pleasure." He glared at the case in condemnation.

"Yeah." Cheryl draped her arm around Roy's hips. "I hate that we have toilet paper up here."

"It's not the same thing. These are living animals encased in an apparatus designed specifically to keep them alive on a voyage through space until they're slaughtered for our consumption."

"So you don't want any clams then?" Gaia popped the lid open.

"Absolutely not!"

"Cheryl?" Gaia asked.

"I'm allergic to shellfish. Thanks though," Cheryl said. "It's weird that they can't grow clam tissue in the meat lab."

"They can," Gaia said. "They grow it the same way they grow chicken and beef tissue."

"Then why bother to order these things?" Cheryl poked at the barnacle-encrusted shell.

"I thought it would be neat for Wave to see what real human clams looked like." Gaia counted her merchandise. "Thirty-six succulent bivalves born in the Sea of Japan." She turned to the rest of the shipment. "I think they shorted us on sanitary towelettes, though."

"It's just barbaric." Roy crossed his arms. "They're alive."

"It's okay, honey. It's for the alien." Cheryl patted Roy's side.

"I suppose," Roy said. "Where is Wave anyway?"

"Wave is concocting." Gaia turned toward the door and hollered, "Wave!"

Wave emerged from the back kitchen bouncing and vibrant.

"Hello! Hello, my comrades. Hello," Wave chimed out. The alien made the O's unnecessarily long and melodic.

"Have you made any progress?" Gaia asked.

"Oh, yes, certainly. I've come up with two snacks that are sure to be pleasant." Wave disappeared into the kitchen and then emerged carrying a tray. "This one snack is called Stunned Snake Snack with Orange and Pickle. Watch!" Wave opened its own personal orb and extracted a tiny wriggling snake. Holding it by the tail, Wave slapped the snake's head against the counter. The baby snake twitched feebly as Wave skewered it to a midget dill with a toothpick, placed it in a paper boat and splashed it with a thimbleful of orange.

"See? It still struggles, but no bites. The pickle-bed and skewer keeps it from running away and the orange is a taste sensation."

Roy's normally rosy cheeks were turning the color of old cheese. "Wave, that is truly disgusting."

"It is?" Instantly, all Wave's enthusiasm faded.

"I think it's brilliant." Gaia kept her eyes off the spasming snake. This was the truth of Kishocha dining. They ate food live. "How much would you sell it for?"

"Two beads," Wave said shyly. The Kishocha stared at Roy with a hangdog expression. "I am disgusting?"

"No, no." Roy tried to recover, but his obvious repulsion hindered his ability to lie. "I'm just scared of snakes."

"You are?" Wave was incredulous. "But they're so stupid!"

"I know. It's like..." Roy stared at the twitching snake.

"It's like bits-o-bakun," Gaia interjected.

"Like that?" Wave's tendrils shot out around its face as they did when the alien became alarmed. Gaia wondered if it wasn't the same sort of reaction as cats getting fluffy when threatened.

Gaia said, "Just like that. Roy will get over being scared, like you did."

"I am not over being scared of bits-o-bakun," Wave said.

"But you will be, I'm sure." Gaia gave Wave a reassuring smile. "In the meantime, excellent work. But I think you should stop with the snake treats for a while and see what you can make out of these." She tapped the case.

As Wave drew near, a beautiful expression spread across its face. It approached the case with reverence and awe. "Are these...human clams with crunchy salty barnacles?"

"They certainly are." Gaia felt ridiculously pleased with herself. "Why don't you take them in back and see what you can make."

"Can I... May I please taste my experiments?" Wave appeared to be holding its breath.

"Do whatever you like. The case is yours. I just want you to come up with a couple of things that are actually good."

"I certainly can do that!" Wave clutched the case to its lean chest and loped on long, spindly legs into the kitchen.

Three hours later, Wave had eaten all three dozen clams, and sucked and chewed the barnacles off as well. Cheryl found the alien in its sponge nest, holding its massively distended abdomen, groaning and farting. She called for Gaia.

"You said you could eat human clams." Gaia was alarmed by the size of Wave's bloated stomach.

"I can," Wave gasped. A huge fart ripped through the air. It smelled like a disintegrating frog. "I will be all right. I made three snacks."

"What are they?"

"Excited Clam with Coffee Syrup. Which is a sweet refreshing treat." Wave paused while another gargantuan wind exited its body. "Then I made Pounded Clam with Orange. Last, I made Sucked Real Human Clam with Tartar Sauce—that was inspired by the Fish Sammich here at Happy Snak." Wave closed its eyes and nostril slits, squeezing out another painful volley of gas. "I think I ate too much mayonnaise."

Gaia coughed. She wished she, too, had contracting nostril slits. "Are you sure you don't need a medic?"

"I will be fine," Wave whimpered. Gaia didn't believe it. In a panic, Gaia went through her bedroom and ordered the shrine door to dilate, hoping to ask Kenjan what Wave might need, but Kenjan was nowhere to be seen. However, Sharkey was clearly visible just walking through the other door. Gaia looked at her watch. Offerings weren't going to begin for hours. Sharkey looked equally startled to see her.

"Why are you here at this time?" Sharkey demanded.

"Why are you?"

"I am retrieving my tooth-sharpening bone which I left earlier." Sharkey bent and picked up the oblong bone. "Why are you here?"

"It's my shrine, I can be here whenever I want." Gaia hadn't spoken to Sharkey since the Gaia-needs-to-be-exorcised incident a couple of weeks before. Now the guard gazed malevolently at her, chewing its sharpening bone. Gaia turned from Sharkey.

"Kenjan?" Gaia called. There was no response.

"Exalted Guardian?" Sharkey said.

"What?"

"Is it you who is making the epic stench?"

"No," Gaia growled and renewed her yelling. "Kenjan!" Again, silence.

"Kenjan hides beneath the surface like an ugly." Sharkey spit out a small piece of bone. "That one cannot hear you. You should splash for attention."

"Did I ask for your opinion?" Gaia snapped. Sharkey

rubbed her in every possible wrong way.

"Oh, I apologize." Sharkey inclined its head. "I thought we were all playing democracy with you. Only Wave is, then?"

"How do you know about that?" Gaia demanded.

"It may be hard for your glorious personage to imagine, but sometimes, when we are out of your presence, we lower Kishocha speak among ourselves." Sharkey shifted its spear to its other hand. "We use only small words, though, so we can understand each other."

"Look, Sharkey, I don't have time to listen to your sarcasm right now." Gaia crossed to the shrine and splashed on the water. "Wave is sick."

"Sick?" A note of genuine alarm crept into Sharkey's voice. "The putrid stench belongs to Wave? What did you feed the servant?"

"A good question," Kenjan inquired from the water's edge. "I am glad to see that Sharkey has absorbed my doctrine relating to rude questioning of your betters. Maybe you can proselytize in my place, Honored Soldier."

"Your words would be nothing but poison in my mouth, Ghost," Sharkey growled.

"Can we not fight now?"

"I'm sorry, but I must. It's part of my perverse and heretical nature." Kenjan shrugged as though it was out of its hands.

Gaia persisted. "Wave's really sick. Is there some kind of Kishocha drugstore or anything where I could buy something to settle its stomach? Wave just ate a lot of clams."

"How many clams?"

"Around thirty," Gaia said. "Wave was trying to make some Kishocha-esque entrees and just kept experimenting until it got really sick. Is there anything I can do?"

"Don't let Wave eat so many clams at once," Kenjan said. "That one will glut itself."

"Careless!" Sharkey hissed at her, then stalked out of the shrine. She heard a splash as Sharkey dove into the waterway.

In spite of how much she disliked Sharkey, the Kishocha's

accusation stung. Gaia felt like she had when as a little kid she'd overfed her goldfish to death. "Should I call the doctor?"

Kenjan replied, "Does the fart odor bother you that much?"

"I'm more worried that Wave will explode."

"Wave will not explode from gas," Kenjan assured her. "And I think Sharkey is returning with a remedy."

"Really?"

"Sharkey has always paid too much attention to Wave. I tried to stop it, but I suppose if I were a soldier, Wave would be quite beautiful to me—" Kenjan lolled in the water. "Speaking of guards, earlier I saw you taking Stinger's gambling piece in exchange for a serving of the orange. Stinger does not understand that you are using it as a money piece, but I do. American Clan Humans like you are always talking about buying things from Kishocha. Now you're trying to sell things as well?"

"Trade," Gaia corrected. "We're tying to work out a barter system. And it's just snacks. It's totally harmless."

"Do you know how the gambling pieces are made, or how Kishocha gambling is done?"

"Of course I don't. Do you?"

"Certainly. I will show you how some time. My Oziru loves playing Bones. I tried to teach my Oziru to play Las Vegas-style poker and blackjack. But the cards kept getting wet so we never got good at playing that game. My Oziru's favorite human game is China Clan Mah Jong." Kenjan sighed. "I wish I could lose to Oziru again."

"How can you gamble if you don't have any money?"

"You make gambling pieces, of course. Or you can have a servant make them for you."

"But are they worth anything?" Gaia leaned forward.

"What do you mean?"

"I mean, do you trade them for other things?"

"Like what?" Kenjan asked.

"Food or clothes or, you know, sex or something?"

"I would never do any such thing. Maybe someone who had

lost their fingers and couldn't carve anymore would have to give love for game beads, but that's just sick. You are a sick and vulgar creature. But since I am perverse, I must grudgingly accept you."

"I'm glad." Gaia scanned the room, checking to see if Sharkey had returned. It hadn't. "Are you sure Sharkey went to get medicine?"

"I am sure." Kenjan deteriorated into its unraveled posture. "Be patient."

Gaia scowled. "I don't like Sharkey."

"No one likes Sharkey," Kenjan said. "Though the guard is an excellent example of the intelligence of the lower castes. One should never underestimate that one, or assume Sharkey to be ignorant in any matter. But here, the guard returns! We are lucky to have a guard-post nearby."

Sharkey strode across the shrine, its feet making echoing wet slaps against the shell floor. The guard thrust a slimy, red, wriggling nodule into Gaia's palm.

"Here is the medicine," Sharkey said.

"Thank you, Sharkey." Gaia tried not to look at the cold thing quivering in her hand. She turned and headed for the door.

"Tell Wave not to eat so much," Kenjan called after her.

Gaia took a deep breath and re-entered Wave's room. Roy and Cheryl were debating the merits of an arcane German stomach remedy and ignoring the customer knocking on the front counter. They were trying to decide if the German stuff would actually kill Wave or give the poor thing some relief. Wave just groaned, and squeezed out a short, squeaky emission. Gaia's eyes watered as she offered the wriggly thing to Wave.

"Oh joy!" Wave gasped weakly.

"Is that medicine?" Cheryl asked.

"So they tell me," Gaia said. The three of them watched Wave pop the slimy nodule into its mouth. Wave began to laboriously chew the rubbery sea creature. "There's someone at the front counter."

"Right." Cheryl's head whipped around guiltily.

"Customers." She abruptly went to serve them.

Roy lingered behind. "Try and think positively and hang in there."

Wave gave a lackluster thumbs-up, which Roy returned before he went to assist Cheryl.

"Is it working?" Gaia sat down on the damp floor beside the sponge nest.

"I think so," Wave said. "Did Kenjan get it for you?"

"No, Sharkey went and got it."

Wave gulped down the last of the nodule. "Sharkey?! Sharkey knows I am making this stink?"

"Yeah, sorry."

"Infinite pain!" Wave curled up into a tight ball. "I am killed by embarrassment."

"It's not that bad."

Wave thrust its muzzle deep into the moist folds of the sponge nest. "It is bad, but I am not sorry. The clams were good. But maybe next time I will not eat them all at once." Wave forced a smile-expression. "See I am intelligent and learn from experiences."

"You sure do," Gaia said gently.

Upon returning to her room, Gaia was not completely surprised to find Sharkey lurking in the shrine doorway.

"Is Wave well?" the guard asked.

"Wave's sleeping."

Sharkey nodded. "Then I will not have to accuse you of cruelty to servants. Consider yourself lucky."

"And because you brought the medicine I will not accuse you of insubordination. Consider yourself equally lucky." Gaia closed the door and flopped down onto her bed.

Sharkey really did pay too much attention to Wave.

Chapter Fourteen: Being Bad

Wave woke up shortly past ten-thirty, after Gaia finished feeding Kenjan, feeling physically better, but mentally worse. When questioned on its morose demeanor, Wave asked for a glass of orange. Gaia loosened Wave's tongue with three shots of dye.

Finally, Wave confessed its confusion over Sharkey. "Sharkey is annoying, yet I think of the soldier all the time. And now I have farted in front of Sharkey! Horror! More orange."

Once Wave's cup was full again, Gaia got herself a beer, then a few minutes later a second bottle, then a third. In an hour, neither of them remembered the day's events. A different subject engrossed them.

"Ketchup," Wave said.

Reality stopped for a moment as the two faced each other across the table. Wave took a gulp of orange. Gaia toyed with the neck of her beer bottle. Then she leaned forward and said, "Mint chutney."

Wave scrunched up its muzzle and narrowed its eyes. The Kishocha tapped the table. Its cranial tendrils vibrated gently.

"Anchovy-Cola Twist," Wave countered.

Gaia stuck out her tongue. "That's disgusting."

"I win!" Wave thrust its fist in the air. "I have invented the most unlikely soft-serve ice cream flavor!"

Gaia was having the best time. No one had ever wanted to play her soft-serve game before. She took a swig of her beer. Wave drained its remaining orange. Shocking streaks of orange dye dribbled down the Kishocha's chin.

"We should do something bad." Wave gazed at Gaia intently. Its mismatched eyes seemed much weirder than usual. The gold one, encircled by Wave's adorable black spot, seemed to be much closer to her than the violet one, which appeared to recede into its head a little.

Gaia said, "You know I think some eyeliner might make your eyes look more even."

Wave cocked its head.

"Just a second." Gaia went into her room, and returned with a black eyeliner pen and a tube of white liquid eye shadow. She'd ordered both a couple of weeks before when she'd first had the eyeliner idea and had forgotten until now to show them to Wave.

"You want to change the markings on my face?"

"Not forever." Alcohol consumption made it easier for Gaia to ignore that this whole enterprise might be insulting or even culturally wrong. "Humans do it all the time. You can do me next."

Wave glanced warily around the room. "Okay. Are you going to make me symmetrical?"

"Yeah! And I'm going to paint eyebrows on you."

"The weird little hairs on you forehead?" Wave asked.

"Right."

"And I will erase yours for a smooth appearance," Wave proclaimed.

It didn't take Gaia long. She used the white to carve out lines in the black spot over Wave's eye and the black to create the mirror image on the white side of Wave's face. She then added swooping eyebrow shapes and drew long thin arcing lines down to Wave's jawline. She ended up with a butterfly-shaped pattern that looked Halloweeny, but was symmetrical. Wave inspected its face in awe.

"So even!"

"You look like a rock star," Gaia said.

"Now my turn." Wave seized the eye shadow and painted Gaia's entire face white. Then, with the thinnest setting on the eyeliner, Wave drew tiny, swirling lines on her cheeks and forehead. The lines were perfectly symmetrical. Wave was cautious while drawing. When Wave finished, Gaia looked like she was wearing an ancient ceremonial mask.

"This is amazing." Gaia seized her hand-held and scooted close to Wave. She took a picture of them together, then one of Wave alone. They admired one another and their own handiwork for a while, exchanging compliments. Then Wave sighed.

"This is very bad, indeed, but it is a secret badness. I yearn to be irritating to others."

"Is that what you used to do with Kenjan?" Gaia asked. Wave snorted, then thrummed loudly. Gaia inferred that this was a laugh-equivalent.

"We mischievously committed many very bad acts of disrespect."

"Like what?"

"Such irritating things," Wave said. "We annoyed people all the time. One time we went to a bridge and played music on banjos and sang songs of protest."

"You play banjo?"

"Not very well. Ineptly played, the banjo is a most distracting instrument. Kenjan wanted to use the banjo because it was the instrument of human-style protest songs. We sang songs about how I could learn in front of where the soldiers were quartered. I thought soldiers would be easy to convince since they are egotistical anyway."

"Did it work?"

"Maybe." Wave leaned conspiratorially toward her. "The guard you named Stinger knows the 'Learning Song'. I heard Stinger singing it one day." Wave leaned back, contemplated the ceiling then lurched toward Gaia. "Oh please, please can we do something? We could bother your superiors just a little... Wait, I know! You are not afraid of talking to the ghost at all, are you?"

"Kenjan?" Gaia asked. Wave nodded. "Not at all. Are you?"

"Certainly, but I have grown courageous with orange. So since neither of us fears the ghost, we should sneak into the shrine and startle it."

"I don't know, Kenjan's already downhearted."

Wave suddenly hunched down and moved close enough for Gaia to smell its scent. Wave smelled sharply acidic, like lemons... Or maybe it was the lemon-scented floor cleaner they'd used to degrease the floor. Gaia couldn't tell. She took a fat gulp of her beer. "Pranks will cheer the ghost. Come now."

Gaia had her reservations, but she also really wanted to do something slightly naughty. It had been a long time since she'd stepped outside the social structure of her work persona. Dimly, old memories swam up through her slightly drunken consciousness. She'd been fun once, before she owned a business. Her fun had somehow been misplaced in the struggle to keep the snack bar out of critical condition. But Happy Snak was clean. All the machines had been put to sleep. Kenjan had been fed earlier, by two shy servant-class Kishocha. It was just past midnight and fun sounded feasible.

The two of them crept back through the kitchen and Gaia's bedroom, each clutching a bottle—Gaia had paused to get a fresh cold beer.

The shrine door dilated. Wave poked its muzzle through the opening, blearily glancing from side to side.

"Kenjan is beneath the waters." Wave had to pause at this point to collapse in a little anticipatory snorting fit before continuing onward. This caused a domino effect of giggling in Gaia. After they'd both composed themselves, Wave straightened up. "We will startle Kenjan now. Gaia, you make splashing noises on the water to attract the ghost. Loud splashing, like terrifying eels breaching the surface."

Gaia slapped her hands brutally down into the water. Massive slapping sounds echoed all around the chamber. She and Wave both jumped at the noise, then renewed their peals of snorting and laughter. Gaia glimpsed Kenjan charging up from the depths and sudden terror surged through her. Was this trick really a good idea?

Kenjan's head broke the water. Suddenly a massively deep voice boomed through the chamber. "*Kaijamfutan*!" The voice throbbed through Gaia like a base drum. It filled her ears completely. A little yip escaped her before she realized the speaker was Wave.

"It is your time of exorcism, *Kaijamfutan*!" Wave bellowed in this deep reverberating tone.

Kenjan's cranial tendrils stood straight on end. Its eyes were huge violet circles. Kenjan looked like a shocked cartoon character. Gaia screamed with laughter.

"PREPARE—!" The thunderous voice broke down to a series of snorting, thrums and grunts. Wave collapsed to its knees on the shrine floor. "...for judgment..."

Kenjan stayed staring at them for a long time. It cocked its head and seemed to finally recognize them. Its cranial tendrils relaxed back into their usual coils. Its eyes narrowed to slits as it swam to the edge of its pool. Gaia's stomach went stony cold. She stopped laughing. She hadn't thought of what Kenjan would think of the face paint. Wave didn't seem to remember that it didn't look the same. The Kishocha held its abdomen snuffling like a winded bulldog.

Kenjan rested its elbows on the edge of the pool and regarded Wave. "You are a bad, bad little fishy."

Wave rolled over onto its side, breathing hard. "You should have seen your cranial tendrils, lovely Kenjan." Wave uncurled its body and lay flat on its stomach, its muzzle even with Kenjan's.

Kenjan's face relaxed into the smile expression. It wasn't a smile, really, but it conveyed the same warmth.

"What perverse thing have the two of you done to your muzzles?" Kenjan seemed simultaneously repulsed and admiring.

"It's just face paint." Gaia relaxed. "It washes off."

"It is amazing." Kenjan leaned close to Wave. "You look so different... Strange patterns though."

“Gaia painted me. I put the markings of the Molten Worm Clan on her. Did you recognize?”

“I did,” Kenjan said. “They look so alien on a human. What do the orange streaks represent?”

Both Wave and Gaia snorted at this question.

“I see,” Kenjan said. “You have been guzzling orange and reaching an effervescent state.”

Wave nodded. “And Gaia has been drinking dehydrating beer!”

“Both of you look funny,” Kenjan said.

“Not as funny as you looked with your cranial tendrils all stiff,” Gaia said.

“Yes. I did Seigata’s voice too well!” Wave stuck its tongue out at Kenjan. Wave’s tongue was very long, and slithered out of Wave’s muzzle for about eight inches before it flopped onto the shrine floor like a brilliant orange slug.

Kenjan began to snort and Gaia to giggle.

“So that was Seigata’s voice?” She seated herself next to Wave. The alien’s tongue retracted into its muzzle.

“Yes,” Wave said in a rolling, deep voice. “I am Seigata. I always keep all my clams to myself. No clams for beggars. Sharkey, go poke that beggar, Wave, with a sharp pole and drive it away!”

“That’s a great impression,” Gaia said.

“Wave can duplicate many voices, even human.” Kenjan’s voice betrayed a good amount of pride in Wave’s talent. “Even that of Oziru.”

“Can you do Fitzpatrick?” she asked.

Wave paused a moment, thinking. “As a matter of fact, Ms. Jones, I can.”

“Oh my God!” Gaia gasped.

“Oh my God!” Wave mimicked her.

Gaia leapt to her feet. “Just wait right there.” She rushed into her room then returned with her hand-held, a notepad and pen, and another beer.

“What new mischief is transpiring, oh my guardian?”

Kenjan craned its neck forward.

"Something very irritating to others," Gaia said. "You'll love it, Wave."

"Another irritating thing?" Wave rolled over closer to her. "What a night this is."

Gaia twisted the cap off her beer and wrote a note. She pushed it to Wave then gripped her hand-held, her thumb hovered above the "phone" button. "I'll dial and when the Superstore answers just read the note in Fitzpatrick's voice."

Wave read over the note. "I don't know how to say this word."

"Champagne."

"Okay." Wave gave her the thumbs-up. "All ready to dive."

Gaia pushed the "dial" icon. A tired-sounding clerk from the Superstore picked up.

"Hello, this is the A-Ki Station Superstore, your one-stop twenty-four-hour shopping center. Please take advantage of our two-for-one special on Roast Beef Dinner tonight. This is Jenny, how may I serve you?"

Wave hesitated, unsure whether it was supposed to speak. Gaia nudged the alien.

"Hello," Wave began in Fitzpatrick's voice. "I need to place an order for myself and my lady friend."

"Okay." Jenny sounded bored. Gaia felt a guilty pang for bothering the clerk, but for the purposes of the prank, it was necessary.

"We'd like two bottles of champagne, a can of whipping cream, a four pack of Pirate 'Feelies' condoms, two ham sandwiches and a coke."

Jenny repeated the order back to them, putting extra emphasis on the words "Feelies" and, inexplicably, "ham". Gaia giggled.

"That's right," Wave said.

"And you want those sandwiches light mayo, no veggies with havarti?"

Wave looked at Gaia quizzically. Gaia nodded. They must

have Fitzpatrick's sandwich order memorized.

"Yes, no veggies, please," Wave said.

"Do you want this delivered to Ms. Jones' residence?" Jenny asked.

"Ms. Jones?" Wave desperately ad-libbed. "Who is Ms. Jones?"

"The person whose hand-held you're calling from," Jenny replied. "She's probably that woman laughing in the background. Take a look and see."

"I am not calling from Ms. Jones' habitation. I am Mr. Fitzpatrick and I need ham now!" Wave used an extra forceful tone, which would have withered a Kishocha servant. Jenny was unimpressed.

"Who is this really?"

"Send ham to me now, lowly servant worm!" Wave shouted into the microphone. Gaia collapsed into giggles. Tears filled her eyes. Her sides ached. Wave continued thunderously, "It is an order from me, Exalted Fitzpatrick."

"Whatever, Ham-Boy." Jenny of the Superstore disconnected.

A few seconds later the reader had an incoming call from Corps Security.

"Don't answer it," Gaia said, though no one had made a move to do so.

"Neither of us would presume to touch your belongings," Kenjan said calmly. "But why does the idea strike now?"

"It's just the Corps Security trying to rat us out for crank calling," Gaia said. "Ha! They won't get me so easily. My answering service will take care of them."

They waited while Gaia's answering service picked up and Lieutenant Singh left a scathing message for the individual making calls from Gaia Jones' hand-held, then disconnected. Once the voice of authority was gone from the room, Gaia started chuckling again.

"I can't believe you told them to send ham now."

"I could not think of what to say," Wave protested. "What

would you have said?"

"I don't know." Gaia wiped away a tear. "It wouldn't have been as funny, though."

Kenjan tapped its finger on the edge of the pool. "What was the point of that?"

Gaia shrugged. "I just wanted to see if we could have that stuff delivered to Fitzpatrick."

"Why?" Kenjan asked. "Is ham a very embarrassing item?"

"No," Gaia said.

"We just wanted to be bad," Wave proclaimed. "And we wanted to annoy our betters, for in annoying our betters we revenge ourselves for our betters annoying us. Do we want to get up and groom the octopi? No. No, we do not. It is very annoying. And yet we must do the hateful deed."

"Go, Wave." Gaia thrust a fist into the air.

Kenjan pulled back slightly. "I had no idea grooming octopi annoyed you so much."

"How could it not?" Wave demanded. "They grasp. They bite with their beaks. They squirt the muzzle-stinging ink."

"Had I the power I would see that you never picked worms from the flaps of octopi again," Kenjan said.

"It is no matter. You are one of the lowly now, beautiful master, and have no powers."

Kenjan looked away. Gaia winced. Wave seemed to become suddenly aware of the awkwardness of its statement, but was at a loss for how to recover.

"And I will never make you clean up after my hamster." Gaia spoke a little too loudly.

After a confused moment, Wave said, "Ah, yes. Gaia does have the mysterious hamster-beast. It digs."

Kenjan nodded. "Some things dig."

Wave wrung its hands. "I am sorry for pointing out your bad circumstance, my master."

"It is fine," Kenjan said. "Gaia Jones?"

"Yes?"

"Since your intention is to be bad, will you carry a message to my Oziru for me?" Kenjan's demeanor was infinitely fragile. The tension of its body, the way its hands failed to move, everything about the alien bespoke loss.

Gaia felt suddenly cold, as though they'd had a hull breach and all atmosphere was being sucked out into space. They had reached the morose section of the evening. Had she been in the habit of having fun recently, she'd have remembered the drinking pendulum effect. The higher the swing into giddy madness, the lower the return into depression. She'd had one too many beers. The room spun gently. Empathy for Kenjan surged up within her, and while part of her knew this was just the effect of liquor, she couldn't stop herself from feeling the powerful urge to help her charge.

Kenjan said, "Please, my guardian. Tell my Oziru I hear its mournful singing, and I ache to be loved as much as my Oziru's arms ache from emptiness. I feel the infinite pain of love."

Gaia's stunted memory capacity couldn't hold that much. She was suddenly annoyed, and her depleted reservoir of tact allowed her to screw up her face in irritation. "Can't I just say that you miss Oziru?"

Kenjan scowled, then smiled at her sour expression. "That lacks poetry."

"But it's short. How much do you think I can remember?"

"Then say to Oziru 'My throat is dry'. Can you remember that?"

"My master," Wave protested. "You are so dirty and mean. Asking Gaia to say filthy, confusing things to Oziru."

"It would be a good joke though." Kenjan pushed away from the edge of the pool. "I think that I may sing tonight."

"You do not like to sing," Wave pointed out.

"No, but it helps to ease me." Kenjan flipped back under the water. Would any of this ever make sense to her? Would she even remember it? Maybe she should write herself a note. Kenjan resurfaced, its expression intense. "Seigata approaches."

"Horror! We have annoyed too much." Wave's expression was miserable.

"Is that bad?" Gaia asked.

"Probably not," Kenjan said. "But you must hide Wave."

"Because I am giddy with orange?"

"No," Kenjan slammed its hand into the water, sending an arcing splash hurtling toward Wave. "Because you have painted your face like a criminal impostor and are too giddy with orange to remember it."

Wave's cranial tendrils stiffened almost as much as Kenjan's had when Wave had been impersonating Seigata's voice. Then Wave's eyes narrowed. "Is this a sneaky reciprocation joke?"

"No!" Kenjan hurled a handful of slimy yellow sea-grass at Wave. "Get out *now*."

Wave leapt to its feet and rushed into Gaia's bedroom. At the same moment, the other door to the shrine opened to reveal Seigata. The alien wore a resplendent collar of woven gold that scooped down low over its chest. As usual, it wore gold bands around the base of each cranial tendril and gauntlets and anklets made from pearls. As drunk as Gaia was, she found it impossible not to stare at Seigata's blank crotch. She knew that she had to get over the idea that the Kishocha were genital-less neuters who shamelessly refused to wear pants. But when sitting down with her head at crotch-level, it was hard to avoid the stare.

"You may rise, Guardian." Seigata mistook her dumbfounded drunkenness for respect. Gaia glanced askance at Kenjan. The alien had disappeared leaving her completely alone with an irritated superior. The room tilted, and Gaia wobbled but kept upright. She felt suddenly childish. She hung her head in shame.

Seigata reached out, lifted her chin and studied her face.

"Are you ill, Guardian?"

Gaia was about to refuse when some independently intelligent internal mechanism recognized the lifeline Seigata offered.

"Yes! I'm not feeling well."

"I thought so," Seigata said. "You smell bad and your face

is ugly. Have you deliriously placed fraudulent markings on your face?"

Gaia wriggled her chin out of Seigata's grip. "I was practicing for a dress-up party. Humans sometimes disguise themselves as other creatures for fun."

Seigata made the smile expression. "Are the other creatures ever fooled?"

"Sometimes, but not by me. I'm bad at disguising myself."

"Yes, you are." Seigata's volume rose while its tone descended. "You are very bad!" Its thunderous voice echoed throughout the circular chamber. Gaia swallowed. She broke out into a clammy sweat. Seigata grew even louder, working on itself like rolling thunder. "The reason I came is that the Corps Security Officer Singh contacted me to find out who had been making annoying calls. The call's origin was from inside the Kishocha area, which was very strange. So I came to the area and found you here, disguised and stinking and holding the hand-held. What have you to say?"

Gaia couldn't squeeze out any words. Seigata's furious voice rang in her ears. She hung her head. She focused on the floor, trying to maintain her balance, then she gathered her breath and slurred, "I'm sorry."

"Are you convulsed with contrition?"

"Sure." Gaia couldn't bring herself to look at Seigata's eyes. Her hands shook. Why did Seigata have to yell at her? No one ever yelled at her. She had no defense against it.

"Good. Be sure to have Wave care for you until your health returns. And promise to make no more foolish calls."

"I promise," Gaia intoned.

"Good." Seigata turned to leave. "I will become angry if I must swim back here again to stop you. But since your crime is only trivial I will say a prayer to try and relieve your malady. It is my greatest desire to never have to chastise you again. Do you understand me?"

"Yes," Gaia said. The Kishocha door twisted shut. Gaia stayed slumped over. She couldn't believe how the evening had deteriorated. She felt sick. The alien didn't return. Gaia looked experimentally up. The room seemed blurry and dim. All the colors looked mushy. The room lurched sideways and she passed out.

Chapter Fifteen: New Product Line

Gaia neither looked nor felt her best the next morning, which began with a second, milliseconds-long gravity failure that nonetheless triggered the requisite flashing lights and alarms.

Not exactly the first sound a woman nursing a hangover likes to hear.

But she rallied. She showered, ate some dry toast and went to the dining room, where she discovered Wave signing for the delivery of the remote kiosk.

It came in seventeen boxes. The words *some assembly required* didn't begin to describe the situation. The kiosk was like a three-dimensional yellow plastic puzzle.

While Gaia perused the instructional pamphlet, Wave lay on the floor with an arm flung over its muzzle, still stained orange from the previous night. Roy arrived and started spraying antiseptic on the dining room tables. Because Happy Snak wouldn't open for another forty-five minutes, Gaia decided to take a run at partially assembling the kiosk. She fitted the plastic-frame tubing together with shaky hands, feeling like she was doing a good job considering the viciousness of her headache.

Slowly the pain and violent nausea were receding, but she still felt like she might die before they completely faded. Gaia had progressed into the silent-prayer-and-bargaining phase of being hungover.

All she could think was: *Please, please, let me stop feeling this way. If this just stops, I'll never drink again.*

Not that Gaia believed in a higher power, she was just following the basic human instinct to mutely beg for relief.

She didn't even know why she was bothering to assemble the awning section of her new Xiao Enterprises concession kiosk. It wasn't going to rain—ever. But somehow the hot dog stand looked bad without the awning. Besides it had the Happy Snak jester logo silk-screened onto its blue and yellow striped vinyl.

As she worked and drank cola, time worked its magic. At last, Gaia was able to engage a cheeseburger.

Attracted by the falling crumbs, a cleaner slid slowly up to her. The cleaners, which had started off as baseball-sized snails, were growing quickly. Now each was easily the size of Gaia's thigh. They devoured a wide variety of molds, mushrooms and black scum which collected around the edges of refrigerator drawers. According to Wave they were supposed to grow to be about the size of Gaia's torso, and strictly feed off refuse. Some human objects confused them. Anything with a battery, for example, had to be locked up. Cleaners were inexplicably attracted to batteries. Gaia also kept the cleaners out of her room, but Wave even let them curl up, like lapdogs on its sponge nest.

Safe in the sphere of his hamster globe, Microbe deftly avoided the cleaner's long, probing antennae, rolled up to Gaia's foot and rammed it. Microbe loved his hamster globe. She knew this because when it was time to come out of the globe, Microbe would roll madly away from her and hide under the refrigerator.

"Hey, Microbe," Gaia said in her sweetest, lowest voice.

"Hey, Microbe." A sweet, low impersonation of her voice rolled out of Wave's mouth. Gaia glanced behind her. Wave lay on the floor studying Microbe with an unseemly intensity. "Hey, Microbe," the Kishocha said again. Microbe rolled over toward Wave, trying to sniff the alien through its clear plastic sphere.

"Do you like my hamster?" Gaia asked.

"Yes, I do," Wave replied. "Watching him is very exciting."

"Do you have hamsters on your world?"

Wave shrugged. "I've never seen one. But my experiences in our home waters were limited."

"What was it like?" Gaia put down the perplexing diagram. She had no idea what it said.

"I remember the water was warm and clear. I pogged around with my siblings in the nursery pool and learned the names of the structures and our clan name, and they told us terrifying stories of the Sharks and of Yellow-Red War Riders."

Roy drifted over to them. Wave watched Microbe.

"All of us pogs in that pool were of noble egg once, but the Yellow-Red Riders came with Battle Sharks and contaminated our parent with their seed. Lots of soldiers lost their limbs in the fight and also after as punishment for letting us seven be defiled," Wave said.

"Amazing." Roy fished a hand-held out of his pocket and set it on the floor near Wave. One of the cleaners slid purposely toward the device. Gaia got ready to poke the thing.

She said, "So you used to be a noble?"

"No, never, except as an egg with only one parent still." Wave dropped its voice even lower. "If I was to still be the child of a noble Kishocha, then my first parent would be the same first parent as the beautiful Kenjan and the wise Seigata. But since my other parent is a Yellow-Red Rider and worse than filth and I am so asymmetrical, I am an orphan-servant, you see?"

"So Kenjan is your half-sibling?" Roy leaned forward.

"No, but if we were humans that is how we would be related. Beautiful Kenjan and wise Seigata pogged together in a previous birthing pool. They are older."

The cleaner had reached Roy's recorder and probed the device inquisitively with its wet antennae.

"Where are your other siblings?" Gaia asked. "Are they on Ki Island?"

"Oh, no, no, no, no, no, no," Wave said. "First sibling and second sibling and fourth sibling all shamefully ran away to join with Yellow-Red Riders. A jellyfish ate fifth sibling. Sixth sibling is, I think, still servant within the Blessed Structure Reliable Sky Embrace on our home world. And seventh sibling teaches pogs."

"What happened to third sibling?" Roy asked.

"Third sibling was won as a gambling prize by the zany Chambered Shell just before that beauty was wedded to Brave Lightning."

"Then?" Gaia asked.

"Then Brave Lightning was chosen to lead the quest for heaven and we all entered the Blessed Structure Shining Heaven's Pearl of Knowledge Island and lifted into the cold void." Wave reached over and stroked the cleaner, who relentlessly sucked the microphone out of Roy's hand-held. Roy didn't seem to notice.

"So Kenjan means Chambered Shell and Oziru means Brave Lightning, and Ki means Blessed Heaven's Pearl of Knowledge." Roy smiled expansively, as though he'd discovered a new purpose in life. "And you are third sibling?"

"Yes. Except that Ki means only pearl, and Kenjan could also be called Nautilus. The beautiful Kenjan once told me that it won me on purpose because I was its half-sibling. But one person overhears our talking and Kenjan's kind words started a terrible fight and that's when Kenjan was first called a heretic. It was before we even met you humans."

Microbe approached and Gaia nudged his hamster ball away from the zealous cleaner. She wasn't sure what it would think of a rodent. "I thought that Kenjan's heresy was human inspired."

"Kenjan was a perverted heretic long before humans were discovered. Humans just gave lovely Kenjan another excuse to be bad. One of the priests said that lovely Kenjan was without pogs because of its bad ways. Maybe I believe that, but maybe I do not." Wave stroked the cleaner again. The striped animal was quivering in a distressing way. Wave reached into the pocket of its smock and pulled out two sets of tweezers. "The cleaner will make droppings now."

"What?" Roy sat up straight and noticed what the cleaner was doing to his hand-held. The microphone was completely devoured. The last of a long blue wire was disappearing into the cleaner's mouth. "Hey, that's mine!"

"Don't worry, Roy. I'll get it back for you, more beautiful than ever." Wave flipped the cleaner over onto its back.

"That's okay, don't kill it," Roy said quickly.

"I won't kill it, I love little cleaners." Wave looked appalled that Roy had even suggested such a thing. "I'll get the microphone back in a couple of days, not this time. This time it's just a normal dropping. See, look, the dropping emerges."

Gaia watched as a tiny, gasping anus seemed to open out of nowhere, and a silvery-gray and glistening nub came into view. The cleaner shook violently. Wave reached down and grabbed one end of the nub, pulling and twisting it expertly. A rank fishy odor filled Happy Snak.

"What are you doing now?" Roy crowded in closer.

"I'm making a gambling piece." Wave focused on manipulating the piece of excrement into an artful position. When the turd was fully extracted, it was about the size of Gaia's thumb. It was cylindrical. The turd dried rapidly, forming a hard, shell-like surface. Wave's attentions to it became more intense.

"Now is the only time its shapeable." Wave paused to blow on the turd. If Gaia hadn't known it was a little piece of dung, she'd have compared this process to shaping molten glass, but she couldn't make that comparison because it wasn't molten glass. It was a little piece of dung.

"What is it?" Roy forgot about his mangled hand-held.

"A piece for gambling," Wave said. "My pieces are in top demand. People are always gambling me for them because I have the beauteous pieces they desire."

"That's what a gambling piece is made of?" Gaia felt her jaw slacken and her upper lip rise in an unstoppable sneer of revulsion. "That's what *all* the gambling pieces in your pocket are made of?"

"Yes!" Wave said.

"You have pockets full of shit?" Gaia felt her blood pressure rise. The health department could never know.

"Don't they disintegrate in water?" Roy asked.

"Never." Wave put the final twist on its gambling piece. By this time the cleaner had righted itself and was slowly pursuing Microbe across the dining room. "It stays hard forever."

Wave explained the intricacies of twisting excrement into art to Roy. Gaia could not listen. How could she salvage her idea now? She'd already bought the kiosk. She'd already put pictures of the jewelry up on the jewelry channel at the station. She had advance orders, sight unseen, for these little pieces of crap. Literally—pieces of crap.

Gaia held her head.

"Is there something wrong?" Wave asked.

"I didn't realize what gambling pieces were made from."

"Not all of them are made from the secretions of cleaners, just the ones for orphan servants and soldiers and peoples like that. We have no gold or ivory so we make these. They last a long time."

Gaia pressed her eyes shut, just to not have to look at the gambling piece anymore. "People don't want to wear shit."

"Were you planning on selling these?" Roy asked Gaia.

"I was going to let the Kishocha use them for money because I thought that humans would think they made great jewelry. I have over a hundred advance orders. I used the money to buy the concession-stand permit and fifty cases of clams. Oh, God."

The three sat in silence. Wave hung its head, knowing it had somehow disappointed Gaia, but mystified as to how. Gaia rubbed her temples.

Roy gingerly lifted the gambling piece. "I don't think you have to tell people that they're made from...feces. I think you can say it's a secretion from a mollusk, or snail or something. It's not slimy or anything and the smell is gone now."

"What about when it gets wet?" Gaia asked. "Does it stink then? I really think I'm going to have to pull the plug. I can't sell people turds to make earrings with."

Wave broke in. "But it's not like the human turd! It's hard, like shell. No bad smells. The pieces are eternal, like gambling itself."

Gaia got the feeling that this was some kind of Kishocha idiomatic phrase. She would have been pleased to note this, perhaps even fantasize about relating her linguistic discovery to Fitzpatrick, if she hadn't been so depressed about the crushing of her dream. How could she unload fifty cases of clams? Chowder maybe?

"Please, Gaia," Wave said. "Please let my other friends buy snacks for pieces. They've never had a snack before. They don't understand what freedom is."

Wave solidly faced Roy, drawing itself up to its full height. "Snacks are freedom, Roy, there is no doubt. If a person has a piece, it can say, 'I want a snack,' and then that person could go and get a snack—any one they want. And all that person has to do is put up a piece and say, 'I want orange,' and it doesn't even have to ask. It could just say, 'Orange!' if it wanted to." Wave searched for the right words to convey this experience. "I want orphan-servants and soldiers to have snacks anytime they want one. As if we were clean and smart."

Gaia felt a pang of compassion. She wondered how Wave could find every chink in her emotional armor without even trying. Maybe it was Wave's sincerity, or maybe it was the Kishocha's alienness. Gaia didn't care much for people. Since the divorce, she had felt like she lacked some vital social quality, whose absence rendered her unable to interact normally. Maybe that quality could simply be described as the desire to care about someone or something. That desire had returned now, with a vengeance. She wanted Wave to be happy. Not because happiness was more convenient for herself, but for its own sake.

Wave was pure, not good or moral, but honest. It said exactly what it thought. Right now, that meant Wave thought that snacks were more than a business proposition, snacks were a whole new way of living. Gaia didn't know if that was strictly accurate, but then, who was she to say what Kishocha thought or felt? Maybe for them even the tiniest freedom was so amazing that it could change the world.

"Gaia Jones." Wave drew nearer. "Fate and the god have decreed that you, a snack seller, are here in this place and time. Could it be for any reason but to give snacks to my people? No, it is your destiny."

Gaia glanced at Roy, who shrugged as if her place in history was all settled.

She said, "Fine, but you have to remember that there are no snacks without pieces, right? Don't go soft on me. And you have to not let people gamble for snacks. This is a fair exchange. One piece for one snack, end of story."

"Absolutely not, that constitutes theft, which creates shrink. I will do as the employee handbook asks and never fail."

Gaia wondered if perhaps Wave should be doing the books instead of her. It seemed to have absorbed all the most noxious accounting lingo in a matter of weeks. Perhaps later, if this venture ever got off the ground. And that all depended on Wave keeping its mouth shut, which might or might not be possible.

Gaia said, "Listen, you must never, ever, ever, under any circumstances tell any human what these gambling pieces are made of. If anyone asks, tell them it's an ancient secret."

"But that's a lie."

"Do you want snacks for your people or not?"

"I do." Wave had a particularly determined look in its eye. "I will lie about the pieces. I will never say that they are droppings."

"Then it's settled. We'll open up the concession stand tonight, as planned." Gaia allowed herself to relax slightly, now that the impending PR disaster had been averted. "Now, what about the menu?"

Wave had devised a menu that it felt would be profitable, according to some restauranteering book it had read. As the menu scrolled up the screen, Gaia began to regain her sense of adventure.

Stunned Snake Snack with Orange and Pickle

Excited Clam with Coffee Syrup

Sucked Clam in Taco Shell with Paste
Live Snake on Jell-O with Orange
Slippery Butter Pats on Paper Squares
Dramatic Chicken Bird Egg in Shell

Lastly, came the mysterious *Prophet's Favorite Snake*, which turned out to be chicken satay with two shots of orange on the side.

"Its a limited menu," Wave said. "But this way I can really perfect my preparation before I expand."

"Expand to what?" Roy asked.

"Full menu treats like Sucked Clam Platter and Quivering Grass Jelly. And also bigger stunned things like Stunned Crab and Stunned Cow Spider. Later maybe I will offer Delicate Kelp and Water Snail in Pool of Seawater. That was lovely Kenjan's favorite Kishocha food. But I'm not a master food maker so it could take some time to learn that. The bowl has to be shaped just right so that the snail does not escape."

"And all these things cost one piece, right?" Gaia clarified.

"Exactly!"

"I'm proud of you, Wave. You've done a great job, and I want this thing to work out as much as you do. So, I think for the first week we'll run a buy-one-get-one-free special to try and encourage business."

"Hooray!" Wave cried. "Two treats for one."

"Now, since I want to make a good impression on our Kishocha customers, I've taken the liberty of getting these." Gaia reached into her pocket and pulled out four velvet bags. She handed one to Wave and two to Roy. "One of those is for Cheryl. I decided that Mickey Mouse wasn't exactly to my taste."

Roy opened his bag and slid the official Happy Snak pit guard out onto his palm. The main body of it was a replica of the Happy Snak jester logo, suspended on a half-inch-thick, flat serpentine 24-karat-gold electroplate chain.

"Oh fabulous heaven! I am blessed by the god!" Wave shouted, then sank into dull repose. "But I cannot wear gold, Gaia."

"I'm afraid this is part of the official uniform now, so..." Gaia shrugged. "If Sharkey bothers you about it, you just send Sharkey to me."

"These are great, Gaia." Roy awkwardly patted her shoulder. "Thanks a lot."

"You're welcome." All her attention was focused on Wave's shaking fingers.

The Kishocha opened up the bag as if it was opening up the Ark of the Covenant. When Wave finally got the pit guard on its neck, Gaia could have sworn that the alien grew six inches. Its face was stern, but its cranial tendrils fidgeted like exited schoolchildren on a crowded bus.

"Gaia Jones? Roy?" Wave addressed them. Both humans regarded Wave expectantly. "I, Wave, have arrived."

Then the Kishocha walked off to its room, leaving she and Roy to ponder what it could have meant.

Chapter Sixteen: Muzzlers

After weeks of nothing, a few Kishocha had finally begun to regularly attend the shrine. The Kishocha had been terrified of her at first but devoted enough to Kenjan to brave her scary presence.

To seem more casual and because the floor was hard, Gaia had purchased a lawn chair for the shrine.

Now Gaia dozed. She'd been sleepy around dinnertime and the prospect of staying up till midnight to oversee Kenjan's feeding was proving to be difficult.

Tentatively, a skinny, asymmetrical Kishocha ducked in the Kishocha-side door. It hunched, still dripping wet from its trip through the waterway. Then the Kishocha padded across the polished shell floor to the edge of Kenjan's pool. It didn't look at Stinger or Sharkey.

By now Gaia knew the drill. Kenjan would not appear. She didn't know why—the Kishocha was chatty enough when they were alone together. But to its loyal disciples Kenjan remained aloof.

The skinny Kishocha knelt and placed its offering to Kenjan (which looked like a large, ragged chunk of fish head) in the special ghost-feeding basket. After saying a prayer, the skinny Kishocha surprised Gaia by scampering over to Mini-Snak and buying a Stunned Snake Snack with Orange and Pickle. Then the Kishocha scurried away, leaving a soiled paper boat in its wake.

Mini-Snak was catching on. Maybe it only had one or two customers a day, but the business was growing.

Over the next five minutes at least ten more Kishocha pulled themselves out of the water. Kenjan was going to get a real feed.

Gaia cracked an eye and regarded the Kishocha with vague curiosity. They were a strange bunch. They were more symmetrical than usual, and rather than giving their offerings right away, they gathered together, talking. Over time, she'd come to recognize a few of the Kishocha who regularly fed Kenjan. This bunch was new. A spark of hope woke Gaia up. Maybe they weren't here for Kenjan at all. Maybe they were here for the concession stand.

Until just now, only a few snacks had been sold, and all to soldiers via Stinger. Stinger itself had become their first regular. The guard ended each night with a Stunned Snake Snack with Orange and Pickle, purchased with one of its many gambling pieces.

Wave stood behind the concession-stand counter, unlidding the ice chest, which was sunk into the countertop. With a flourish, Wave produced a case of fresh Real Human Clams. It arranged the bivalves carefully, standing them up on their sides as if they were a series of soldiers at attention. Wave admired its handiwork for a moment, and then seemed to suddenly notice the crowd that had assembled.

Wave clapped its hands. "Please everyone! I'd like you to know that you can trade gambling pieces for snacks."

The small crowd of Kishocha seemed startled by the attention.

"You, oh Honorable Scholar!" Wave called. "Would you like to try a treat? It's two for one piece today. A special day. I have a delicious snack called orange. Would you like to try?"

Gaia frowned. She didn't know Wave was still trying the two-for-one thing.

The Kishocha whom Wave addressed pulled a fist-sized glob from under its vest. Gaia shuddered to think of the size of cleaner that had laid that monster. Wave scowled and waved its hands. “No, Honorable Scholar, we don’t accept rocks. Gambling pieces only. I see you have many. Please trade me for some orange.” The scholar shifted so that its back was to Wave but kept looking over its shoulder at Mini-Snak.

Gaia smiled to herself.

Wave took the job seriously. Since it had received the pit guard, there had been a change in Wave. Gaia caught the Kishocha deliberately not groveling on three separate occasions. She could tell when Wave was resisting the urge to grovel because Wave always stood extra straight.

As usual, Wave wasn’t wearing its pit guard. It never wore it in front of any other Kishocha. Should she make Wave go get the thing or just forget about it once and for all? After one moment’s thought, Gaia decided to be cruel.

“Wave?” she called. Her voice upset one of the offering-bearing Kishocha so much that the alien dropped to the floor. Gaia tried not to notice.

“Yes, Gaia Jones?” Wave said.

“You aren’t in uniform.”

“Oh, really?” Wave tried to act casual, but its hand instantly went to its throat. Caught.

“Go get it.”

“Yes, Gaia Jones.” Wave slunk quickly out the side door. Gaia took a long draw on her Frosticcino and turned to Stinger. For the last couple of weeks Gaia had focused on befriending Stinger. Unlike Sharkey, who was alternately sarcastic and formal, Stinger had grown willing to share its thoughts with Gaia. She knew, for example, that Stinger was chosen to be a member of Oziru’s household chiefly for its looks. It was apparently quite good-looking for a soldier. Stinger pointed out that though its markings were solid, with no swirls, they were symmetrical. Also, Stinger’s lighter orange eyes were a sought-after feature.

Stinger’s soldiering career had been lackluster, and mainly focused on gambling and spitting red kelp. It had only been in one fight, and that was with a band of raiders it called “The

Squids". Once, when Sharkey was on an eating break, Stinger had confided that it found Sharkey rather pompous and conceited, and didn't agree with it at all about Gaia's concession stand. Stinger insisted it wanted the concession stand, especially for the orange and the Snakes on Jell-O with Orange. Gaia felt she'd made a major breakthrough.

Stinger was an amazing gambler. Stinger had strands and strands of gambling pieces hung around its neck. And the individual pieces changed quite frequently, as Stinger lost some and won others. The soldier was a high roller, with Lady Luck on its side.

Did the Kishocha even have a Lady Luck? Well, that was just one more conversation she could have with Stinger, wasn't it?

"Is there some kind of lucky spirit for you guys?" Gaia tried not to look at the newest Kishocha who'd come to give Kenjan its offering. It crept along, clearly making an effort to not be heard. "You know, for gamblers?"

Stinger frowned at her. "I do not understand."

Sharkey stepped over. "Gaia means who is Lucky Bones."

"Lucky Bones." Stinger smiled. "Lucky Bones is on my side."

"I can see that." Gaia indicated Stinger's pieces.

"Lucky Bones is all white and glows like a jellyfish in the dark," Sharkey said.

"Lucky Bones likes me because my face is all white and my eyes are dice colored, and jellyfish is in my name," Stinger said. "Lucky Bones hates Sharkey. See that gambling piece around Sharkey's neck? That bellystabber has had the same old gambling piece ever since before we left home."

"I'll show you bellystabber," Sharkey murmured.

"Sharkey's such a bad gambler," Stinger continued, "that even cleaners have more gambling pieces."

"I am not a bad gambler," Sharkey said. "I abstain from the game."

"You abstain because you're so bad that pond pogs won't gamble you because they find the game too unchallenging,"

Stinger said.

Gaia snickered.

At that moment Wave stepped through the open door like a prince entering the camp of his enemy. Wave's head was aloft. Its new pit guard gleamed in the dim light. Instantly, Sharkey sprang forward but seemed to hesitate when it saw that Wave's pit guard was made of gold. Sharkey looked appalled.

Gaia preemptively jumped in. "Before you even start, Sharkey, that necklace is part of Wave's official uniform, and I've ordered Wave to wear it, so you just keep your comments to yourself, okay?"

Sharkey spun around, startling three timid Kishocha servants who were hesitating near the door. "This is heretical."

"It's not heretical, it's human," Gaia corrected.

Sharkey snorted. "All the same."

"You have to admit though, Wave looks blasphemously beautiful in that pit guard," Stinger said. "It's too bad you're a red-yellow orphan-servant, Wave. Your cranial tendrils are so beautiful I'd share my pit with you. What color is your tongue anyway?"

"You are so vulgar," Wave said, though it clearly responded to the flattery.

Sharkey stepped between Wave and Stinger. "You need to try your hunt elsewhere."

"I don't need to hunt at all. I had a harpooner last week. We should all three share sometime. This harpooner's pit was so deep. You could have fit your whole muzzle into this pit. And fragrant! You could—"

"Do you want a free orange?" Wave broke in, derailing the conversation. Gaia was annoyed. She was curious about Kishocha sex and thought Stinger's tales of conquest would be an excellent way to learn about it. Fortunately, Stinger ignored Wave.

"Do you have a muzzler, Gaia Jones?"

Before Gaia could answer, Wave stepped forward. "Stinger means, do you have an object of your affections?" All three Kishocha stared at Gaia expectantly. "Humans have objects of their affections, yes?"

"Yes, but I don't."

"So you have a dry throat?" Stinger shook its head. "Its painful to have to always prod your own throat like an ugly."

"I don't prod my throat." Gaia didn't know if she was claiming to never masturbate or trying to explain human anatomy. Maybe both. "And I'm not ugly."

"No," Wave hastily put in. "You're very symmetrical."

"You never prod your throat?" Stinger couldn't believe this. "Why not?"

"Because there's nothing to prod," Gaia said. "Human...love parts aren't there."

"I knew that!" Wave turned to Sharkey. "See! Gaia Jones is not a no-sex." Sharkey shrugged and looked away.

"Where are they?" Stinger asked.

"They're between my legs," Gaia replied. All three Kishocha looked directly at her crotch, Stinger and Sharkey in puzzlement, Wave in triumphant glee.

Stinger cocked its head. "Then where is your excrement hole?"

"It's down there too," Gaia said.

Stinger recoiled. Sharkey looked disgusted, and Wave looked sad and embarrassed.

"Right by your love parts?" Stinger's horror could not be masked.

"Exactly." Gaia was growing more and more uncomfortable with this conversation, and with the aliens' shameless crotch-staring.

"But how can you tell an egg sac from a piece of filth?" Stinger persisted.

"Humans don't have egg sacs. They have babies, you know, live young?" Gaia said. The group of Kishocha who had come to make offerings to Kenjan was about twelve strong now and had gathered at the edge of the water, but weren't sliding their offerings into the basket. They seemed to be just standing there, whispering and glancing over at her. She wondered if they, too, were marveling at the disgustingness of the human reproductive system.

Sharkey asked, “You mean the young grow inside you?”

“Yes,” Gaia answered.

“The pogs are protected by your body?”

“Usually only one pog at a time is born. But yes, that’s how it works. I’ll check out a media disc and show it to you, and you can see how it happens, okay?”

Sharkey quickly raised a hand in refusal. “It sounds like a good way to protect pogs, but I do not care to see.”

“I do,” Stinger jumped in.

“Good,” Gaia said. “So will you ever make pogs?”

“I am not a breeder,” Stinger said matter-of-factly. “I will never have permission to lock my stamen with another. So I will express no egg sacs. Too bad, I like little puddle jumpers.”

“I’m sorry.”

A Kishocha inched curiously toward Mini-Snak. Gaia nudged Wave. “Shouldn’t you be over there?”

“I will tend the store at once.”

Sharkey stared after Wave with a predatory fascination that discomfited her. Was this what she’d call love or what she’d call stalking? The soldier watched Wave load a fresh gallon of orange into the dispenser gun and set the portion at one fluid ounce. Sharkey drifted nearer while Wave inspected the snakes for vigor, discarding two limp floaters on the surface.

“I think,” Stinger whispered to her, “Sharkey’s dry for the orphan-servant.”

“Wouldn’t Sharkey be wet for it?” Gaia whispered back. Stinger snickered.

“You’re almost as filthy as me, Gaia Jones.” Stinger shifted closer. “Its always the way with the rigid ones.”

“How do you mean?” Gaia asked. Sharkey leaned on the concession stand and poked at the clams with profound disapproval. Wave stood too stiffly and told Sharkey to stop it at once, if it pleased.

“Well,” Stinger said, “that one stares at Wave. Do not think

I spit at Sharkey for this. Wave is too beautiful to be an orphan-servant. And it is so exotic."

"I never knew Wave was beautiful."

"Wave's cranial tendrils." Stinger yanked on one of its own finger-length tendrils. "They are almost as long as a noble caste."

"I see."

"And with its pit covered..." Stinger paused to exhale forcefully, its nostril slits widening to big round O's. "With its pit covered, Wave even makes my throat wet."

"You keep your hands off. Wave is too nice to be going with a gambler like you," Gaia said, laughing.

"I have a harpooner anyway. So, Gaia Jones, when you have a love object, do you have a boy-type-human?"

"Yeah, I generally prefer the boy-type-human."

"And they are different from you in your love parts, so Wave tells me," Stinger said.

"Right."

"But girl-type-humans are the same as you." Stinger held itself as though it was making closing arguments before the Supreme Court.

"That is correct." Gaia felt like she might know where this conversation was going. She'd get a human reproduction media disc when she obtained "The Miracle of Birth".

"Then why would you have desire for the different one?" Stinger's simple question derailed her. She had been preparing a brief speech, complete with the usual in-and-out pantomime to explain intercourse.

"Wouldn't you rather have the girl-type-human?" Stinger asked. Gaia hesitated and Stinger panicked. "You are a girl-type-human aren't you? You're not a boy-type, right? They have the face hair, correct?"

"That's right," Gaia reassured Stinger. "I am a girl-type."

"It doesn't bother you that the boy-types are different? Don't they look deformed?"

"No." Gaia couldn't stop herself from laughing. "I mean,

they did when I was a little kid, but I got used to it."

"Then you can understand how a soldier could adore beneath its caste." Stinger nodded.

Sharkey was criticizing Wave's Happy Snak smock. It covered too much of Wave's body and that, Sharkey claimed, was unacceptable. Wave stood so stiffly its cranial tendrils were practically standing up, which was a feat for tendrils as long as Wave's. The alien looked like it had set its tendrils in fat hot rollers. Wave's yellow and violet eyes glinted.

"Unless you wish to trade your gambling piece for a snack, I would like to ask you to step away and make room for paying customers." Wave lifted its muzzle high. Sharkey looked for one moment like it was going to physically attack Wave, then suddenly dropped its head in a half-bow.

"I exist to serve only you." Sharkey's eyes lidded.

Wave hunched down, its cranial tendrils wiggling frenetically. "You do?"

"There's nothing I want to do more in life than obey you. It would complete my life to hear your wisdom as my own gospel as well."

Stinger winced at Sharkey's sarcasm. Gaia felt a small, burning surge of empathy for Wave. Wave was nicer than anyone she'd ever met and didn't deserve the abuse Sharkey dished out. She didn't care if Stinger's love theory was true. Or rather, if it was true then Sharkey was an even bigger ass than she already thought. She watched as Wave's cranial tendrils sank.

"I hate you, glorious Soldier Sharkey."

"That is your right, most pure and lovely Wave Walker, and yet I serve and love you anyway, like the filth I am," Sharkey said. "How sad my life is. I may have to sing a mournful song."

"Then go sing it to Stinger." Wave pointed toward them. "Because I do not feel sympathy for you."

"I hear and obey." Sharkey shrugged and padded over to them. "Wave is most certainly not at all egotistical or above itself. In fact, I think that being with Gaia Jones has made Wave Walker more humble and agreeable to its station than Kenjan's great experiment did. Thank you, Gaia Jones, for steadfastly upholding the tenets of our great society."

"You're an ass, Sharkey," Gaia said. "Wave's too good to even stun your snakes."

Sharkey lapsed into uncharacteristic silence, then crossed to the Kishocha-side door and took up its usual position.

"What was that about?" Gaia asked Stinger.

Stinger shrugged. "Mysterious."

Gaia glanced away from Stinger just in time to see a large rock hurtling through the air toward Kenjan's island. The rock crashed through the delicate latticework window, bounced off something inside the house, then landed with a wet thud on Kenjan's bed.

"Honorable Scholar!" Wave cried. "Why must your school criticize in death as well as life?"

In the moment she had to think, Gaia thought, *What?*

The scholar ignored Wave, raised another rock and hurled it at Kenjan's house, bellowing, "Go away, Ghost!"

Stone after stone flew through the air. The Kishocha bellowed out epithets along with their missiles. "Heretic! Barren! Curse to you!" The shrine echoed with the crashes of breaking coral and wood.

Sharkey and Stinger remained motionless and silent.

She couldn't believe this was happening. Wave also stood still, but seemed rooted in horror, rather than just complacent like the guards.

Gaia rounded on Stinger.

"Do something!" She seized Stinger's upper arm and tried to drag the Kishocha out.

"It is their right to express anger at the ghost."

"They're destroying Kenjan's house." Gaia jerked Stinger's upper arm again. "Go out there and stop them."

Stinger sighed and stepped forward. "You! Honorable Scholar and servants. You must be orderly. You must throw rocks one at a time."

The assembled Kishocha seemed to find this request

reasonable and lined up to stone Kenjan's house. Gaia found this totally unacceptable. Her fear of being hurt by the crowd was overpowered by her desire to beat at least one of them senseless. Her restraint evaporated. She charged forward.

"You get back! You get out of my store!" Gaia grabbed her own drink and flung it at the scholar. The waxed paper cup bounced off the Kishocha's shoulder then spilled onto the floor. The scholar launched its next rock directly at her. The other Kishocha let loose a barrage of rocks and clam shells. Gaia couldn't possibly dodge them all. She shot up an arm to try and protect her face from the onslaught. Nothing hit her. Looking up she saw that Wave had stepped between her and Kenjan's detractors. Wave doubled over as a baseball-sized rock smashed into the Kishocha's abdomen. A clamshell grazed the side of Gaia's face, scraping the skin away.

"You keep away from Gaia Jones." Wave was enraged. "You go home."

"Stand down, Servant," the scholar shouted.

"No! You have no right to criticize her with stones."

"Disobedient," the scholar roared, hurling another stone at Wave. Wave didn't dodge. It took the impact in the throat, howling out a terrible scream of anger.

Gaia rushed to the concession stand and grabbed the clam-pounding mallet. Reason had fled. As she spun around to attack the scholar, she saw Sharkey step forward and smash the blunt end of its spear into the scholar's head with a wet smack. Sharkey whirled, bringing its spear across the back of the scholar's knees forcing it to the ground. The other Kishocha simply dropped to the floor, terrified and supplicant. Again, Sharkey brought its weapon down, this time across the scholar's shoulders. Gaia thought she heard something snap. Stinger moved in after Sharkey, blocking another brutal blow to the scholar's head.

"Sharkey!" Stinger said.

Sharkey stopped and looked over to Stinger.

"Our Lord Oziru has proclaimed that any Kishocha who hurts a human is charged with death." Sharkey spun, and before Stinger could intervene, Sharkey drove its spear into the scholar's back, pulled back and with one arcing motion severed the scholar's head. Black blood rushed out across the floor, hissing and steaming. Gaia scampered back from it, gagging on the smell.

Sharkey surveyed the blood and steam. "Motions of treason," it said.

Gaia felt sick. She flung an arm across her mouth to keep the smell out, and the horror and bile in. Wave lay on the floor clutching its throat. Wave's breath came in shallow gasps, like a person trying not to cry. Gaia went to it, but she didn't know what to do.

"It's okay, Wave." She was afraid to touch Wave. She gagged on the smell of acid.

Stinger looked irritated. "All of you go and take the body back to the school. Leave the head."

The other Kishocha rose, cowering as they did so. They picked up the scholar's body and dragged it out. When they were gone, Stinger grabbed the head by its cranial tendrils. It turned to Sharkey. "I will go explain to glorious Oziru. You stay—and see to Wave. I think that one is hurt."

Sharkey nodded, then knelt and pulled Wave into its lap. "Pull your hands away," Sharkey said, not cruelly, but decisively. "Let me see your wound."

Wave complied, leaning its head against Sharkey's chest and shoulder.

"Is it bad?" Gaia crouched down beside them. Her throat hurt from the fumes. Irritated tears welled in her stinging eyes. She pulled her smock over her nose and mouth.

"No, the impact was taken by this blasphemous jewelry." Sharkey studied the latch of Wave's pit guard, then unhooked and removed it. Gaia could see where the pit guard's edges had bitten into Wave's skin. "The god must love you, Wave."

Wave shook its head.

"It's true. The god armored you in unfit garb, to bear the wrath of the unholy—just like in the stories." Sharkey stroked the side of Wave's muzzle.

Wave's cranial tendrils curled weakly. It seemed to perk up, although the reference was beyond Gaia.

"Can you talk?" Gaia asked.

"Yes, but it hurts my neck."

"Then remain silent," Sharkey said.

"Can you take Wave back to its room?" Gaia asked Sharkey.

"Yes, I am strong enough to bear the weight," Sharkey said.

Gaia thought at first that Sharkey was being sarcastic again, but then realized that Sharkey had genuinely misunderstood her intention. "Please take Wave back to its room and wait with it."

"That would leave this place unguarded," Sharkey said.

"I command you to do it," Gaia said.

"Then I will obey." Sharkey took Wave's pit guard and handed it to Wave, then gathered up Wave and carried the Kishocha into Happy Snak. Gaia followed long enough to retrieve her mobile breather pack. She fitted it over her nose and mouth and returned to the vacant shrine. Careful to avoid stepping in the steaming pool of blood and acid, she crossed to the Kishocha-side door and closed it.

The room was even more still then, and more empty. Gaia walked the rim of the circular pool and searched for Kenjan beneath the water. Finally she caught sight of a shadowy movement in the depths. Kenjan seemed to notice her at the same time and swam up. Its head broke the surface of the water.

"I take it the criticism is over," Kenjan said.

"Yes." Gaia sank to her knees. Her voice sounded muffled.

"I taste blood in the water. Who is hurt?"

"Some guy Wave called 'scholar'," Gaia replied. "Sharkey killed it."

Kenjan nodded, as if this was to be expected. "But no one else?"

"Wave got hit with a rock, but Sharkey's taking care of it."

Kenjan surveyed the damage done to the grotto. "I suppose

I should begin to repair my house."

"Do you want me to help?"

"No," Kenjan sighed. "It is my lot to live like a dog now, with no servants. By the way, have you given my message to Oziru yet?"

"I haven't seen Oziru since you gave it to me."

"Then this criticism is not a reprisal—that is good." The alien drifted away from her. As Kenjan pulled itself out of the water, Gaia thought she could hear it singing a cheery tune, but she didn't know why it would do such a thing.

Chapter Seventeen: Humans

After Gaia left Kenjan's shrine, her shock and numbness wore off. It was easy for her to be brave in front of other people, but alone in her room fear overtook her.

Gaia crumpled onto her bed. She curled beneath the thin blanket like a kid trying to hide from monsters. She was scared and shaking. Tears leaked out of her eyes. She wanted her mom. She took a few deep breaths, found her hand-held and entered her mother's number. She waited, biting her lip.

"Please answer the phone, Mom."

Her mother's answering service picked up.

An unexpected, convulsive sob choked her. Her mother wasn't there. Gaia gulped. It was stupid to cry about something that was over. She'd only been scratched. Wave wasn't badly hurt. Kenjan wasn't touched. The only person mercilessly decapitated before her eyes had been disturbing the peace. The image of the scholar's open neck gushing black blood rose up before her again. She'd been able to see the Kishocha's spinal column. Its cranial tendrils had still been moving when Stinger picked up its head. Another pathetic sob broke out of her clenched teeth.

She was done. She was glutted on aliens and alien ideas and explaining sex to aliens and trying to understand aliens. She didn't want any more cultural expansion. Mini-Snak wasn't doing well enough to put up with execution by stoning. A jolt of nausea shook through Gaia's abdomen, sending her running to the bathroom. She coughed, gagged and vomited up her dinner. Panang curry splashed wetly into the chemical toilet. Gaia coughed and whimpered at the humiliating pain of puking. She hadn't thrown up for at least a decade, then she became involved with aliens and was instantly afflicted with permanent nausea.

She had to quit. She wasn't a cultural anthropologist or a gravitational physicist or even a particularly good or empathetic listener. She just sold snacks.

After rinsing her mouth and splashing her face with cold water, Gaia tried her phone again. If she had been able to reach her mother, her mother would have said to stop all this and come back home. Gaia dialed Blum's office, but no one was there at twenty to one in the morning. For some reason, Gaia could not bring herself to resign to an answering service. She needed a real person to quit to. She had one real person's private number. She dialed it.

A sleepy male voice answered. "This is Fitzpatrick."

"I quit!" Gaia shouted. "I don't even care about any of it. Find somebody else to put up with this shit." With each word, Gaia's voice degenerated closer to unintelligible sobbing.

"Ms. Jones?" Fitzpatrick's voice was gravelly and deep.

"What?"

"Your visual's not on. Would you engage it, please?" Fitzpatrick cleared his throat and coughed once.

"No." Gaia's hands shook too much to grip the hand-held anymore. She set it down.

"Well, my visual is on if you want to switch to your main screen."

Gaia sniffed, swallowed and switched over. Fitzpatrick sat on the edge of his bed, shirtless, tousled and unshaved. He wore a pair of flannel pajama bottoms. He removed an actual pack of cigarettes from his nightstand drawer and lit one.

The sight of it momentarily surprised Gaia out of her misery. "Why isn't your smoke alarm going off?"

"I disabled it." Fitzpatrick took a deep drag of smoke.

"Executive privilege. I take it you're tired of your job?"

"I want to quit." Gaia held her voice steady.

"I see." Fitzpatrick reached over to a hot-drinks dispenser and got himself a coffee. His dispenser was the fancy European kind that was recessed into the wall. He took a sip of the coffee. Gaia was jealous. She wanted to have a hot coffee and a personal cabin that had clearly been professionally decorated. She wanted blue and gray striped flannel sheets. She didn't want the impressionistic winterscape Fitzpatrick had chosen for his wall, but she could block that out.

"Traditionally when one quits, one usually gives a reason why." Fitzpatrick addressed the camera, even though there was no visual of her. All he saw was blank screen.

Gaia said, "I'm tired."

"What of?" Fitzpatrick's voice remained calm.

"Them."

"Them..." Fitzpatrick took a gulp of his coffee. "Yes, they can be quite the test of patience. What did they do?"

"They threw rocks at Kenjan, then Wave and me, then Sharkey cut the scholar guy's head off." Gaia paused for a moment, before continuing. "I want to go home."

Fitzpatrick's cigarette and coffee were forgotten. His shocked expression filled Gaia's screen.

"That sounds awful. I am so sorry." He knocked the column of gray ash off his cigarette and crushed it out. "Are you hurt?"

"No."

Fitzpatrick lit another cigarette. "So am I correct in assuming that you feel you are in danger from the Kishocha?"

"Sharkey cut a guy's head off today." Gaia knew she'd said that already but words didn't seem to convey to Fitzpatrick how it felt to watch that happen. "And just a few weeks ago Sharkey had that thing pointed at me. When that guard jabs a spear at you, it's not bluffing."

"I understand that you feel threatened, but Oziru assured us that you would not be harmed by a Kishocha on pain of death, and I think we know that Oziru's not bluffing when it makes a statement like that," Fitzpatrick went on reasonably.

"So what?" Gaia shouted. "So Sharkey gets executed for killing me. Big fucking deal, I'm still dead. And what if it's not Sharkey? What if it's some other Kishocha just following its master into the barren, scorching desert because orange is blasphemous? What then?"

Fitzpatrick stared into the camera, as if by sheer will of concentration he could turn on her visual. "You are making very little sense right now, Ms. Jones."

Gaia took a deep breath. "I know."

"Do you really think Sharkey is going to kill you?"

"I don't know. But I'm not only worried about myself. Kenjan's not safe. I'm supposed to take care of it. I can't do it. There's only one of me."

"Within its own society, Kenjan's position is really precarious," Fitzpatrick said. "There's nothing we can do about that."

"You didn't tell me this would happen." Gaia heard the whine in her own voice and winced.

"We didn't know it could happen. You're the first one on the inside."

"You should get someone else. Maybe you could do this. You're good at talking to people."

Fitzpatrick sighed. "I'm not the guardian."

"I don't want to be the guardian anymore!"

"I know. It's hard on you." Fitzpatrick was a perfection of soothing reassurance. Gaia wished she didn't want him to be that way, that she could scoff at him for being insincere. But right now she wanted, more than anything else, to be comforted. "Oziru wouldn't allow anyone else. We tried very hard to dissuade Oziru. We tried to get a trained person in there, but Oziru wouldn't allow it. Being a guardian is a sacred calling. When Kenjan asked for you and you accepted, the pact was sealed. The fact that you didn't know the consequences of your words was irrelevant to Oziru."

"I'm a free human being."

"I understand, but we really need you to stay there if there is any way that you can. I know it's difficult for you—"

"Sharkey cut someone's head off!" Gaia yelled into the receiver. "Head off! Cut it off! What don't you understand about this?"

"What happened after that?"

"What?" Gaia's concentration was thrown.

"What happened after that?"

"Sharkey went to help Wave, who'd been hit by a rock." Gaia slumped, remembering how tenderly Sharkey had lifted Wave. "Sharkey pays too much attention to Wave."

"Meaning?"

"I don't know. That's what all the Kishocha say. I guess it means Sharkey's got a crush on Wave."

"Sharkey wasn't aggressive to you?"

"No," Gaia said, dully.

"What about the other guard?"

"Stinger picked up the head and took it somewhere," Gaia said. "To Oziru, I think."

"And Kenjan?"

"Kenjan hid the whole time." Gaia sat down on her bed. "Some of its stuff got broken. I think Kenjan needs a new hand-held."

"I'll get one tomorrow," Fitzpatrick said. Silence drifted between them. It was as if by yelling Gaia had exorcised all her emotions. She felt drained and mute. Fitzpatrick peered into the camera, trying his psychic-manipulation trick again. "Are you still there, Ms. Jones?"

"Yes," Gaia murmured.

"I can't force you to stay. I can only beg you to try. We need this."

"Who's we?"

"Everyone living one the station who isn't you. Kishocha technology could make a big difference for us."

"Sure." Gaia pushed out one syllable in response. She didn't want to give in to Fitzpatrick just yet. He could console her for a little while longer.

Fitzpatrick seemed to recognize and accept his role and

kept speaking in a smooth, collected tone. "What you need to do is tell me what I can do to make you feel safe."

She let out a short, bitter laugh. "Get me a Norton shock pistol."

"Done."

Gaia's eyes widened. She switched on the visual, leaning in close to the camera. "I can have a stun gun?"

Fitzpatrick smiled. "It's good to finally see you. You can have two stun guns if you want. I have amazing latitude with regard to your continuing happiness."

"Can I have a customized Mitsubishi liquid oxygen rebreather?"

"Yes," Fitzpatrick said.

"And surveillance cameras for the shrine?"

"Absolutely."

"And can I borrow a rebreather from building maintenance in the meantime?"

"If you decide to stay, then yes." Fitzpatrick took a long, final drag on his cigarette before rubbing the butt out. "What do you think, Ms. Jones? Will you stay?"

"I don't know." She wanted to turn her visual off again, but once it was on, she couldn't. It would be rude.

"I've got an idea. Why don't you meet me tomorrow night at the Embassy Club. We'll have dinner and talk more then." Fitzpatrick's voice was bright and professional, and repelled Gaia slightly. Had he been sincere earlier? Was Fitzpatrick that good of an actor?

"What time?" Gaia felt withdrawn and mechanical.

"Is eight fine for you?" Fitzpatrick's tone softened as he read the discomfort in her expression.

"Are you paying?"

"Yes."

"But you'll be reimbursed," she said. "Because taking me out to dinner is your job, right?"

"Does it really matter?"

"If you're being reimbursed then there's no way that this

can be a date. You're not asking me out to a romantic dinner when I'm irrational, right?"

"I'll be reimbursed," Fitzpatrick assured her.

"Good. Then it's a date."

Chapter Eighteen: Black Dress

Gaia twisted her arms behind her back, fumbling for the tiny metal tag of her zipper. She'd managed to drag the zipper from her tailbone to her bra strap before losing it completely. The top of her dress hung open and let in chilly drafts.

She wore a black dress, made of clingy, shiny fabric with a fitted torso, a low neckline and a very long zipper. She wore it once a year to the Merchant's Gala. The rest of the time, she wore her Happy Snak smock, on the theory that if she didn't promote her business, no one else would. The smock made getting dressed in the morning easy.

The black dress interested Wave. Wave had read that the dress was the traditional garb of the human female, but had seen few women wearing them. Wave was also fascinated by Gaia's shoes, which were of the patent-leather low-heeled dress variety. Wave found human feet grotesque. They were freakishly small to the Kishocha, and the pointy toes of the dress shoes only accentuated this feature. For an hour or so, Gaia tried to be a good ambassador of women's fashion, but she had finally tired of Wave's questions. Wave sensed this and wandered away to help some customers, leaving Gaia to carry on her battle with her zipper alone, while thinking obliquely about the traditional costume of her gender.

It had a kind of significance even though Gaia didn't know what that significance was. She knew she was a black-dress woman. She was neither a white dress nor a red dress female. She was neither vulnerable nor passionate, yet still decidedly a woman. So the black dress it was.

There was no way she could explain that concept to Wave. As Gaia finally found the zipper and yanked her garment mostly closed, she found herself pondering the yawning abyss that separated their species. There must be millions of ideas too integrally Kishocha to be explained, like singing when you're sad or not-really-dead ghosts.

When she tried to imagine what more she could not know or ever understand, Gaia experienced a sudden vertigo. She couldn't imagine. She couldn't understand even a fraction of what it was like to be Kishocha. They were so utterly alien.

Until now, she'd never understood the profound meaning of that word. She ran her fingers across the scrape on her cheek, where the deceased scholar's clam had grazed her flesh. She felt confused and cold. The enormity of the task she'd taken on came rolling at her like a tidal wave. She felt like she'd blacked out in some foreign bar and awakened to find herself married to a stranger.

She knew she shouldn't have taken off the Happy Snak smock. The Gaia who wore that smock was a person she was comfortable being. The black-dress Gaia was as mysterious to her as her new identity, Shrine Guardian Gaia. The only way she could stop feeling lost and confused during the next few hours was to pretend to be wearing the smock—pretend to still be at Happy Snak pondering the benefits of Readi-seal deep-frying cartridges.

"Readi-seal, the seal that never leaks." Gaia mumbled the slogan to herself. She grabbed her bag and headed out. She hoped to pass through Happy Snak with minimal commentary.

Cheryl was the only person in the back kitchen. She sat on a green stepladder, chewing some Nico-Nico gum and leaning against storage locker fourteen. Past Cheryl, Gaia could see Roy pumping orange cheese onto a paper boat full of blue corn nachitos. Gaia couldn't see Wave, but she could hear it arguing with a customer about soft drinks. The woman had ordered her drink without ice, and when Wave dispensed her beverage, the cup had been only two-thirds full. She wanted a full cup. Wave explained that ice displaced one third of the drink, so a cola with no ice should fill only sixty-seven percent of the cup. Full Drink Woman reasserted her demand for a full cup. Wave responded more forcefully that would cause loss to the beloved Gaia Jones in the form of over-poured beverages.

Full Drink Woman demanded to see Gaia Jones. Wave replied it was not possible for her to have an audience, that Gaia Jones was far too important to speak about portioning soft drinks and that Full Drink Woman would have to learn the rules before she tried to buy anything at Happy Snak. Full Drink Woman began to curse Wave.

Gaia rubbed her eyes. She didn't want to enter the fray, but it pained her to listen to Wave destroying any chance of a return visit from Full Drink Woman. Cheryl didn't move either. She rolled her head tiredly toward Gaia.

"Wave's got some flexibility issues," she told Gaia, "and it doesn't really understand the customer-is-always-right rule."

Gaia nodded, listlessly. "Can you finish zipping me up?"

Cheryl hauled herself off the stepladder and closed Gaia's zipper. "Nice dress," she said, then returned to her seat and stared in a glazed way, at nothing. Gaia hoped Cheryl was on break.

Roy came to Wave's rescue. Roy was a natural at customer relations. He got Full Drink Woman the full drink that she coveted, then listened to her complaints about Wave, Happy Snak and A-Ki Station in general. Roy sympathized without being condescending. Full Drink Woman left smiling.

Wave chewed its lips in confusion. Its cranial tendrils hung flat and forlorn, indicating a conflicted mental state about possible wrongdoing.

Roy told Wave not to worry about it, then asked if Wave knew what the word "bitch" meant. A beeper went off. Cheryl stood and removed twenty pounds of chicken from the Safe-T-Thaw, pausing for a moment to jam a thermal probe into the translucent flesh. The light flashed green. The meat was thirty-five degrees Fahrenheit, right on the edge of the bacterial danger zone.

Cheryl padded over to the prep table and started threading chicken onto skewers for chicken satay. "You going out with somebody?"

"Fitzpatrick." Gaia put on a small handful of jewelry: a dress watch, two rings, a set of earrings. She disliked necklaces.

"Fancy." Cheryl worked the chicken flesh onto its skewers in rhythmic knitting motions.

"It's not a date." Gaia tugged at her thigh-high stockings. She wondered if one of them was inside out. It kept falling down. She took her shoes off to check the seams. Both stockings were inside out. Gaia pulled them off.

"Too bad. He's pretty good looking."

"He called my store Crappy Shack." Gaia pulled her left stocking back on.

"Was that the old location?"

"Yes."

"Right." Cheryl finished a skewer. "You have to admit that wasn't the nicest-looking store on the concourse."

Anger flared up in Gaia. Her cheeks got hot. She focused on successfully donning her right stocking. "It was the best I could afford."

"Exactly. It didn't fit in with the corporate clones on the station. It was original. Now you've got a really nice place that's just as original without the second-hand stuff. I bet he doesn't call it crappy anymore."

Being chronically early, Gaia arrived at the club fifteen minutes before Fitzpatrick. She acquainted herself with the lobby. The club resided at the top of a twelve-story tower perched atop the thirty-six-level complex that formed the main compound of A-Ki Station. The club's floor rotated slowly, so that patrons could enjoy their drinks while gazing out at the splendor of human life in space. Diners were offered a circular panorama of the corporate tower complexes with massive radio arrays and flamboyant signs advertising their sponsors. On the perimeter of the towers, rank upon rank of black obelisks ringed the station like a surrounding army. Solar panels.

As Gaia surveyed the familiar ugliness of the human buildings, she found herself looking past them, at their foundations. Now that she knew the station was comprised of shell, she wondered how the buildings had been anchored to it. She was thinking of the clock-mounting incident, when she'd hammered a nail into the living flesh of her wall. The injury had healed over the next few days, but left a pock-marked scar.

The surface of the station was not dusty or rocky. It looked almost like coral. Wide shiny fingers reached up from the surface, and gripped the foundation of the Coke building like hundreds of massive hands. Why hadn't she seen this before?

It struck her as strange that she'd never looked at the ground. She'd never thought about the fact that it wasn't rock and concrete securing them to the station. They were being held in the grip of a massive sphere packed full of water and aliens.

Humans were either parasites or pets. Gaia couldn't figure out which one. The last time she'd felt this disoriented she'd been signing her divorce papers. In a sudden regression into childish insecurity, Gaia felt like calling her mother again. She suppressed the urge.

She looked at her watch. Fitzpatrick was one minute late. The door of the club slid open and there he stood—without his briefcase. Fitzpatrick wore a suit, but no tie. Somehow, Fitzpatrick looked more casual and simultaneously snappier than he usually did. Gaia suddenly wished that she were a sufficiently assiduous student of fashion to determine the exact location of this subtle difference.

Fitzpatrick saw her, smiled and walked forward in a confident, manly way. What was it about him that seemed so masculine tonight? Maybe it was all the time that she was spending with the Kishocha. They were genderless, but she found herself boorishly assigning gender roles to them anyway. In fact, to her, they all seemed male. The most ambiguous of the aliens was Wave, to whom Gaia could not assign any kind of gender at all.

Gaia found herself, for the first time, admitting that she enjoyed the sight of Fitzpatrick. He moved with a certain grace that, while not weak or effeminate, had a note of refinement. His blond hair seemed rakishly adventurous. His jaw, square to the point of being silly, looked good to her.

Gaia breathed deeply. Maybe Fitzpatrick's disheveled attentiveness the previous night had eroded her defenses. Or maybe, as Stinger had suggested, she needed to find someone to muzzle with. Gaia suppressed an internal shudder. She was only microseconds away from considering sex with Fitzpatrick, based on the criteria that he was human and also male. Could she be any less discriminating?

And yet Stinger's comment tugged at her. She had been "prodding her own throat like an ugly" since she'd been on this station. Still the idea of Fitzpatrick as a sex partner made Gaia slightly ill, in an aroused kind of way.

"Ms. Jones, so good to see you." Fitzpatrick shook her hand warmly. This was nothing new. He always shook her hand warmly. Why should she notice it especially tonight? She suddenly pictured him naked. For some reason, even clothed in nothing but fluorescent light, Fitzpatrick was holding a briefcase. Gaia suppressed a giggle. Was she cracking up from the pressure? Her moods seemed to be beamed into her head by a hostile alien intelligence. One moment she was morose and maudlin, the next aroused, the next completely giddy. One thing was for sure. It wasn't the Kishocha implanting these ideas. If it were the Kishocha, she'd be thinking more of clams and decapitation.

"Hi." It was all Gaia could manage.

"Enjoying the view, I see?"

"I was just looking at the foundations of buildings."

"Does structural engineering interest you?"

"Not really," Gaia replied. All urge to sleep with him dissipated. "Let's go get a table."

"I have one reserved."

She followed Fitzpatrick to their table. After perusing the club's menu, Gaia decided to go with two appetizers and no entree. She wasn't into overpriced plates of lab-grown meat. She knew what it cost to buy all the ingredients at the club and found their markup breathtaking.

Fitzpatrick ordered the lab-grown veal, sautéed in marsala with tiny red hydroponically grown potatoes and sugar snap peas. The veal was garnished with real slices of lemon, which had to be shipped from the Sunkist complex on Mars. He also ordered wine and a salad. Gaia had a dark beer, which was brewed locally by a guy who used to be on the custodial crew of the Coke Tower.

"So," Fitzpatrick began, once the server had withdrawn. "Are you doing all right?"

"It's going pretty well." Gaia broke a hunk of bread off the miniloaf in the center of the table. "I've decided to stay."

Fitzpatrick reached into his inner suit pocket and retrieved a slim cigarette case. He popped it open, pulled out a stick of Gitanes cigarette gum, and began to chew it thoughtfully. Gaia warmed to him again, but wasn't sure if it was just another hormonal surge.

"Why did you want the rebreather?"

"I want to be able to go in the water, so that I can find Kenjan if I need to. The water is too deep for me to feel comfortable without an oxygen supply."

"Are you a good diver?"

Gaia nodded. "I've got a lot of hours underwater."

"Yes, it says so in your file."

"If you already know that, why did you ask me?" Gaia scowled.

"Just a little small talk." Fitzpatrick straightened his cuffs. The waiter arrived with their food and silence settled between them. Gaia tore off another hunk of bread, while Fitzpatrick started on his salad.

Gaia poked at her appetizers and ordered more beer. Because she constantly saw people chewing, Gaia had developed the habit of rating people's attractiveness on how they ate. Fitzpatrick looked good eating. She imagined this was the reason she was attracted to the refined guys, even though they were out of her league. Maintenance guys, who definitely were in her league, were universally atrocious chewers. They also tended to leave small piles of garbage wherever they went. Even coffee generated a tiny monolith of crushed cream packets, sugar envelopes and broken stir sticks. Fitzpatrick, in contrast, was an unfailingly neat eater. He even secreted the foil wrappers of his Gitanes cigarette gum in his pocket.

Gaia suddenly realized that she really didn't want to talk about the Kishocha or any important matter. She wanted a break from them. Yet, she still had to negotiate the main course, dessert and cigarette gum. She decided to just ride it out in silence, then abruptly ruled out that course of action as inexcusably rude and bitchy. Besides, Fitzpatrick had done a lot for her and though she hated to admit it, Gaia wanted him to like her.

"So," Gaia said. "Are you married?"

Fitzpatrick, at first startled by this question, recovered quickly. "No, neither am I gay. Yourself?"

"You know I'm not married."

"A lesbian then?" Fitzpatrick finished his salad and set the fork down.

"No. I'm divorced."

"That doesn't preclude your being a lesbian."

Gaia scowled. "Are you recruiting for them or something?"

"Not at all, I'm just making conversation. I'm also divorced."

"Before you came into space, or after?"

"After. Space life didn't agree with my wife's career. She's a ceramic artist. The shipping costs were astronomical—literally."

"I bet. You should see the bill for a case of Earth-grown clams."

Fitzpatrick nodded. "And your husband?"

"What about him?"

"Did you to decide to end it before you came here?"

"Yeah, we split up in Washington, before I started Happy

Snak. He was a public defender turned corporate mega lawyer. He was a bitter man."

"How long were you together?"

"Only a year." Gaia toyed with her empty vegetable skewer. "Then I couldn't stand it anymore."

"My wife and I were together for seven years."

"Any kids?"

"None, we were waiting to be more established."

"That was smart, I guess." Gaia's second plate of appetizers arrived, along with Fitzpatrick's entree.

"You know the reason I like eating here is that they do such a good job with inferior ingredients," Fitzpatrick said.

"What do you mean inferior? They use top-of-the-line stuff. Those parsley leaves have *Boeing Arboretum* written all over them." Even across the table Gaia could make out the deep green letters.

"Yes, but it's nothing compared to the flavor of food actually grown on Earth. Speaking of which, did you really order clams from Earth? I heard something about that from the woman at receiving."

"I thought they'd be a neat experience for Wave. Wave had eaten one at an embassy banquet and couldn't get over how weird they were," Gaia said.

"In what way?"

"They looked different, and tasted different, and were salty in a different way... I guess you'd have to eat a lot of live, raw sea creatures to become a connoisseur." Gaia nibbled on a frog leg.

"As opposed to dead, cooked amphibians?"

"Frog meat's the best up here. It's from real frogs. That's why it's so expensive."

"Do you think I might be able to purchase a couple of your clams?" Fitzpatrick asked.

"For yourself?"

"I've been having a real craving for chowder, and canned just won't do."

“So is chowder your dish?”

“How do you mean?”

“All guys have a certain dish they make, and it tells a lot about their personality. For example, if a guy’s signature dish is a breakfast dish, like an omelet, you know he’s used to cooking for women in the morning,” Gaia said.

Fitzpatrick seemed amused by this. “Excellent theory. What do you think chowder says about me?”

“You’re from the northern coast. You’re used to going to ski lodges and dating girls who wear sweaters and curl up to you for a bowl of steaming hot chowder?” Gaia guessed. “You use the coziness stratagem.”

“Very good, Ms. Jones.” Fitzpatrick smiled over his fork. “And what is your dish?”

“Anything that can be breaded, wrapped in waxed paper or eaten off a stick.”

“So you attract a male with bright colors and eye-catching graphics, use him quickly while on the go and dispose of him neatly in any convenient trash receptacle?”

“I like convenient men.”

“Kenjan certainly isn’t convenient.”

“Kenjan’s not a man,” Gaia replied. “And besides Kenjan is convenient. It’s right there, twenty feet away from me at all times. Wave is practically in my underwear with me. All in all, the Kishocha are pretty convenient. It’s just that they’re also foreign and scary.”

“It’s a lot of work to understand them, but it’s worth it in the long run,” Fitzpatrick said. “Do you think they’re going to like the Mini-Snak?”

“I do. I’m thinking of building a customer base. I want them to be happy, and I want them to have snacks. That’s the whole idea of Happy Snak. Do you know that they don’t even have the basic concept of snacks? It’s kind of sad.”

“That they don’t like fatty, salty food?”

“No! They don’t have the concept that they deserve a treat. It doesn’t have to be greasy and salty. It could be sweet or wriggly or crunchy or slippery, but it has to be fun. It has to be cheap and special. It's the—" Gaia faltered, remembering what Wave had told her and suddenly feeling the truth of her words. Owning them. "It's the most basic personal freedom."

Fitzpatrick paused for a thoughtful moment then said, "I suppose you're right. Put that way, snacks are really rather subversive to their culture."

"I'm not going to stop though. I love watching them try new things, and then decide for themselves whether they're horrible or wonderful. Most of them have never gotten the chance to choose anything for themselves. It's all virgin territory. Many of the soldiers and servants really are curious about humans and human things, but they just aren't allowed to try them out under normal circumstances."

"Is that why you and Wave were discussing human sex practices?" Fitzpatrick asked innocently.

"How do you know that?" Gaia reddened.

"One of the embassy secretaries overheard Wave telling Roy about it. He was dying to know how the Kishocha do it. Because of you we're all learning so much more about them than we ever would have."

"I think I might be learning a little too much."

"It's not uncommon to experience culture shock when going from one human country to another. I can't imagine what you must be experiencing, but I suggest that you talk to Oziru about what happened to you. The alien has an interest in making you feel comfortable and safe."

"I guess," Gaia said.

"You really should, if only to have bragging rights on being the first human allowed into the Kishocha sector. Plus you'd have an excuse to request a rebreather. And if you did go to speak with Oziru, you could do me the very great service of asking about the cause of recent gravity failures."

"I wouldn't understand the answer, even if Oziru explained it." Gaia gave a short laugh. Physics had never been her strong suit. "Can't you have one of the scientists call them and ask?"

"If Oziru was answering its phone, that's exactly what we would do. Alas, the ruler of the Kishocha has been incommunicado since Kenjan has become a ghost."

"Did you try reaching Seigata? I know that at least the security forces have no trouble at all contacting that alien." As soon as Gaia asked, she realized how futile asking the priest for help would be. Fitzpatrick's expressive eye-roll communicated volumes.

"Seigata said that Oziru might be punishing us for allowing Kenjan to die, but I don't know if I buy it. Did Wave ever mention that Oziru might hold a grudge about that?"

"Never. Wave would have mentioned something like that." Gaia folded her napkin and laid it across her plate. "Is that why you really asked me to dinner? To talk me in to finding Oziru?"

"Not at all. I asked you to dinner because I'm hoping to seduce you. Being able to discuss the gravity issue is merely a fringe benefit of my lecherous initial plan." Fitzpatrick finished the last of his veal. "Shall we order dessert? It's something cheap and special, and for no good reason."

Gaia smiled. "Sure."

They finished dessert and cigarette gum, which Gaia didn't usually chew, but the evening seemed special enough to indulge in a few excesses. When they left the restaurant, it seemed normal to go back to Fitzpatrick's embassy quarters for another drink. Then it seemed perfectly reasonable to sleep with him, if only to try out his sheets. It had been a long time since she'd enjoyed that variety of human comfort.

She was on top. He was a good lover. They fell asleep for a while. She dreamed she found a soft-serve ice cream that was perfectly clear—so clear that it was almost invisible. While the idea delighted her, it also disturbed her. She couldn't figure out what it was made from, or how it could be as clear as water and still taste like fresh raspberries. The more she looked at it, the more alien it seemed. But the more unnatural it became, the more utterly she desired it.

Gaia pulled her eyes open and sat unsteadily up.

The clock read eleven fifteen and she hadn't fed Kenjan. She left Fitzpatrick asleep.

When she got back to Happy Snak, there were two messages for her. One was a note from Roy saying that he and Wave had taken care of Kenjan. The other was a voice-only from Fitzpatrick, wishing her good night.

Chapter Nineteen: Deep Water

When Kenjan heard Gaia's plans to see Oziru, the alien asked for paper. Gaia gave Kenjan a pad of paper. Kenjan rejected her offering. It wasn't Kishocha paper. An argument ensued about Kenjan asking for things Gaia could not get.

Wave had vanished then reappeared with some thin, flat, purple sea creature. Kenjan took the creature and started cutting what she now recognized as Kishocha letters into its skin. Gaia shuddered and joked about living documents. No one laughed.

Gaia received and installed surveillance cameras the day after the attack. She looked in on the shrine several times a day, both to ensure Kenjan's safety and out of idle voyeuristic curiosity.

She also practiced diving with her Mitsubishi rebreather.

The company had expanded into heavy underwater equipment during the suboceanic development boom in Tokyo Bay. Her gear was on loan from the maintenance crew. They used divers to access the bottom levels of station buildings, which remained permanently flooded. The woman who brought it over had pointed out the rebreather's individual quirks, and questioned Gaia pointedly about her actual diving ability.

Gaia had taken up diving during her marriage. While she was underwater, her husband couldn't talk to her, not even by phone. This resulted in her racking up copious hours at

Keystone and other locations in Puget Sound, a trip to the Great Barrier Reef and serious consideration of underwater welding as a career.

Wave was upset by Gaia's presumptuousness. It simply couldn't imagine that Gaia was going to see Oziru uninvited. When Wave had suggested that it go ahead to beg for an audience, Gaia had forbidden it, explaining that she didn't want Oziru to have the chance to deny her. This further upset Wave, who expressed its extreme reluctance to take her. Gaia said she'd go by herself if Wave didn't want to go.

This made Kenjan laugh.

Wave fretted. The alien's twelve bony and elongated fingers knotted together as if holding on to one another for comfort. At last Wave agreed to take Gaia to Oziru.

Gaia checked the straps of her flippers. They were far uglier than Wave's naturally aquatic feet. Her flippers were stiff and yellow. Her wetsuit was garish red.

The document lay in a shallow bucket. Kenjan's incisions had gradually sealed up, leaving deep blue scars. Kenjan's signature took up at least one quarter of the available writing space.

Wave gazed at Gaia's Mitsubishi flippers with serious intensity. "I like this formal shoe better than the other one. The other shoe made your foot look too little and stumpy. This shoe is a pretty yellow color."

"Thanks." Gaia checked the seals on her equipment. "Are we ready to go?"

"Yes please." Wave shoved the document into a net bag where it dripped and struggled weakly. Gaia pulled her mask over her face and flopped stupidly along the floor, making at least three times as much noise as Wave did. Until now, she had never noticed how the Kishocha could pull their toes together to muffle the slapping noise. She glanced over at Kenjan, who chuckled behind its hand.

"Laugh it up," Gaia muttered.

When they reached the waterway, Waved dived in. Gaia followed more slowly, easing herself through the initial transition from breathing gas to liquid. The first draw of fluid always made her gag a little, even after so many times.

The Kishocha water was warm, and except for the cleaners gliding through it on their translucent, undulating mantles, rather empty. The cleaners looked a lot better underwater than they did sliming along the walls. In the water they had grace and speed. Moving like miniature flying carpets, they swept past Gaia's legs and disappeared into the deeper water. Visibility was higher than she expected, but compromised by the overall dimness in the waterway.

Wave sat on the shell floor, waiting for her. Its cranial tendrils drifted casually around its head. Fully unfurled, Wave's feet were bigger than her flippers. Wave's ribcage began to expand. Vibrant, red gills opened alongside of the alien's chest cavity. Gaia's eyes widened.

Wave made an enormous smile-face, and then Gaia heard a series of clicks and high squeaks. It sounded like feedback or dolphins.

Gaia tried to find the source of the sound. Wave tapped her arm and the same sequence repeated. She realized Wave was talking to her. Gaia gestured toward the surface and swam up. Wave followed. Once she'd coughed the oxygenated fluid back into her rebreather mouthpiece, she took a shuddering breath of air.

"What did you say?" Gaia bobbed in the gentle waves.

"I asked—show me your gills, please."

"I don't have gills," Gaia said, laughing.

Wave was astounded. "How do you breathe?"

"I breathe through this thing on my back," Gaia said. "It has special human breathing liquid inside."

"I thought it was some kind of formal dress."

"It's a life-support apparatus."

"You do not ever breathe water?"

"No." Gaia spat out the remainder of the rebreather fluid.

A look of startled knowledge crossed Wave's face. "You mean you are a drownable thing?"

Gaia snorted and accidentally inhaled a gulp of water, which she immediately coughed back out. "All humans are. Didn't you know?"

"All humans drown?"

"Yes."

"You should get out of the water right now, Gaia Jones. Water is a drowning atmosphere."

"It's okay, Wave. I have this." Gaia showed Wave the mouthpiece.

"But it takes a long time to swim to Oziru's garden."

"How long?" Gaia asked. "In human minutes?"

"Maybe twenty."

"This has six hours of oxygen." A thought suddenly struck Gaia. "Oziru's garden isn't all underwater is it?"

"No, there are flying things in it."

"Then it should be okay. Just lead the way."

"Okay." Wave made the okay sign.

"One more thing."

"Yes?"

"I can't understand you when you talk underwater."

"Oh, I understood that with my intelligent deduction. You don't speak underwater Kishocha language. Okay now, let's go please?" Wave dipped below the water. It waited for her to submerge, took a few lazy kicks then, when Gaia followed, Wave darted suddenly downward and sped away. Gaia kicked as fast as she could, but quickly lost sight of Wave when the alien rounded a corner. Gaia tried to follow and felt a current pulling her toward a dark downward bend. A cleaner undulated by below her, was caught in the current and sucked out of sight. The shell walls glowed eerily phosphorescent green and purple. She could barely see.

A sudden fear jolted through her as she realized that she hadn't bothered to reset her orientation device at Happy Snak. She assumed that Wave would be beside her the whole time and it had just slipped her mind. She knew A-Ki Station was big, and she didn't know how deep this hole below her was, or where it went, or if Wave had even gone that way. She was a hundred yards from Happy Snak and nearly lost already. She focused on keeping her breathing steady. If she went down that hole she could easily be pulled too far downward to ever find her way home. And she was a drownable thing.

She felt the current suddenly pulse, jerking her downward nearly twenty feet. Gaia swam up with all her strength. For a moment, she swam in place before finally crawling back to shallow water.

This was a disaster. She wasn't going to be able to see Oziru. Bruising disappointment burst through her chest.

The surface glimmered a few feet above her. Gaia swam toward it with a sense of crushing defeat. Then she caught the sound of Kishocha being spoken. It seemed to be coming from all around her. She twisted around, trying to see who was talking.

Downward and to her left, a black Kishocha hand beckoned her.

It wasn't Wave. Wave's hands were white. She kicked through the water, until she reached a cavelike opening in the shell wall. A spiderweb-like grate made of red shell blocked the entrance. Kenjan floated on the other side. Kenjan's chest had expanded to cartoonish proportions. The flesh inside its gills was violet. Kenjan's cranial tendrils, lacking any sense of obedience to the laws of gravity, floated around the Kishocha's head in a spectral way. The white bands around its cranial tendrils and the markings of Kenjan's muzzle glowed faintly blue.

Kenjan looked just like a ghost. The alien beckoned to her. Gaia drifted forward, determined to not be given the creeps. Many underwater creatures had phosphorescence. Kenjan's simultaneous undeadness and glowing were coincidental. Gaia repeated this to herself.

Kenjan reached out. Gaia extended her hand. Kenjan pressed a flat, thumbnail-sized object into her palm while mouthing the word "Oziru" in an exaggerated way. Gaia nodded. Kenjan withdrew into the darkness of the cave as quickly as an eel.

Gaia didn't open her hand. She desperately didn't want to drop this object. This thing had to be important. Why else would Kenjan feel it had to pass it to her from the shadows of some kind of drain? She felt bad because she wasn't going to be able to deliver it.

As she swam toward the surface, Wave returned. Oddly, the alien approached her from the opposite direction. They both surfaced. Gaia tucked the mysterious object surreptitiously into the leg of her wetsuit.

"Gaia Jones," Wave said seriously. "Can you swim?"

Gaia heaved out the liquid for the second time in five minutes. She felt ill. Her nose ran freely. "Yes, of course."

"Please show me swimming if it is convenient for you."

Gaia complied in an amused way, swimming in a circle around Wave. "There."

"So you are an honorable slow cripple swimmer."

"Well, I can't swim as fast as you," Gaia said, huffily.

"I will carry you," Wave pronounced. "I will be your swiftly kicking feet."

Gaia scowled, disliking this idea, but unable to find a good reason not to agree to Wave's plan. It would be safer, but she wanted to have time to look around. She hadn't allowed herself to even dream of what it would be like to swim in alien water, because the likelihood of it had been nil. Now she was here and wanted a chance to meander. Then again, she would have time to meander when her own scuba gear arrived.

Wave continued, "I will take only shallow waterways in case you are drowning. Then, I'll push you to the surface. Does that please you greatly?"

"How long would it take to get to Oziru's garden swimming at my speed?"

"I do not know, but maybe we would grow old and die before we reached our exalted destination," Wave said.

"Then I guess you can carry me."

They submerged again, and Gaia waited while Wave

arranged her under its body, facing downward. With no regard for Gaia's breasts, Wave wrapped its sinuous arms around her chest. The alien took a few experimental kicks, then she felt Wave's body convulse. Together they shot through the water, whipped around the curve, caught the downward current, and plunged into the dark tunnel. Phosphorescence surrounded her, but they swam so fast that Gaia couldn't make out where it came from. They curled past a startled Kishocha, made a turn and sped on, downward. Gaia had a moment to glimpse a school of silvery fish before they plunged through them and scattered them like leaves. Another corkscrew turn and they were in a lighted waterway.

It was as wide as a highway and full of swimming creatures and sound. Clicks, squeaks, squeals, and long, low growls overlapped each other into an impossible noise. Kishocha stopped to stare at them. Huge, torso-sized fish with fins resplendent and colorful as kites ambled by. Unlike the floor of the waterway near Happy Snak, this one teemed with life. Anemone-like creatures undulated far below her on the sandy floor. Spidery crabs scuttled through a twisting forest of submerged tree roots, swinging like armored monkeys. An alarmingly large eel with a mouth crammed full of teeth lunged out at them. Wave paid no attention to any of it. They burst up from the water. Wave pulled her halfway out.

"Are you drowned?" Wave yelled. She turned and removed her mouthpiece.

"I'm fine." Gaia was annoyed, yet touched by Wave's concern.

The walkways alongside the waterways were crowded and silent. Kishocha of every describable marking, who moments ago had been going about their arcane duties, stopped and gawked at Gaia as though she had arrived from Mars.

She had arrived from Mars, but that was only a layover, which she didn't think warranted this kind of staring. She stared back at them. A giddy, childish feeling of excitement surged through her.

Spiraling openings of mysterious chambers perforated the

shell wall. Vibrant purple and green foliage dripping with humidity drooped down across the water's surface. Fist-sized insects flew from the centers of enormous fleshy flowers that dotted the walls. Slender trees grew up toward the mossy roof. Gaia gaped at a group of little half-sized Kishocha pogs with cute, nubby cranial tendrils. The pogs screamed in terror when she laid eyes on them.

Then she saw a huge, red octopus in a tree. It slithered like a collection of glistening snakes from one branch to another, caught one of the iridescent insects flying past and devoured it in one gelatinous gulp. Its large luminous eyes swiveled from side to side and then it flung itself out of the high branches into the air. Gaia's eyes widened in horror at the imminent death of the confused mollusk. They widened still further when the creature stretched out all its tentacles, caught the air in its webbing and popped open like a parachute. It drifted gently down to the water, swiveled beneath the surface and was gone.

Gaia noticed that she was drooling and crying simultaneously. Her jaw had dropped open for so long that a thin trail of saliva dribbled down her lip. Her eyes stung. She blinked and wiped away the drool then the tears.

As if her movement released them, the Kishocha around her began to move again. They talked quietly as they jostled past each other. None of them went into the water near her. Several of them got out, though.

Then the guards arrived. At least twenty of them dove into the water from all sides, harpoons in hand, circling her and Wave. Wave went limp. Wave's white body floated like a corpse beside her. All around, and even beneath her, menacing guards pointed their harpoons at her. The water went quiet except for the sound of one voice. Face down and limp, Wave chirped pathetically. Gaia hoped Wave was explaining their presence here. Wave's speech went on for some time. Gaia did not move. She floated, flaccid, just like Wave. She'd seen what happened when one provoked a guard.

Suddenly, a low grumble filled the water, and all noise but the popping of her rebreather ceased. The low sound increased, filling the water entirely, like the bellow of Tibetan horns. The sound kept coming until Gaia could feel it in her bones. Her ears rang and even her blood shook. The guards around her floated passively to the surface. The anemone-things darted back into their tubelike bodies. Fish scattered. The red octopus Gaia had seen before lunged backward into a crevice.

Looking down the waterway, Gaia saw a massive shark round the corner. Its skin was glossy black. It swam with an open-mouthed frown, row upon row of teeth curling back into its huge jaws. Gaia's heart began to pound, hammering against the sheer power of the sound and the terror at the sight of the shark. The beast approached, then sank to the bottom, circling.

Once she pulled her eyes away from the shark, Gaia realized Oziru had arrived. Oziru wore bands of pearls wrapped around its arms and legs, and gold around its throat. It floated toward her upright, like an angel might float downward from heaven. Behind it swam two smaller sharks festooned with huge diaphanous fins, like angelfish. The black shark beneath her still circled.

How could she have thought that she could just come into the Kishocha sector and casually ask Oziru about the stoning? How could she have assumed that she could ask Oziru anything? When the Kishocha was on land it was statuesque, but in the water, Oziru was like a god. Oziru's eyes locked on hers. Two other high-pitched notes cut through the low bellow. Pain shot through Gaia's eardrums. Then all sound abruptly ceased.

Gaia thought she might be deaf.

Two round, higher notes rang through the silent water. One thin, high, popping note emerged from Wave. Oziru drifted upward to the surface. Gaia felt the alien tap her on the head. She lifted her face from the water, disengaged her mouthpiece and disgorged her liquid in an unlovely retch.

The once lively corridor was dead silent. All Kishocha lay prone on the walkway, like corpses on a battlefield. The water was thick with Kishocha bodies, just floating there. No one moved. No one spoke. The only people even daring to breathe were she and Oziru.

Oziru's head floated above the water's surface, its cranial tendrils writhing slowly atop the water.

"This is very unplanned, Gaia Jones." Oziru's voice was low, but didn't make her bones throb and quiver. She was still frightened, though. Her mouth, in spite of all the water around her, felt dry.

"I—" Her voice came out in a whisper. She cleared her throat. "I needed to see you."

"In regard to what thing?"

"I have something to give you." She couldn't make her voice any stronger. She reached under her wetsuit and pulled out the object Kenjan had given her. It was a shell or tooth with a single character scratched into it. She handed it to Oziru, who took it, then stared at it for a long time. Gaia's heart felt like it was going to burst. She could see the water rippling around her chest each time her heart beat. Her body stiffened and she began to sink.

Oziru seized her painfully around the arm and pulled her up to the surface. "You should relax in the waters, Gaia Jones, or you will sink, and you are a drownable thing."

Two of Oziru's tentacles slithered out and around her body and held her upright. Their grip was crushing.

"I was—" Gaia began, but Oziru raised a silencing hand.

"Do not speak. We will go to my garden, and you will tell me your reasons there."

Chapter Twenty: Motions of Language

Oziru headed their procession, swimming more slowly than Wave had during their initial descent into the Kishocha sector. Gaia gripped Wave's forearm, reassured to feel its touch. Wave held her tighter than before. They swam in the shadow of the black shark. Behind them, the ranks of Kishocha guards swam like a school of heavily armed fish.

Gaia had been near sharks before but was never complacent with the idea of them. The shark above them was clearly much more intelligent than the Earth variety. It obeyed Oziru's orders. It had a spotted tongue. It was named Sudden Red Crush.

Before they'd submerged, Wave had warned Gaia against making any quick motions toward Oziru while Sudden Red Crush was in attendance.

Gaia squeezed Wave's arm again. Secretly, she hoped Wave would hug her back, but Wave didn't. Belatedly, the thought seemed to occur to the alien to squeeze Gaia back. Wave clenched its arms in a short, mechanical way as if it was practicing some new language that it didn't understand.

Because of Wave's soft demeanor, it was easy to imagine that the Kishocha's body would be correspondingly giving. It was not. Nothing but sinewy muscle composed Wave's body.

Gaia watched the shark's tail swish lazily through the water. The procession swam this way for a while, keeping close to the surface. Then they dropped downward into a swift current. Gaia guessed that this was the highway of the Kishocha sector. They moved so fast that Gaia couldn't focus on anything that wasn't straight ahead of her. A few minutes later they pulled up from the current.

Wave tapped her arm and pointed ahead to a massive purple and orange siphon. It hung like a flaccid cave, but rather than being dark inside, it was gloriously bright. Oziru swam inside, trailed by Sudden Red Crush. Gaia and Wave followed, riding the shark's powerful wake.

The water grew clearer as they progressed. It became invisible as air—if air had been almost indiscernibly pink. The inside walls of the siphon glowed phosphorescent blue. The procession emerged in a massive chamber, so deep and so tall that Gaia could see neither the floor nor the ceiling. The water darkened beneath her to a deep red-violet. Sudden Red Crush veered downward, descending until it became nothing but a tiny black silhouette against a field of red-violet darkness. Huge spiraling structures rose from the unseen depths. Wave swam toward one, and Gaia realized that the structure was quite distant and bigger than her original estimation. It was easily the width and breadth of the Coke Tower, and much higher. Each twisting shelf was engulfed with life. Pink and orange sea fans adorned the edges like lace on a cuff, while bulbous, thick-trunked trees grew from the upper ledges.

Oziru came to rest on the edge of one of the shelves. She and Wave alighted beneath Oziru. The incline was very slight, as if she stood on a low hill. Water lapped at her shoulders. The normalcy of something solid beneath her feet was relieving. Gaia tried to pull away from Wave, but the Kishocha held on to her, waiting.

Oziru sang out a series of long, piercing notes of gradually descending pitch. Its cranial tendrils moved in a kind of synchronicity just as the copious arms of an Indian god might move. They formed signs, twisted and formed other signs. Gaia realized suddenly that some of the shapes were like the motion of Kishocha letters.

Wave directed her vision downward. Far below them, Gaia saw a huge siphon gasp open. One after another, other siphons yawned agape.

The water pulled downward. Gaia clutched Wave's arm and looked back up to Oziru's form silhouetted against the light at the surface. She felt as though she was rising, but the water level was dropping. Oziru twisted once and the downward current of the water intensified. She saw Wave's toes gripping the bumpy coral on which they both stood.

Oziru continued to sing, its tentacles signaling in an arcane language. Oziru began to slowly spin, gradually increasing in speed like an ice skater until the alien was nothing but a whirling blur. Gaia felt herself being pulled off the ledge. One of her feet slipped. Instantly, Wave pushed her down flat against the coral and lay atop her. She gripped on to the rough knobs of coral. Gaia's arms shook from exertion. Then she was no longer underwater. She could still hear singing. She looked up and saw Oziru, whirling in thin air, six feet above the ledge where she and Wave lay.

Gaia spit out her mouthpiece, coughed and looked back again. Oziru floated in midair. Oziru's tentacles flung themselves straight out and the alien slowed and descended, coming to rest an arm's length from her.

Gaia looked down over the edge and saw the water's surface just below them. The air suddenly filled with wet popping noises as the octopi that had been stranded out of the water leapt outward and drifted, like a shower of vibrant umbrellas, toward the water. The creatures rained down from far above, where a thick white mist obscured the chamber's ceiling.

"I thought," Oziru said, "that you might be more comfortable in the dry." Gaia looked back at Oziru but was too overwhelmed to say anything. Wave shifted off her but remained prone.

The knobby coral Gaia desperately gripped began to vibrate. She let go, and it sprang open. Brilliant, fleshy yellow petals burst out of it. The whole bed of coral suddenly wiggled and shook, exploding into bloom. Color spread like a stain all around her, curling up the gentle incline until it twisted out of sight around the curve. Enormous white butterflies launched themselves out of crevices Gaia had not seen. They fluttered in reckless craziness out among the still-descending shower of octopi, who ate as many as they could catch.

Looking out across the vast chamber, Gaia counted at least ten islands like the one she stood on rising up through the heavy mist. Some of them were nothing but hazy gray shadows; others loomed closer. She couldn't see the outer walls of the chamber.

She should sit up and say something intelligent. Sitting up was easily accomplished, but she could neither find words nor the impetus to speak. She'd thought that her capacity to be amazed into stupidity had been fully extended in the corridor. She'd been wrong.

Gaia jumped at the sound of an enormous splash, then another. She turned and behind them she saw that the nearest island was, unlike the others, utterly black and devoid of life. It protruded from the water like a decayed tooth. As she watched, a whole side of the coiled shelf cracked and a house-sized chunk plunged into the water below. Gaia felt a light spray from the huge wave that rippled across the red water.

"I suppose it is natural for you to stare at the lovely and dead Kenjan's home, though it is a mournful place to rest your vision." Oziru's voice was only inches from Gaia.

"I'm sorry." Gaia was surprised she could still speak. "I didn't mean to stare." But she didn't stop. At the base of the blackening pillar, a new pink column twisted upward, its tip just breaking the surface of the water. At the top Gaia saw a blue siphon from which pink water gushed. "Is that structure a replacement?" Gaia pointed to the new spire.

"When it is finished it will house my next consort," Oziru said.

Next consort? She didn't think she'd inform Kenjan. She thought of the letter dangling in Wave's loose grip and hesitated, considering for the first time whether this was in any way appropriate. "Have you picked the new consort?"

Oziru looked at her for a long moment, and Gaia wondered if she hadn't just made some terrible blunder. Finally it spoke. "I do not choose. The stars decide this. I have spoken to the priests in our home waters. They say Seigata is fit to bear young."

Gaia didn't know whether to say "Congratulations" or "I'm sorry" or nothing at all. She chose the last.

The letter flopped and struggled.

Gaia swallowed, then held out her hand to Wave. Wave knew what she wanted and gave a moment of silent resistance before finally passing the bag to her. "Oziru. I have a letter for you."

She handed Oziru the letter. The Kishocha unfurled the letter across its lap, holding the edges to keep the letter from struggling. As it read, Oziru's cranial tendrils curled around in front of it, almost like a child curling a hand in front of a note written during class. Oziru hunched. Then the Kishocha stood, walked the few feet to the edge of the shelf, knelt and put its head underwater.

Gaia glanced askance at Wave, who lay prone on the ground.

"Exalted Oziru is calling someone, maybe," Wave whispered.

Oziru pulled its head out of the water and hunched protectively over the letter again. It turned briefly to stare at Gaia as if she was a dangerous contagion, then turned back to the note.

She broke out in a prickling sweat. "Am I in trouble?"

"No," Wave said.

"Are you sure?"

"No, Honorable Gaia," Wave said.

"So you don't know who Oziru called?" Gaia sensed she was beginning to babble.

"No, I do not." Wave shot her an evil glare from between the petals of a fleshy flower. Wave gnawed nervously on one of the inner leaves.

Gaia lapsed into silence. Oziru continued to ignore her.

According to her watch six minutes and forty-five seconds passed.

Gaia began to relax. She leaned back and stared up. This could not possibly be sunlight, yet the light that radiated down from the ceiling was very like sunlight. Though diffuse and not warm, the light was enough like the sun that Gaia had the glorious feeling of being outside. Even the breeze felt natural. She felt like she was again sitting on an enormous boulder on the shores of the Pacific—if the Pacific had been bright red and full of flying octopi.

Gaia felt a tug at her tank. She expected to see Wave subtly trying to get her attention. Instead, a purple-spotted octopus sat next to her as a large, expectant dog might. One sucker-intensive arm curled up around her diving tank. The octopus looked her in the eye and yanked on the hose again.

"Hey!" Gaia grabbed the tentacle. It curled around her hand. Gaia jerked backward. The octopus jerked her forward. Wave lunged forward and flicked the octopus on the head.

"No treats for you. Bad beast. You go." Wave kept flicking the octopus between the eyes, not hard, but persistently. "No tug-tug game." The octopus gave one last, listless tug at Gaia's arm then undulated into the water.

"How long is Oziru going to read that?" she asked. Wave shrugged and lay back down.

Gaia stared at the disintegrating black ruins of Kenjan's former home. The section that had sheared off had exposed a string of interior chambers. Most looked like furniture of some kind, but one chamber was full of large cogs. Gaia squinted, as if that would sharpen her already perfect vision. The cogs and gears were connected to each other in a medieval-looking fashion.

She asked Wave the purpose of this rambling machine. Wave told her that it had no purpose, except to move itself.

"Lovely Kenjan liked to play with human technology. It said that to understand one must go back to the beginning. Lovely Kenjan's favorite toy was a printing machine. It is in a lower chamber so you can't see it. Lovely Kenjan was carving the holy Kishocha letters so that it could print. It made letter blocks for noble Oziru's name and its own name and for love, and printed it."

"That's really sweet." Gaia thought obliquely of Fitzpatrick. She should call him, but what would she say?

"It was defiance-sweet." Wave's voice dropped lower. "The Holy had called for Kenjan to give reason it should continue as consort when Kenjan was barren as the void. Kenjan printed this letter many times, each exactly the same without making a single holy gesture. It printed on dead-things—worse than dead-things. It printed on something, which had never even been alive. This was very blasphemous like—" Wave searched for a metaphor. "Like...I cannot think of anything so bad as this that one could do in Happy Snak."

"What did it print on?"

"Plastic sheets, like the ones in front of the cold-case of Happy Snak," Wave said, sighing. "Those make me so nostalgic."

"Kenjan never accepted the holy words of priests as from the lips of the god," Oziru interrupted. Gaia's cheeks flushed in embarrassment. She hadn't realized the alien was listening or could hear them. Oziru remained sitting in its hunched position. "My beloved Kenjan thought it understood the god better than they did."

Oziru ran its hand across the surface of the letter. The letter trembled.

"No surprise that Kenjan should still struggle after death. This letter is proof that a disobedient spirit continues to resist through eternity." Oziru straightened up. "Gaia Jones, you will never bring writing done by the ghost to me again. You will never tell anyone of this letter's existence. You will forget that you saw it."

"I didn't read it."

"Of course not, you are not a priest and have no knowledge of holy letters, as is right and natural. But as the guardian of the ghost you must not allow its blasphemy to seep out of the confines of its chamber. If the ghost continues to be rebellious, it will be exorcised and your Mini-Snak will be no more. If you see the ghost making holy letters, you should discourage it."

"How do I tell holy letters from regular ones?" Gaia asked.

"All Kishocha letters are holy. They are not like your human dead-sound marks. They contain the motions of divinity. The ghost must not be allowed to defy the god again."

Gaia said, "I understand."

Wave mashed its face further into the petals of a flower.

Oziru continued, "Is this blasphemous letter the sole reason you demanded my attentions?"

"No." All liquid in her mouth evaporated. She felt the profound urge to fling herself down flat and play dead. Wave definitely had the right idea.

"What then?" The timbre of Oziru's voice hit her like a physical force. Goosebumps rose up, and the muscles of her arms began to infinitesimally quake.

"I..." She trailed off. Gaia knew that she'd come with grievances, but she couldn't think of any words. Her thoughts scattered like a flock of pigeons being assaulted by an excited dog. "I need..."

Oziru regarded her imperiously, its cranial tendrils lashing slowly from side to side. "Wave!"

Wave flinched. "Yes, my glorious lord?"

"What does Gaia Jones want?"

"She begs for a divination." Wave's hands shook as it spoke.

"What for?"

"To know that Mini-Snak is a righteous endeavor, and so Gaia Jones can understand what the god wants of her."

"Why would the god have any care for a human?" Oziru's eyes settled on her.

Gaia managed to locate her voice, but her intellect lagged fearfully behind. "The god let Kenjan choose me as a guardian."

"Perhaps the god wanted all Kishocha to remain uncontaminated by the dead. Perhaps it was never the god's intention at all, but Kenjan's last defiance."

"Maybe it was," Gaia said. "But without a divination, I won't know for sure why it happened."

Oziru narrowed its eyes. Its cranial tendrils halted, mid-lash. "There is no logic behind those words."

Gaia choked. She had to think of something to say, something that had nothing to do with Kenjan.

Gravity. She was supposed to ask about the gravity. That had nothing to do with Kenjan.

"There have been microgravity failures in the human sector that have caused some damage, and I'm worried that people will be killed if this continues." Gaia felt her intellect resurrecting itself.

Oziru took its time responding to this statement, and when it did its voice was slow and perplexed, as the alien tried to follow Gaia's reasoning.

"Why would you need a divination about that?"

"Wave told me it was a holy force. I thought that meant it was the power of your god."

"It's regulated through the songs and motions which I perform," Oziru said.

"So, you haven't been punishing us humans?"

Oziru started aback. "No, I have not."

"But the gravity..." Gaia trailed off again.

"I have had sorrow sickness and have not danced some days." Oziru stroked the letter again, which Gaia thought would be dead by now. It wasn't. It curled weakly at the edges, still trying to escape. "This doesn't matter so much inside the orb of Ki Island, but Seigata had told me human structures need to be always held with heaviness. So I dance though I have ill, acid nausea."

"I'm sorry."

"There is no reason to ask the god about gravity," Oziru ended.

"That's a relief." Gaia forced a little perkiness into her tone. "I'll just be on my way."

"No, you may not leave. I will call Seigata to divine your purpose, since you want to know," Oziru said. "I can see that you are clever to wonder about it."

"If it's only me then, please, don't trouble Seigata." Gaia wanted nothing more than to go back to Happy Snak, crawl into her bed and maybe leak a few overstressed tears.

Oziru rose and bellowed out a series of sharp ascending notes. Instantly, the anvil-shaped head of Sudden Red Crush rose out of the water behind Gaia. She bit her lip to keep from moving or screaming. Residual fear made it easy for her to freeze. The shark floated inches from her body. Gaia barely breathed. Its teeth were bigger than her hands.

Without ceremony Oziru tossed the dying letter into the shark's mouth. Sudden Red Crush swallowed it whole.

Chapter Twenty-One: Smoke and Abortion

Gaia clenched her fists. This was awful. She should never have come. She hadn't even assembled the courage to ask Oziru to prohibit other Kishocha from throwing rocks at Kenjan. Oziru's attitude toward its former consort was heartless. Apart from getting an answer about the gravity, this visit was a complete failure.

Wave wouldn't look at her. Gaia didn't know if Wave was scared or sad or just angry. But Wave had curled in around the emotion coursing through itself and refused to give her any support. So Gaia silently waited. Time passed. Alternating washes of fatigue, cold and dullness wore her down to a state of inert inoffensiveness. She sat, passive as a closed clam.

Seigata finally emerged from the red water glistening and wrapped with strand after strand of yellow pearls. Its throat was ringed from jaw to sternum in an intricate collar that not only covered the alien's pit, but also managed to obscure any hint of the pit's existence. Golden rings circled the base of each of Seigata's cranial tendrils.

Seeing that Oziru was seated, Seigata collapsed immediately to its knees, which left it sunk up to its hips in water. Behind Seigata, Gaia could see an entourage of a dozen other Kishocha waiting just beneath the surface. Only minute differences in their facial swirls defined one from the other.

"You have summoned me," Seigata said.

Oziru hands curled inward, as if it were still holding the ghost of Kenjan's letter. "Gaia Jones of my house has asked for a divination."

"For what purpose, my noblest master?" Seigata's elongated, singsong accent confounded Gaia. She wondered if the alien really was singing its words for some reason.

"To discover her place in the currents of the god's will." Oziru laced its fingers together. Gaia remained still and silent.

"Come to me, then, Gaia Jones." Seigata extended its hands, wet gold rings glistening against its fingers. The priest tilted its head slightly. Its palms were open to her. She held out her own hands and Seigata folded its warm fingers around them.

Oziru lay down on its side. Its long, heavy cranial tendrils dangled in the water. Gaia wondered if sitting or standing upright in air was a strain on its neck muscles. The spotted octopus that had previously tried to dismantle Gaia's rebreather latched onto one of Oziru's tendrils and seemed to be riding it.

"Gaia Jones." Seigata sighed enormously, as if deflating. "Gaia Jones is a difficult question to ponder."

"Yes." Oziru flipped the octopus into the air. The octopus flew up, popped open and drifted gently back to the water.

Seigata released her hands. "I would like to try a different technique of divination from the normal Kishocha, simply to be sure I am not mistaken in the god's intent."

The octopus had wrapped around Oziru's tendril again, waiting.

"This uncertainty is uncharacteristic of you," Oziru commented.

"Forgive me."

Oziru flipped the octopus into the air again.

"What method will you perform?" Oziru played a listless game of tug of war with the octopus.

Seigata said, "Since the human soul is made of fire, I will use smoke and abortion."

Gaia glanced at Wave. Apparently all the Kishocha believed this to be true of human souls. She deliberately ignored the word *abortion*, since she couldn't even hazard a guess what that would be. She unsuccessfully tried to comfort herself by thinking of the "pain and suffering" payment which she was sure to receive for this encounter. The impending cash infusion didn't quell her alarm.

Oziru said, "So extreme? You must feel very unsure."

"Yes, glorious Oziru, I do. I beg this of you." Seigata stretched itself out across the coral. Its jewelry clicked against the hard shells.

When Seigata lay fully prostrate, Oziru said, "Fine, you may divine this way if you choose." Oziru turned its attention to her.

"Gaia Jones."

"Yes, glorious Oziru?" Gaia found herself bowing her head reflexively.

"You have already used my time and favor past the point that I can spare it. When Seigata's divination is over, Wave will take you back to Happy Snak. We will confer over Seigata's holy findings at a later tide. I have much work." With that, Oziru slid into the red waters.

Gaia said, "I'm sorry," but Oziru was already far beneath the water. She turned to Seigata who looked much more formidable than before.

"Follow me. Leave your servant."

Seigata drew Gaia away from Wave. It climbed the gentle incline silently and slowly, which was lucky for Gaia since the carpet anemones were slippery.

They ascended higher, into the heavy curtain of mist. The coral slowly gave way to soft, spongy moss. Thin, willowy trees grew around the edge of the structure. Bells and chimes dangled from their branches. Gaia thought she saw a dove. It turned out to be something like a small, white pterodactyl.

Seigata motioned that she should sit, which Gaia was grateful to do. The sensation of moss beneath her feet produced a sharp pang of homesickness within her. The pterodactyl-thing came to rest on a bell-laden branch, which chimed eerily under its weight.

Seigata walked into the misty trees, then reappeared

carrying a pink egg. It sat opposite Gaia and asked her to hold out her hands. The priest cracked the egg into her upturned palms.

If a huge spider or slimy crustacean embryo had slid squawking from the egg, Gaia would not have been surprised. But the egg's interior was very ordinary. It held clear albumen with two orange yolks floating in it. One yolk had broken, and leaked thinly through the albumen. Seigata leaned over it, regarding the yolks.

"I no longer need smoke," Seigata announced. "You may reunite these with the waters." It indicated the yolks. Gaia walked to the edge of the spire, which was dizzyingly far above the water level. She scraped the egg off her hands. When she returned Gaia found that Seigata had made itself comfortable, leaning against a conveniently shaped rock. Seigata looked much less formal and scary. Gaia sat opposite it.

"The aborted egg indicates that there are two paths that you can follow. One leads to order and the other to chaos," Seigata said softly. Gaia didn't have to think too hard to figure out which egg yolk indicated chaos.

"Okay." This divination told her nothing but she was strangely glad. Gaia disbelieved divinations, but when one is told a fortune, it's always hard not to be affected by it.

"This may be hard for you to understand, but your desire to know the god's will for you is misplaced. Neither you, nor any other human has any part in the god's plan. That is why one of the yolks is broken. When a thing has no place in a pattern, the result is disorder and chaos. Disruption is the only result. Because you have no purpose here, any action that you make inside the god's pattern is wrong."

Gaia hadn't expected her fortune to be "everything you do is bad". She'd done a lot for Kenjan, and more than that for Wave, and Mini-Snak was gaining popularity by the hour. Happy Snak was becoming a destination establishment, instead of just a cheap replacement for Treat Bonanza, and she'd finally made some friends. That was not wrong. She reminded herself that she didn't believe in mysticism, and then decided to use it against Seigata anyway.

"But how can that be true, when the god made me Kenjan's guardian?"

"Kenjan no longer has any place in the god's order either. The god killed Kenjan to protect the righteous from living amid its heresy. The god made Kenjan a ghost to keep that one from reaching heaven. And last, the god made Kenjan choose you, a human, its guardian to keep the ghost from being able to pollute any more Kishocha. This decision was made by the god not to draw you into the Kishocha waters, but to keep Kenjan from ever getting back to them." Seigata took a deep breath. "You understand, maybe?"

"And yet, the opposite seems to be happening. How can that occur without the god's consent?"

Seigata's eyes narrowed. "Many things occur without the god's consent. They are named evil."

"So I am evil?" Gaia kept her expression innocent, earnest. Maybe she would get out of here with her body and dignity both intact.

"No, Kenjan is evil. You are merely Kenjan's servant. That one is very evil."

Gaia felt her ire rising. "Seigata, I don't serve evil. I serve snacks."

"Snacks, too, are evil."

She could not let this slur pass. "Snacks are not evil. They're tasty. And they're some of the best things about life."

"About human life. Snacks are not for Kishocha. Snacks corrupt. Snacks impersonate truth."

Gaia had no idea how that could happen, and said so.

Seigata had an answer ready. "They offer cheap satisfaction while the soul swims to hell. They blur that pattern, replacing sustenance with venal urges for orange. They take the divine mystery of carbonation and transform it into a sticky poisonous brew of black vice. Your people build temples to blasphemous carbonation. The Coca-Cola building, where you, yourself originate."

Gaia thought about trying to explain that Coca-Cola was

not a religion, but felt it went outside the range of the current argument.

"So you are against snacks, and you think that humans are evil."

"I am against snacks, but I do not think humans are evil. You are simply not ready to travel in the god's ocean yet, and we should not aid your progression into a mystery you are not yet able to understand."

Seigata had obviously thought this whole thing through. "We have intruded on the god's pattern for your people. Making contact and encouraging you humans to live on our island like worms biting into the skin of a great shark. That was the worst of the heresies of Kenjan. For the god's pattern, I believe that we must separate. We must undo the contamination, which we have done to ourselves and to you. You have not mastered the skills to traverse the great ocean and survive. You do not know gravity. You do not know how to call back to your home quickly. The human goal in the ocean is to go searching for nothing. Kishocha know what they want and seek it singularly."

"The god, right?" Gaia felt like she'd really gotten the gist of the conversation now.

"Exactly. Our search is for the god. We should not be here going around this red planet. Our search must go on."

"Can't you stay here and send other people out?"

"We are the ones who were sent out. And here we are, going in circles around a red dry hell that is going in circles around a yellow sun. Confusion is compounded upon confusion. We must go on. The students of the scholar, True Current, know this. I know this. Only Kenjan did not believe this. But you can help us correct our path by taking Kenjan to your world."

"To Earth?"

"Or to Mars." Seigata waved the difference aside. "I think the god may have intended for Kenjan to be on Mars."

"If I could even get permission to do that, which I don't think I could, Kenjan would die," Gaia said.

"Kenjan is already dead."

"Well, then Kenjan's already out of the way and doesn't

have to go to Mars."

"Many do not agree," Seigata said. "It is well known that we would not be here with you humans if Kenjan had not been charmed with you. Kenjan argued that the god led us to meet you for a reason that we Kishocha must discover before going on. We had to learn from you, said Kenjan. We know now that you were simply a temptation, to which that one weakly succumbed. There is nothing to be learned from congress with mammals."

Gaia was not prepared to give up Happy Snak or her dream of an ideal life in space, which included congress with aliens. She also felt that Seigata was not the kind of person who could be argued with about matters such as personal freedom.

She said, "I am not going to take Kenjan to Mars. It's just out of the question. I don't have a visa for Mars, or a business permit, and they don't allow ghosts."

"So the humans are also worried about contamination from Kenjan? They are at least that insightful. I can understand. Kenjan is persuasive. This makes me respect the human piety more. Not all human priests rush to embrace wrong ideas."

Gaia nodded. Another human would have found the nod noncommittal and lackluster, but Seigata didn't seem to notice. She wondered what nuances of conversation she was missing.

"I have given you the divination as Oziru commanded, but now I humbly beg that you assist me." Seigata shifted forward.

"What do you need?"

"When Kenjan died in your original Happy Snak, some things were left behind."

"Yes, the motions of dying." Gaia allowed herself a little beam of satisfaction at knowing the Kishocha so well that she could predict what they would say.

Seigata went on to immediately deflate her sense of worldliness.

"I mean some material possessions of Kenjan's. There was a wrist cuff, a pit guard and three tendril adornments that were never found. These are precious items and I would like to find them."

"I can't help you with the tendril adornments or the wrist cuff, but I've got the pit guard."

"This object is a symbol of rank. I will need to wear it when I am made the consort of Oziru. So could you please return it to me?"

"Yes, of course. I'm so sorry. I had forgot I even had it. I haven't even thought of it for months." Gaia's skin prickled. Did Seigata think she'd kept Kenjan's pit guard on purpose? No wonder the alien had a low opinion of humans.

"Ignorance must be forgiven, or all servants would be beaten to death."

"I'll get the pit guard back to you. I promise. And Fitzpatrick might be able to help me find the other things. They're probably just in a locker someplace."

Or being auctioned off to the highest bidder, but no. As far as she knew she was the only person auctioning Kishocha items. Then again, there were many illegal auctions out there... She hoped she could make good on this promise.

"The sooner you can return these items to me, the better," Seigata said. "But that is trivial and easily taken care of. Just pass them to Sharkey tomorrow. More importantly, you must control the ghost. Many call for Kenjan's exorcism. They call to me to cease the ghost songs permeating our waters. They cannot sleep for fear the ghost will enter their minds. Many sleep out of the waters or with ear covers."

"I'm sorry about that, I'll talk to Kenjan."

"It is my decision to silence Kenjan or not," Seigata said. "And Kenjan is unruly and disruptive. Kenjan sings all night. If you could hear it, you would know that Wave is the only Kishocha who ever sleeps now. This song so upsets Oziru that it does not sing, then your Coca-Cola temple almost breaks free adrift in the great ocean."

"The gravity failure is not Kenjan's fault. Oziru said it was just sick with sorrow."

"Oziru would not shirk its sacred responsibilities if Kenjan did not force it."

"But really, Kenjan might be annoying—"

"Do you suggest that hounding Oziru is a forgivable thing?" Seigata interrupted severely.

Gaia suppressed her every immediate urge. She was being pointlessly argumentative. She forced herself to think like Fitzpatrick. What would he say?

"No, absolutely not. Oziru is the undisputed master of Ki Island."

"I am glad to hear you say it," Seigata said. "I was beginning to suspect that you had become sick and possessed. You must understand that you are an advocate only for the ghost as a dead thing and not for Kenjan as though it was still a person."

"Yes, I understand." Gaia held tight to the working vocabulary of her internal Fitzpatrick.

"If you have the power to make Kenjan stop singing, you must use it soon. I cannot explain how important this is. Oziru must be able to sleep and dance. Oziru provides for all of us. Kenjan is dead and selfishly wishes Oziru to join it in oblivion, but if that happens, we will all wither and die."

"I understand," Gaia said. "I will do as you ask."

"Excellent." Seigata lifted a hand and formed a strange sign in the air. "I bless you, and wish you all success."

Chapter Twenty-Two: Isolation

Gaia hunched on the edge of the waterway, coughing and retching up fluid. Her arms shook with exhaustion. Her throat ached. Her nose burned. She felt leaden and ill. This was the way she always felt after diving. While she was in the Kishocha sector she just hadn't noticed.

She had a lot to do before she could slide into torpor. She couldn't allow herself to think too hard about today. Numbness slipped over her and she accepted it. Numbness would help her get through the next few minutes with Kenjan. Then she'd be able to try and locate Kenjan's missing jewelry.

She rubbed her eyes and looked around for Wave. She saw wet footprints preceding her into the shrine. When she entered she followed the tracks to their terminus—her closed bedroom door. Wave had gone ahead without her.

Strange.

But maybe Wave had been just as scared as she'd been.

Kenjan was in its grotto staring at its new hand-held. Lights flickered across its muzzle.

"Kenjan!" Gaia called across the water. "I delivered your letter."

The Kishocha set its hand-held down and emerged from its little house. "What did my beloved say?"

Gaia took a deep breath. Words failed her.

Kenjan moved closer, to the edge of the black and red

island. "Tell me what Oziru said."

"Oziru said that I shouldn't bring any more letters from you."

"No! That is not true. Are you sure you gave the letter to Oziru? Did the Kishocha have big cranial tendrils?"

"I know what Oziru looks like."

"Who else saw the letter?" Kenjan said. "Was Seigata present?"

"Only Wave was there."

"No one else?"

"Sudden Red Crush ate it," Gaia said. "Does that count?"

Kenjan clenched and unclenched its fists.

Gaia sank down to the floor at the water's edge. "You've got to start acting like you're dead."

"Be silent!" Kenjan snapped.

"You're going to be exorcised if you don't." Gaia didn't have the energy to be affronted by Kenjan's imperiousness.

"I will not bow down," Kenjan bellowed. "You were the one who told me I was not really dead."

"Not by human standards. But you know damn well that the Kishocha expect you to act like a ghost."

"I do act like a ghost. I act like a vengeful and restless spirit. I will not let Oziru forget me."

Gaia had to admit she hadn't thought of this—that Kenjan would be deliberately "haunting" Oziru. It made perfect sense, though. "If you don't shut up, Seigata is going to exorcise you."

Kenjan's muzzle curled into an animalistic snarl. "When did you begin to live in fear of Seigata, oh my beloved guardian?"

"This afternoon when Seigata told me, straight out, that it was going to kill you if you didn't stop singing."

"Why were you talking to Seigata at all?" Kenjan asked.

"I was having a divination." Gaia winced at the admission.

"A divination? To see what? There is no point in a human having a Kishocha divination." Kenjan began to pace. Its cranial tendrils lashed against one another. "There is no point in anyone having a divination from Seigata. The priest only knows how to repeat what it has been told. It has no vision."

"I had to think up a good reason to be there."

"So you chose divination?"

"No, Wave did," Gaia said. "I couldn't think of anything."

"I see. And what did Seigata say about your place in the god's great ocean?"

"That isn't relevant. What matters is that Seigata told me that your singing was disrupting everything on Ki Island and I should either stop you or take you away."

Kenjan stopped pacing. Its cranial tendrils hung limp. "Take me away?"

"To Mars or Earth."

"Seigata asked you to take me from the waters?" Kenjan crouched down on the edge of its island.

"I said it was impossible. But really, it's not. You're just lucky Seigata talked to me and not Blum."

"Oziru would never allow me to be removed from the range of its song," Kenjan said. "No matter how melancholy I made Oziru, my beloved would not let me be taken away."

"I don't know about that. I saw your old house."

Kenjan didn't reply.

"It's falling down," Gaia said. "Big blackened chunks of it are falling into the water."

"Do you enjoy tormenting me, Guardian?" Kenjan didn't look at her.

"And there was this new spire growing up right beside your old place. Oziru said it was the house of its new consort."

"There is no other on Ki Island who is of the blood," Kenjan said.

"Oziru said that the priests on your home world designated Seigata as Oziru's new consort—"

"Be silent!" Kenjan sprang to its feet. "I order you quiet!"

"No," Gaia shouted back. "I order you quiet. Stop singing. Stop trying to get Oziru's attention. It's over between you two."

"I will never believe that. Our love is stronger than the bonds of death. I will never let go." Kenjan started to steam.

Gaia bolted to her feet.

"Stop that right now. If you steam, I'm leaving."

"Then leave, revolting Guardian," Kenjan spat. "You do not serve me."

"No, I don't," Gaia coughed. The chemical reek tickled the back of her throat. "I protect you—even from your own stupid ideas. If you sing tonight it will prove that Seigata is right and you need to be killed. Do you have a death wish? Would you rather be eaten and shit out by cleaners than stay quiet for just one night? What is wrong with you?"

"I am lonely," Kenjan bellowed back at her. "I want to be with my beloved."

Gaia retreated to the back wall, next to her bedroom door. The fumes hadn't permeated the air there yet.

"You would not understand," Kenjan said. "You are always alone. You cannot feel how I feel."

"Maybe I can't understand how you feel, but that doesn't mean I'm wrong." Gaia hefted her rebreather.

"Sound travels vast distances in water. I can hear Oziru, and Oziru hears me. Our voices can entwine in harmony. Even if our bodies may never again touch. It brings me momentary comfort in my isolation. Do you think I could bear to hear Oziru's love song mingling with Seigata's? Do you think I could live through the torture of hearing the tiny voices of their progeny learning to sing?"

"It's not worth dying over."

"I am already dead," Kenjan said. "Everything else is just the wait before oblivion."

Gaia's thought's spiraled down to a dark dead-end. Kenjan was going to sing. There was no stopping it. The alien didn't care about itself, her, Wave or anything else. A warm ball of red anger spun deep in her chest.

"You self-pitying bastard," Gaia said. "Go ahead and die. You obviously want to."

"You still cannot accept that I am already dead, deluded Guardian."

Gaia groaned. "I'm so tired of talking about you. I have a

life too."

Kenjan cocked its head. Its cranial tendrils perked a little at the ends.

"So you do," Kenjan said. "When I am exorcised you will be able to continue your life."

"When you are dead, I won't have the life I want. Everything I have is dependent on you being here. I want to see more. I want to dive Ki Island. My hope is tied up in you, you suicidal jerk."

"I am sorry I am not a better master."

"You could be. All you have to do is shut up."

"That is all I had to do to not be killed at all, and look where I am now," Kenjan said.

Gaia had to admit that this was, in fact, true. Annoying, but true. "So what you're saying is that you can't learn? Wave can learn things, but you can't. Are you sure you're the one who's superior?"

"I will never learn to be compliant."

"Please, Kenjan." She heard her voice almost begging. "Please. All I'm asking for is one night. I'm not asking you to change who you are. Sing like hell tomorrow night. Just don't sing tonight. I promised Seigata I could get you to be quiet. Let me keep my word."

Kenjan ran its fingertips across the water's surface.

"Well?" Gaia held her breath.

"Very well, I will not sing for one night, but do not make a promise like that again. I will not continuously sacrifice my integrity for yours."

Gaia sagged in relief. "Thank you very much. It means a lot to me."

"I see that. But now you also know that singing with Oziru means everything to me?"

"Yes, I do."

"Then we will not argue this matter again?"

Gaia shook her head. This was all such a waste. "After tonight, you can sing your way to oblivion."

Chapter Twenty-Three: Today's Entrepreneurial Woman

Gaia collapsed onto her bed. She mashed her face into her dry, soft pillow. Her cool, dark bedroom provided an octopi-free safe zone. After a rest, she'd call Fitzpatrick and ask him to help her find Kenjan's things.

She closed her eyes, but didn't sleep. Her eyeballs rolled beneath her lids. Something was bothering her. She checked her alarm.

Was she late for something? She couldn't be. She didn't have any plans. Her stomach fluttered nervously. Her eyes popped open. She'd forgotten to place the fresh-produce order, and Happy Snak was going to run out of cherry tomatoes, not to mention lettuce. And she hadn't placed the meat order either.

The protein lab was closed to orders for the night, but produce could still be procured. She dialed up the arboretum and was informed that Cheryl had already ordered the cherry tomatoes, along with everything else that Happy Snak needed.

Gaia lay back down, relieved at the averted tomato crisis, but annoyed that Cheryl had done her job so efficiently. Gaia pulled her blanket up over her eyes. Worthlessness washed over her. She'd failed to complete any of her specified duties today. The only actions she'd accomplished were delivering a forbidden letter and incurring the wrath of a flying omnipotent god-king.

World: one. Gaia: zero.

She curled up tighter in her blankets and dragged a pillow

over her face. If she could sleep, she'd regain confidence. Anxiety gnawed at her.

She was hungry and thirsty, and her bladder was uncomfortably full. She might as well just get up. After a trip to the bathroom, Gaia dug through her snack stash. She found a warm box of PowerWoman!! brand athletic nutritional drink and a mostly full carton of chocolate-covered fortune cookies. Armed with these supplies, Gaia queued up her message center.

Fitzpatrick had left a message asking her about her day. Gaia jabbed the erase button. Then the arboretum called asking about the produce order. This message was followed by another from the arboretum confirming Cheryl's online order and saying that they'd have to substitute yellow cherry tomatoes for red, since red was temporarily out of stock.

Gaia's mother had called to effuse about the style and popularity of the alien jewelry that she'd just received. She chided Gaia for calling the necklaces "pieces of shit" then talked for five solid, enthusiastic minutes about her marketing plans.

New Earthling, an Earth-based talk show, requested an interview with Wave Walker. Gaia saved the contact number.

Fitzpatrick called again to request that she refrain from doing media interviews without first talking to the embassy liaison and asking her to instruct Wave Walker against them as well.

What was he? Psychic?

Fitzpatrick also wanted to hear from her at her first convenience. Gaia bit into a cookie. It wasn't convenient yet. The next five messages were all wordless disconnects from Fitzpatrick.

Finally, the Frymaster Corporation sent a text message to say that her replacement parts had been shipped, along with interactive instructional media that explained how the new valves were to be installed. The valves were under warranty only if a certified technician performed the installation. The company regretted deeply that they were not able to send an authorized technician to her service area. Frymaster Corporation encouraged her to take their online test and become a certified

Frymaster technician herself. Gaia demurred.

Messages accomplished, she went rifling through her drawer for the pit guard. It lay next to some Sparkle Lady barrettes, and gave off a faint, bacon-like smell.

Gaia donned a clean Happy Snak smock and dropped the pit guard into her pocket. Should she talk to Wave? Wave had been upset by the day's events, although Gaia didn't know exactly what part of the day had distressed it. Was it Oziru's callousness toward Kenjan's letter? She supposed she'd saunter by Wave's door and see if the Kishocha emerged. Gaia walked to her door, slid it open and jumped back with a startled yelp. Fitzpatrick was right there sitting on a plastic chair, looking drowsy.

"Glad you're back safe at last, Ms. Jones." He flipped open his case of cigarette gum.

Happy Snak was dark and quiet.

"It's the middle of the night." Gaia didn't bother to ask how he got in. "What are you doing here? Did Cheryl let you stay in here?"

Fitzpatrick raised an eyebrow. "She and I fed the ghost together. After that I decided to wait for you, but it seemed inappropriate to hang around in your bedroom, so I've just been here."

"Come in then." Gaia stepped aside.

Fitzpatrick seated himself in Gaia's only chair.

Gaia rubbed her face. "I figured out that gravity-failure problem everybody's been talking about."

"And?" Fitzpatrick leaned toward her.

"Oziru was just depressed and didn't feel like gravitizing the place, so it didn't."

"I don't follow you," Fitzpatrick said.

"Oziru makes the gravity work by singing or dancing or something."

"Is that what Wave told you?"

"No, I saw it happening."

Fitzpatrick toyed with his cigarette gum case. "You should

tell me everything that happened."

She gave a brief outline of events beginning with the letter and ending with Kenjan's bleak announcement. Fitzpatrick listened seriously, only taking out his hand-held once to make a call about Kenjan's missing possessions. Apparently the entire floor of the previous Happy Snak had been sectioned and given to the station's exobiology department for further study. No one was at the lab, but Fitzpatrick described the missing articles and politely requested that they be returned. Easy as that.

Watching him calmly and expediently solve her problem, Gaia felt the strong urge to fling herself into Fitzpatrick's arms. She resisted, though, as fatigue had clearly made her sentimental. A man being able to competently complete a phone call didn't make him Prince Charming.

He disconnected. "Do you feel safer now?"

"I guess—I don't know. It doesn't matter. Once Oziru gets remarried, I think Kenjan's going to kill itself anyway. I don't know what's going to happen then. Maybe we'll all have to leave."

"These are some very worrisome statements," Fitzpatrick said.

"I know. It's depressing."

Fitzpatrick regarded her evenly. "Do you know how painful it is for major ambassadorial personnel to be informed of critical events via snack bar managers?"

"Sucks to be you." Gaia rose and opened her door. "Now I really have a lot to do."

"Just one more thing." Fitzpatrick's demeanor softened, and he took a step closer to Gaia. "Do you regret having spent the night with me?"

"What?"

"Since you haven't returned my calls I thought you might be bitter about it. I thought you might be angry with me."

"But I never returned your calls before I slept with you either," Gaia said.

"Yes, but it didn't hurt my feelings then."

Gaia snorted with laughter. "Oh, please."

"I'm serious." Fitzpatrick reached out and gently caught one of Gaia's hands. "I really enjoyed our evening together and I was hoping to have another."

Gaia sobered. She did want to see him again, but felt ridiculous developing a crush on Fitzpatrick just because he never had food in his teeth. She hoped that they'd be able to be real lovers someday...but not today.

Finding the strength to trust, hope and love again would have to go on the back burner. Since she was today's entrepreneurial woman, Gaia had a legitimate excuse to avoid meaningful congress with another human being: She had to work. She pulled her hand away.

Fitzpatrick stared dejectedly at her discarded box of PowerWoman!!

"I would like to see you again," she said. "You know, sexually."

Fitzpatrick's eyes widened in vague amusement.

"I suppose that's a start. Maybe after we have sex for a couple of weeks, we can begin to have a romance?"

"Maybe. Now beat it. I promise you that we'll talk in a day or two. I'll tell you everything."

"And we'll have sex again?"

"Probably sex first, then a power nap, then talking," she said. "Does that sound okay to you?"

"I'll put aside three hours." Fitzpatrick pressed a quick, warm kiss to her cheek then left her alone. Gaia watched him let himself out. He was awfully convenient.

As she passed Wave's door, she noticed a piece of paper adhered to the outside of her door. The note informed the Happy Snak management that Wave Walker would be sick tomorrow and thus unable to work.

Who told Wave about calling in sick?

Roy had some explaining to do.

Chapter Twenty-Four: Cold Snap

Wave remained secluded in its room the entire morning. Gaia pulled cold drinks and fielded constant questions about the alien's absence. Wave's regular customers were mostly maintenance guys. They wanted to know what exactly was wrong with the alien. A girl from the loading dock left Wave a get-well card.

Roy and Cheryl inquired about the previous day. Gaia remained noncommittal. When pressed she said it was none of their business. Rebuffed, the couple drifted away into their own world of bickering and private jokes. Gaia had made herself extraneous. And the level of bitterness she felt about it surprised her.

Before she'd met any of these people, she'd been safe. Now she acutely felt the vacancies in her life. What she'd considered comfortable insulation metamorphosed into emptiness. Most painfully she felt Wave's sudden withdrawal. It even overshadowed the budding hope of intimacy with Fitzpatrick and the discovery of the new alien world. She wanted Wave to emerge from its self-imposed exile and be meaninglessly happy. In Wave's absence, disappointment descended like a mass of arctic air, making every experience sharp and painful.

She cursed Wave for ignoring her and cursed herself for ever allowing herself to emotionally rely on some alien she'd practically just met.

After lunch, she prepped for dinner. At four o'clock, she ate a hot dog that tasted like cardboard. Dinner came and went. She told another dozen people that Wave was sick. Roy and Cheryl left at eight. Gaia closed the restaurant alone.

She'd closed down hundreds of times before, but today the cleaning seemed to stretch on for hours. Each section of Happy Snak, from the reeking, curry-spattered counter to the greasy hot dog rack revolted Gaia. Wave made cleaning more fun. But no fun was to be had tonight. Gaia mopped alone. Wave always made an elaborate show of moving obstacles out of the way of her mop. Gaia had to move the trash can herself and felt lonely. Wave's door remained closed. No new sick note had appeared. Gaia took heart that Wave would return tomorrow and rescue her from her solitude.

Ten thirty approached, and Gaia prepared to fake her way through a night cooking at Mini-Snak. She didn't want to stun snakes and wouldn't be sucking any clams. Sucked clam would have to be 86'd. Maybe the Kishocha could stun their own snakes. Even armed with a jug of orange, Gaia balked at her duties. She didn't want to enter the shrine without Wave.

What sort of mood would Kenjan be in now?

Gaia still had ten minutes. Why not feed Microbe? She coaxed her hamster out. Microbe sat in her hand, eating a pile of green pellets and dehydrated carrots. As Microbe chewed, he stared warily at Gaia. Microbe was a very fastidious hamster. He only smelled a little like dank wood shavings. He kept his hindquarters spotless and soft. His black eyes glinted like obsidian beads. His tiny toenails clutched onto her palm. When he was finished he cleaned his already pristine muzzle.

"Good boy." Gaia petted Microbe's tiny, petal-like ear. Microbe's small body stiffened and the shrine door dilated. Sharkey and Stinger stepped into her bedroom. Spooked, Microbe dived into Gaia's smock. Sharkey and Stinger and their weapons took up most of the small room. The guards looked confused. Gaia felt a spark of anger igniting in the pit of her stomach. Just before the shrine door clenched shut, Gaia saw Oziru standing at the edge of the water.

"What are you doing in here?" Gaia cuddled Microbe to her

stomach.

"Oziru has ordered us out of the shrine. This was the closest door," Stinger said. "Sudden Red Crush is at the waterway."

Sharkey repeatedly jabbed the "open" icon on Gaia's door, trying to get into Happy Snak. "This door won't open. Even though I press the correct picture."

"That would be because I didn't want anyone to come in here and bother me." Gaia made no attempt to restrain the nastiness in her voice. They'd ruined her Microbe moment. Now her hamster shook violently against her. All sense of serenity had been shattered.

"I apologize for this bad intrusion in your dry eel nest. Oziru is in a strange and complicated state," Stinger said.

"What do you mean?" Gaia momentarily lost Microbe within the folds of her Happy Snak smock.

"Kenjan did not sing last night," Stinger said. "I think the ghost may be finally tired of haunting. Oziru has come to check."

"That's good, isn't it?" Gaia asked.

"Who knows? But we must not be with them, and neither should you. Do not attempt to enter the shrine. Oziru is unattended."

"Where can we go to sit?" Sharkey stepped between them. "This room smells like death."

Gaia unlocked her bedroom door. "The dining area's through the kitchen, where the chairs are."

Sharkey and Stinger jostled through the door. In the middle of the kitchen, Sharkey turned toward Wave's room, sniffing.

"Honorable Gaia Jones, is Wave Walker curling to rest here?" Sharkey poked the closed door with the tip of its spear.

"Wave's not in the mood for guests. Go to the dining room." Gaia closed the door behind them, leaving the guards to amuse themselves in Happy Snak. Microbe burrowed toward her bra. She knew from experience that it would require several minutes to extract him from her clothing. This accomplished, Gaia regarded the forbidden shrine door. She activated her surveillance cameras. She felt guilty, but what was the purpose of having a surveillance camera if not to spy? A tingle of exhilaration and shame rushed through her. Oziru sat at the edge of the water and listened to Kenjan's animated harangue. Kenjan splashed water everywhere. Oziru did not move, except to duck a cracked clamshell, which Kenjan had hurled at its head.

After watching this pantomime for a few minutes, Gaia grew tired of trying to imagine what the two were saying. She decided to tackle the audio. Gaia met with little success.

If Oziru and Kenjan were anything like she and her ex-husband had been, they would be arguing all night long. She'd have ample time to discover how to work the sound. She flipped through the manual and came to the conclusion that she needed someone who could really follow instructions.

Gaia went in search of Wave.

Gaia peeked out of her door. She didn't want to attract the guards' attention. Stinger stood in front of the Cherry Bomb console, intently watching the graphics. Sharkey paced the length of the dining room lost in its own thoughts. Gaia slipped across the back of the kitchen to Wave's room and tapped gently.

Wave cracked the door open.

"Hi, Wave," Gaia said.

"I am very busy right now. Please call again at another time." The Kishocha closed its door.

Gaia knocked again. When Wave didn't answer, she kicked the door. "Wave, I really need to talk to you." The door slid open.

"What do you want me to do?" Wave intoned dramatically. "Oh, please command me, Gaia Jones. You are so powerful that I must be obedient to you."

"I'm not going to command you," she said. Wave's sudden transmogrification into Sharkey-like sarcasm confounded her.

"So you are tired of commanding me? I am so sorry. Can I help you regain your strength to command me more?" Wave's cranial tendrils thrashed in agitation.

"What are you talking about?"

"You are just playing a game like Kenjan. You still command me even though you say I have become manager of Mini-Snak. It is all the game to you and fun at the expenses of my pride." Wave's voice grew louder with each new thought. "And why? My hope is too cheap. Will you take all my money pieces away now? I am no employee, any longer. Such a charade."

Gaia expected Wave to be upset about Kenjan, but Wave was angry with her.

She hadn't thought Wave was capable of real anger, especially toward her. She and Wave shared a special relationship, didn't they? She appreciated Wave in a way that no one else did. Wave gave her its immediate trust and she'd reciprocated with instant warmth. Of all the people on A-Ki Station, Wave was the only one she was always willing to tolerate.

Something fragile snapped inside Gaia. Her composure deteriorated.

"Are you trying to quit?" Gaia's voice was breathy and high.

"Why should a person as me need to quit? I am only a slave to be at your command and grovel like a low worm," Wave hissed. "I hold two regrets in my chest. One is that I let Sharkey do muzzling with me and the other that I believed you."

Gaia eyes stung. Tears blurred her vision. She couldn't believe it. Would she be crying every day now? She didn't dare look to see if the guards were watching. How could they not be looking? She wiped her eyes with her forearm. "I don't understand what I did."

"Who cares what you did?" Sharkey said from behind her. "Why are you regretful of our slippery closeness, Wave?"

Both Gaia and Wave turned toward Sharkey. The guard stood between freezer locker seven and the prep table. Gaia might have been touched by the concern in Sharkey's voice if she hadn't been so humiliated.

She said, "Will you please leave?"

Wave kept its face turned slightly away. The ends of Wave's

cranial tendrils twitched. “Soldier Sharkey, I am fighting with Gaia Jones. I will fight with you when it’s your turn. Egotistical!”

Sharkey nudged Gaia out of the way. “I will fight with you right now, Wave Walker!”

Wave straightened. Wave was taller than Sharkey, though more slight. Wave’s cranial tendrils writhed; each tendril lashed the next into a more violent frenzy. Wave resembled Kenjan more than ever. They seemed to be connected on a quantum level. Did Wave have a projectile clamshell too?

“You will not,” Wave said. “And do not shove Gaia Jones like you were more important.”

Sharkey inclined its head to Wave. “I will await your orders, my noble Lord of Orange. Call me to your presence when you see fit.” Sharkey stormed away to join Stinger.

“You muzzled with Sharkey?” Gaia asked Wave.

“It is nothing of your concern. I need not ask you for permission!” Wave’s mismatched eyes frightened Gaia. She caught her breath in a sobby hiccup. “Do not express acid as though I have beaten you.”

“I’m not expressing acid. I’m crying.”

Wave seemed perplexed. Its cranial tendrils slowed to a sluggish churn. “Why?”

“Because you’re mad at me and I don’t know why.”

“I just told you why! You are commanding me. You kick my door and demand to enter even though I paid my rent money pieces, just as promised. No kicking then.”

Gaia sniffed. “I’m sorry I kicked your door.”

“Good. You should be. To be so rude.” Wave glanced sideways at her.

“But you were mad at me before I even kicked the door. Actually, you seemed mad at me ever since we came back from Oziru’s garden.”

“And well I should be.”

“But why?” Gaia’s voice dropped.

“Because you were only playing a game of democracy with

me, but I believed us to be friends and equals. You hurt my heart."

"That's not true at all," Gaia said. "You are my friend. We are equals."

"Then why make me go back to grovel like a servant in the garden of Oziru? Do you think it pleases me to lie on my belly like a crawling worm?"

"If you didn't want to come you should have told me."

"And leave you to wander the bowels of the island until your breathing machine ceases to function? You did not know what you were doing." Wave looked down. "You are a slow cripple swimmer. You were swimming down stupidly, like you knew everything."

"I'm sorry I made you go with me. But I didn't want to take Stinger or Sharkey. I don't trust them enough."

"And then you kept asking me questions as though I would know or was allowed to speak in the presence of Oziru." Wave's tone grew whiny.

"I'm sorry for making you do what you didn't want to do. I was asking you questions because I was scared. I wanted to know things were all right." Saying this out loud, knowing that Stinger and Sharkey were probably listening, nearly killed her, but she knew she had to make it right with Wave.

"Things were not right."

Gaia closed her eyes. "I know that now."

"Are you going to begin to cry more?"

"No, I'm not going to cry more," Gaia said.

"Are you certain? Your eyes are red, and nose is running. These are crying symptoms."

"They'll clear up."

"Oh." Wave straightened back up, awkwardly glancing around the room. Its cranial tendrils hung limp. "I am sorry to yell at you and make you do crying."

"That's okay. I just had a hard day." Gaia wiped her nose on the bottom of her Happy Snak smock. "Thank you for not abandoning me when I didn't know what I was doing. I could have died in there."

Wave accepted Gaia's thanks. For a moment they stood, relaxing into their reconciliation.

"So," Gaia said. "Why are you mad at Sharkey?"

"I cannot say."

"You don't know?"

"No," said Wave. "I cannot tell."

"Oh. It's a secret."

"It is the biggest secret." Wave slumped against the doorframe. "I want to love Sharkey. For many reasons, I want to shout, 'Love!' But Sharkey is bad. So bad. You do not know."

Sharkey paced through the dining room shooting angry glances in their direction.

"Could we talk somewhere else?" she asked.

"Not in the shrine. Kenjan would overhear."

"That's not really a problem right now." Gaia crossed her arms. "Oziru's in there talking to Kenjan. Oziru sealed the whole shrine off. Why do you think the guards are hanging around in the dining room?"

"Oziru is speaking to Kenjan?" Wave's eyes widened. Gaia nodded. Wave cocked its head. "But the door is closed. How do you know this?"

"I have a surveillance camera, remember?"

"And you have it on?"

"Yeah," Gaia said.

"So you are spying on the Divine Oziru as it breaks the sanctity of the shrine and talks to the ghost?"

"I was trying to see if Oziru was going to be done soon, because I have to get in there." She didn't want Wave getting mad at her again. "I couldn't understand what they were saying."

"Do they know you can see?" Wave's voice was hushed.

"I don't think so."

"Can you hear their words?" Wave was so close to her that its cranial tendrils brushed against her face.

"I couldn't figure out the sound," Gaia admitted.

Wave snorted. Its cranial tendrils quivered and she saw the familiar sparkle return to its eyes. "So you came for me to connect the sound?"

"Well," she said. Wave's tendrils fell. "Yes."

Wave's tendrils perked up again. "Gaia Jones, this idea of spying on our betters that you hold is sick and wrong."

"I'm worried. Seigata told me to make Kenjan stop singing, and I did, but now Oziru is there. I have to know what they're saying. I don't want Kenjan to be exorcised."

"You are so inappropriate...I may love you," Wave said. "Not like Sharkey. Different love. No muzzle love."

"I understand."

"I will help you fix your spy camera."

Chapter Twenty-Five: Perverts

Wave scanned the Plexiglas corridors of the hamster maze until it located Microbe. The alien did not tap on the tunnel or attempt to attract the hamster's attention. Wave seemed pleased just to watch Microbe cleaning its ear. Finally, Wave turned its attention to Gaia.

"Your room smells bad."

"I haven't had a chance to clean. Have a seat." Gaia indicated the end of her unmade bed. Wave eyed Gaia's bunk dubiously. Her duvet hunched on one corner. Her discarded jeans lay splayed across the bed's midsection. Her pillow sagged against the wall. Gaia yanked the bedclothes into a more palatable formation.

"It is too dry," Wave said.

"But it's soft."

"Do you have a damp towel?" Wave knotted its fingers. "When I go to Roy and Cheryl's to watch a film, they give me the damp towel to sit on."

"Okay." She dampened her bath towel, folded it in quarters and handed it to Wave.

"Do you have a garbage bag?"

Gaia supplied one. Wave spread the garbage bag out on Gaia's bed, then smoothed the moist towel over it and sat down.

"Do you have the Book of Instructional Wisdom?" Wave asked.

Gaia tossed the booklet across the bed.

As Wave perused the manual, the Kishocha stroked its cranial tendrils absently. Gaia randomly pressed combinations of buttons on the remote. Wave asked for the remote control and, after a few seconds of flipping through various menus and settings, handed the control back to Gaia.

"I just can't get the volume control to work," Gaia said. "You want to try again?"

"No need."

"I knew you could figure it out."

"Did you read any of the Book of Instructional Wisdom?" Wave asked.

"Sort of."

"No, you are a liar. You have read none of it. If you had read, you would know that this product's sound system is sold separately. There is no sound. This 'no reading' problem of yours is why you do not have command of the Frymaster brand fryer either, while I, having read the Book of Instructional Wisdom and passed the Tests of Competency, will be receiving my certification from Frymaster Corporation. I will fix the Frymaster then."

"You took the correspondence course?"

"The label said that only a certified repair person could fix the machine, so I asked for certification," Wave said. "Now I may also fix the Frymaster in the Embassy Club which has been acting irrationally."

"How do you know?"

"Frymaster Corporation master controller referred them to me to fix their machine. I will do this on Tuesday and be paid many money pieces. But I cannot fix the sound because there is no sound part to fix."

"Well, we can still watch without sound." Gaia reached for the surveillance remote control, but paused at Wave's expression. "Are you sure you want to spy? You don't have to."

This startled Wave out of its reverie. "Oh, yes! I want to do the spying."

"Why are you looking like that, then?"

"What am I looking like?" Wave asked. Gaia mimicked its soulful expression. "It is Sharkey. I am attacked by melancholy."

Gaia screwed up her face. "I don't like that Sharkey."

Wave's eyes narrowed. "And so?"

"I just wanted to mention that I don't like Sharkey." Gaia rummaged through her refrigerator for some snacks. "And when did you muzzle with Sharkey anyway?"

"On Wednesday, when you were at Electrical Authority to pay the fine. It was the morning of Kenjan's criticism by the scholar True Current. Roy and Cheryl were busy with customers and Sharkey came to find me."

"Why?" Gaia popped open a bag of pickled iguana eggs. She'd purchased them specially to try out on Wave, but had forgotten until now.

Wave looked at her blankly. "To muzzle me, of course. Are you hearing my story?"

"Sharkey came just to muzzle you?" No wonder Sharkey had known how to open up her door.

"Yes, very honorable. Guard Sharkey did not pretend to gamble with me, then slip and fall and jam its muzzle into my pit like some people have tried." Wave looked thoroughly disgusted. "Sharkey said to me, 'Wave, I wish to muzzle with you. I have brought spicy squid suction cups to show my intention,' and there was a heap of suction cups with stinging jelly and I said, 'Come in Sharkey, and give to me the suctions.' And I was shy, but I pretended to be wise and sat in my sponge nest like it was the regal bed of anemones."

"Was it your first time muzzling?" Gaia asked. Wave snorted and yipped. Gaia interpreted this as laughter.

"No, I have muzzled before, certainly. I am an adult for longer than you have been swimming alive."

"Sorry." Gaia offered Wave an iguana egg, which the alien savored before continuing.

"But it was the first time muzzling with Sharkey, whose tongue is so agile." Wave kneaded the moist towel.

"I thought you said that Sharkey hated you."

"No, I just said Sharkey was arrogant. Now I know that Kenjan would not let Sharkey court me because Sharkey is Seigata's servant."

"So?"

"So Sharkey would tattle on Kenjan to Seigata, as was its duty as a servant." Wave's face convulsed in sudden misery. Gaia held out her bag of eggs. Wave shook its head. "Sometimes a servant's duty is the cruel, wrong thing to do."

"Kenjan was right to bar Sharkey from ever entering our garden." Wave curled its knees up to its chest. "Sharkey is bad."

"Did Sharkey do something to you?" Gaia sat next to Wave. Dampness seeped into her pants.

Wave suddenly seized the remote control. "We should see what Kenjan and Oziru are doing now."

"Right." Gaia stood. The wet fabric stuck to her thigh.

"Do you always spy?" Wave asked.

"Only when I'm worried about someone."

"Are all humans peekers and perverts?"

"Perverts?"

"Because these cameras are made just for spying, lots of people must be peekers," Wave said.

"I suppose so."

"Even you have set up a camera to peek."

"I set up the camera so I can see if something bad is happening," Gaia said.

"Something bad is happening. They are yelling and spitting acid. But nothing serious will come of this. I know, I've seen them fight before often. You should not worry. Let us have fun spying."

"So you don't mind if I turn the camera on now?"

"Please do feel free! We can peek at the fighting faces of Oziru and Kenjan and laugh together like friends at the misery of our betters."

"I was trying to figure out when Oziru might be leaving so that I could get in there." Gaia pressed a button, and the picture assembled itself, slightly out of focus.

"Oziru will feed Kenjan tonight. No need to go in, but exciting to spy anyway."

Gaia sharpened the visual.

Oziru reclined right on the edge of the calligraphy line. Kenjan leaned as close as possible without breaking the barrier. They were within an inch of each other.

Wave shook its head. "This is not the demeanor of a person who has forgotten its great first love."

"Especially since Oziru's going to be remarried," Gaia agreed.

"I know, Sharkey told me. Well, Oziru and Kenjan are not fighting any longer."

"That's good, I guess." Gaia poked around in the iguana eggs, looking for one that wasn't already broken. "Maybe Oziru will leave soon."

"I do not think Kenjan will let Oziru leave. Great surprise! Forbidden contact!"

Oziru lunged across the line and swept Kenjan into its embrace. Oziru's tentacles lashed around Kenjan like the coils of an aggressive constrictor. Oziru seized the shell pit guard, which Kenjan had crafted, and ripped it from Kenjan's throat. Loose shells scattered across the shrine floor. Kenjan threw its head back. Oziru buried its muzzle deeply in the folds of Kenjan's pit.

"Wow!" Gaia's eyes popped wide open. Wave's jaw hung slack. Oziru continued its ravenous molestation. Thick, red goo began to bubble and drip from Kenjan's throat. The less-than-ideal camera angle prevented Gaia from inspecting Oziru's pit for similar goo. Kenjan seemed willing, but because the alien was completely encased in Oziru's tentacles it was hard to tell for sure.

"Is that normal?" Gaia asked. Wave didn't answer. "Wave!"

"I am not peeking!" Wave yelped, then looked around. "Oh. I forgot it was you."

"Is that red goo normal?"

"Yes, very lubricated. Kenjan is always most fragrant. Honey-makers always buzzing around it for sweet smell."

"Can Oziru get its whole muzzle in there?"

"Mostly," Wave said. "I wish I could hear."

"They're not saying anything."

"Kenjan's tongue moves." Wave pointed to Kenjan's muzzle. Gaia zoomed in on it. Blurry, wet, striped flesh filled the screen. Wave jumped back. "Too close."

Gaia pulled the camera back to a head-and-shoulders shot. Kenjan's tongue was, indeed, moving. Gaia squinted hard at Kenjan's muzzle. What was she doing? She couldn't read lips even when humans were speaking English. Her chances of deciphering the panted exclamations of passionate aliens were slim. "I bet Kenjan's just talking about how big Oziru's tendrils are."

"Certainly that, but Kenjan has always gotten its way with Oziru during muzzling," Wave said.

"Really?"

Wave's head bobbed in verification. "When Kenjan first wanted to talk to humans and Oziru said no, Kenjan muzzled and begged until Oziru says, 'Fine, talk to the uglies. Just give me you for piercing.' And then the first contact was made." Wave popped another yellow iguana egg into its mouth.

"Kenjan's highly persuasive, huh?"

Wave never took its eyes from the screen. "They really cannot see us, can they? I feel so..."

"Perverted?"

"Yes, we are big perverts. It is so wrong to peek at muzzling, especially forbidden ghost muzzling."

"Do you want me to turn it off?"

"No, surely everyone has peeked before, but never at something so shameful as this."

Oziru pulled its muzzle from Kenjan's throat. Oziru's muzzle was shiny and sticky with red ooze. It looked like blood. Oziru's thick tendrils relaxed a little, so Gaia could see Kenjan a little better. The former consort lay, cradled amid Oziru's cranial tendrils. The purple flesh of Kenjan's pit was engorged. Four turgid prongs of swollen flesh protruded from the slick petals of delicate tissue near Kenjan's collarbones. Each was as long as Gaia's thumb, bulbous and shiny. The flesh along Kenjan's sternum had swollen, vaguely pink under its white skin.

Slowly, Kenjan lifted a hand, pushing its fingertips steadily up Oziru's chest until it reached Oziru's pit guard. Kenjan didn't remove the guard; rather it slid its fingers underneath the ornate jewelry. Oziru's eyes closed; then it pulled Kenjan's hand away. They seemed to pause to have a brief, sexy argument.

Kenjan ran its tongue around the edge of Oziru's pit guard. Oziru's cranial tendrils flexed around Kenjan's body. Oziru pulled its own pit guard from its neck. Thick strings of red fluid dripped from the guard as Oziru flung the jewelry away.

Gaia peered at Oziru's pit, which looked just like Kenjan's, only the skin around Oziru's sternum was not swollen. As Gaia watched, the same four prongs of flesh stiffened under Kenjan's attentions.

"Holy Waters!" Wave pointed at the screen. "They are going to pierce."

Oziru and Kenjan entwined themselves. Their throats locked together. They barely moved, except to quiver against one another. Abruptly, they both relaxed. Oziru disentangled itself brusquely. Kenjan reached after Oziru, but Oziru retreated too far. Kenjan sprawled at the water's edge, its tentacles splayed out on the floor. Oziru slumped against the far wall. Oziru said something. Kenjan held out its hands.

"I did not know Kenjan knew how to beg," Wave whispered.

Gaia felt sick and sorry.

Pathetic silence filled the room. They watched in vile fascination as Oziru left.

Wave hunched, hands over its face. Wave and Kenjan had a complex relationship. Was it painful for Wave to witness Kenjan's humiliation?

"Are you all right?" Gaia asked.

"They will cross seed, and Kenjan will make pogs." Wave's cranial tendrils hung limply down its neck. "Ghost pogs... And then Oziru's violation of the dead will be revealed. All evil will be revealed."

"No it won't. Kenjan is barren."

"Kenjan is not," Wave said.

"What do you mean?"

Wave failed to answer or even move.

"Kenjan said all its pogs blackened and died within a day," Gaia said.

"That's true. They have all died before."

Gaia smelled a faint tang of acid that rose from Wave's skin. Her hands started to hurt.

"There won't be any evidence this time either. We'll take care of the bodies."

"No." Wave sank to the floor and pulled the damp towel over itself. "Because the others died of poison attack."

"What?" Gaia demanded. "What are you talking about?"

"This is Sharkey's secret that I learned. Sharkey poisoned all of Kenjan's pogs with Holy Blackening Poison. It is the purifying poison that smells like bits-o-bakun. Sharkey killed every last one."

Gaia felt like she'd been punched in the stomach. Sharkey wasn't her favorite person, but she'd never thought it was a baby killer.

"Sharkey was ordered to be the executioner of Kenjan's pogs," Wave said. "Sharkey told me this because its heart was squeezed with regret at murder."

"Who ordered Sharkey to be an executioner?"

"Sharkey's master, Seigata. And now I have told you, like I promised I would not. I am bad."

"You're not bad." Gaia absently felt through her pocket for Kenjan's pit guard. "But Sharkey is."

The pit guard still gave off that faint smell. The scary smell of bacon. She held it out to Wave, who recoiled from it.

"Do not, Gaia. It is contaminated."

"So, Sharkey put poison on this too?"

"No, Sharkey said that Seigata did that itself."

"How did Kenjan not smell the poison when it put this on?"

"It hid the poison in a capsule made from gel. It knew

Kenjan planned to go into the human sector and would be far from Kishocha waters by the time the capsule dissolved so there would be no one to help it." Wave kept its eyes fixed on the jewelry as though it were a snake that might suddenly strike. "To make sure I would not be in attendance, Seigata sent Sharkey to delay me. It was how Sharkey and I first met each other."

This pit guard wasn't a symbol of rank. It was evidence. No wonder Seigata wanted it back.

Wave continued, "Seigata ordered that Sharkey should kill Kenjan's pogs. Did Sharkey do right by following its master even into the barren desert? Or is Sharkey evil for blackening pogs and keeping Oziru without descendants?" Wave radiated distress. "Am I bad for telling what I promised I would not?"

Gaia wished that she had remained ignorant. But knowledge had come, and it colored everything. Wave was the only true innocent in this affair.

"We've got to tell Oziru." Gaia stood.

"No!" Wave shoved Gaia back onto the bed. "Sharkey will be executioned."

"Sharkey deserves to be executioned."

"I love Sharkey!" Wave yelled.

"No you don't." Gaia hurled her empty PowerWoman!! box at Wave. "You don't even want to look at Sharkey."

"Do not tell me who I love." Wave caught the box and hurled it back at her.

"Sharkey murdered Kenjan's babies, Wave."

"Sharkey only followed the orders of its master, nothing more. That is what is right and natural. That is what makes the order. Sharkey is honorable." Wave looked like a vengeful gorgon. "Sharkey does not have free will."

"So that's okay then? Because you love Sharkey it's okay that Kenjan is dead now?"

"Why should servants suffer for doing what they are told? What if Sharkey had disobeyed Seigata? Then Sharkey would be dead, and I would be without love."

"You'd find other love," Gaia said. "Better love."

"You know nothing of Kishocha. Do not dare to make statements about our love. Already I am lonely for my half-sibling. Why make me lonely for a lover as well?"

"It isn't fair for you. But it's even less fair that Kenjan's murder is never brought to justice."

"And so?" Wave said. "Maybe Seigata is brought to justice, but my Sharkey is also executioned from good loyalty to an evil master, and Kenjan is still dead. Do you know that Oziru did not sanction Kenjan's death? No, you do not. Maybe Oziru wanted Kenjan to die. Maybe only we will be executioned to keep the peace."

"Can you really look me in the eye and tell me you believe Oziru authorized Kenjan's death?"

Wave snarled and collapsed back. "I concede. Oziru did not want Kenjan to be made dead."

"Kenjan isn't dead. It's sitting in there alive, fucking Oziru, moaning sad songs all night, and eating hundreds of dollars of chicken satay. That alien is alive."

"You make no sense."

"Kenjan gets to be alive again. I'm going to make it happen. Open!" she bellowed. The door stayed firmly closed. "Open." She began pounding on the clenched sphincter of her door. "Dammit. I'm calling Fitzpatrick. We'll get in the other door. Where's my phone?"

"Gaia." Wave wailed from behind her. Gaia spun around and found Wave huddled on the floor behind her. "I beg you, Gaia, do not kill my Sharkey. I beg you please, Gaia. Please, please do not do it. You cannot bring Kenjan back from the dead. You can only hurt me."

Gaia swallowed in revulsion at Wave's pitiful display. "Stop begging, Wave."

"Will you not do it?" Wave still huddled on the floor.

"If I don't, what's going to happen when Kenjan has pogs? Are we going to shove them down the garbage disposal?"

"We could hide them in an aquarium."

"Aquarium?"

"Yes," Wave said. "Pogs are only as big as the Cajun

chicken sub sandwich. They will all fit into a big aquarium. It will be good."

It took Gaia a few moments to process the idea that putting babies into an aquarium was good. "I did see one listed for sale used in the classifieds. From that sushi place that went out of business on Boeing-4."

"I'll call right away." Wave started for the phone.

"Wait." Gaia grabbed Wave's arm. "Say we put them in an aquarium and sprinkle food on top every day like they were goldfish or something. What are we going to do when they grow? What are we going to say?"

"I will claim them as mine," Wave said. "I am Kenjan's sibling. No one will have knowledge of it."

"I thought you needed permission to make pogs."

"You are my master. Give me permission."

"This is insane."

"No one ever has to know of Sharkey's crime. And I can live happily, no longer in slavery. Please do this one thing for me. I beg you."

Gaia rubbed her eyes. This plan was ludicrous, but she couldn't think of a better one. She loved Wave and Wave loved Sharkey. Even though she hated Sharkey, she owed it to Wave to keep Sharkey alive.

Wave bounced up to its feet. "Gaia, we must move quickly."

"Why?"

"Because the pogs are being born now." Wave indicated the surveillance screen. Kenjan was alone in the shrine, hunched over on its island convulsing. A long red strand of flesh squeezed out of Kenjan's pit. The pulpy tube was, indeed, about the size of a Cajun chicken sandwich. Kenjan pushed out three more tubes, along with a massive extrusion of thick mucous that enveloped the four pog pods in gelatinous fluid. Kenjan curled around them. Wave shook its head. "Kenjan is willing them to die."

"What?"

"The pogs must be into water within the hour, or they will die."

"Maybe," Gaia ventured slowly, "maybe that would be for the best."

"No, I have decided. They will live and be mine."

"If they die, we don't have to do any of this. And it's what Kenjan expects to happen anyway." Hope glimmered within her. Maybe everything could go back to the way it had been before she'd known how humanly sordid the Kishocha were.

"I want nothing more to die," Wave said.

"Not even Seigata?" Gaia asked.

"Not even that one. Dying must stop before life can resume. It is not for me to judge Seigata. It is for the god's consideration."

She took a deep breath. "Okay... We'll...find some way to raise pogs in an aquarium. What should I do with this?" Gaia held up the pit guard. "Seigata wants me to return it."

"Then return it. And this ripple will go unnoticed. Now we must enter the shrine to get the pogs."

Gaia held her head, pressing both hands hard against her cranium as if her skull would burst without constant pressure. If she'd actually believed in the god, or any god, the injustice of this situation wouldn't bother her so much. Could she live with this?

If she gave Seigata the pit guard back and erased forever the evidence of the alien's deceit, Seigata would become Oziru's consort. Gaia would have to allow Kenjan to be exorcised eventually, but that's what Kenjan wanted. Life would go on as usual. Wave would have pogs, and there would be trouble, but not much and not for long. Sharkey would claim to be the proud coparent. Happy Snak would prosper. Fresh Peace Corps workers would replace Roy and Cheryl. Maybe she'd start seriously dating Fitzpatrick. Maybe they'd even love each other.

Gaia knew that this plan wouldn't play out the way Wave wanted. She could recognize impossible fantasy when it so blatantly presented itself. Failure was highly probable if she acted on Wave's instructions, yet if she did nothing failure was certain.

"Please go into the shrine and collect the pogs," Wave said.

"Please let me have this my way."

"Why don't you go get them?"

"I am not the guardian. Kenjan will not obey me."

They'd need something to put them in until the aquarium arrived. The big stainless steel prep sink would have to do. And she'd also need something to carry the pogs in.

"I'm going to get a bus tub," Gaia said.

"I will call for the aquarium."

Gaia slipped into the backroom and grabbed the tub, leaving the door open. She feared the pogs would be heavy and awkward, and she didn't want to drop them.

Chapter Twenty-Six: The Truth

The shrine door opened. An odd musty smell drifted into her bedroom, mingling with the acid distress that already permeated the air. Microbe burrowed furiously into his pile of dank wood chips. Gaia's hands ached badly, especially at the wrists.

"Kenjan!" Gaia called across the water. The Kishocha gave no response. It lay, hunched around the gelatinous mass. Gaia didn't know if the alien was trying to hide or cradle the egg sacs. "Kenjan, come on, talk to me. Don't make me swim out to the ghost island."

"Leave me." Kenjan's voice was nothing but a growl. "I feel sick."

"All I want to do is get the pogs into some water."

Kenjan's head rose slightly. "I knew that you were spying on me. I heard the camera lens moving."

"No you didn't," Gaia said. "It's sound-proofed."

"To you, maybe. To Kishocha ears it hums."

"I worried that you weren't all right."

"Well, now you know that I am not all right." Kenjan lay its muzzle down. "Do you feel satisfied to see me humiliated?"

"I don't want your pogs to die," Gaia said. Wave hung back, just inside the bedroom door. "Wave is going to take care of them."

"No need. They will die. Wave knows this. They might as

well die quickly, before they begin to move."

"Maybe this time they'll live."

"They always die. I should just crush them now." Kenjan's voice was barely audible.

"No!" Wave cried. "Please Kenjan. Do not!"

There was no getting around it. Gaia dived into the water. Her legs felt unusually heavy. She reached Kenjan's side quickly and pulled herself up on the scaly surface of the ghost island. She sat there and dripped.

Kenjan seemed haggard. Its throat was still bare, and its pit was swollen and distended. Kenjan's usually massive chest looked sunken.

"Hey, Kenjan."

"Go from me, I beg you," Kenjan said.

Gaia ignored Kenjan, instead focusing on the pog pods. They looked like any other kind of large egg sac. A fine webbing of veins covered the outer skin of each one. They pulsed as blood pumped through them.

"These look pretty lively."

Kenjan looked at her sideways. "How would you know?"

Gaia's eyes narrowed. But she said nothing.

"Do you see that larger one?" Kenjan asked. "It is a noble flyer. If it were to live, it would resemble Oziru."

"Then we should really get them in the water."

"They will blacken. Truly, it does not matter."

Gaia tapped her fingers on a glossy, black rock. Already Wave's plan was going awry. No one who understood anything about genetics would ever believe that an orphan-servant and a soldier would spawn a flyer. She stared hard across the water at Wave's averted face. She wished that she could mentally force Wave to meet her gaze and admit that this surrogate-parent idea was absurd.

"Do not look hatred at Wave, my guardian," Kenjan said. "The servant means well, but it is impossible, in any way."

"It is not impossible!" Wave shouted striding forward. "Why give up when the god has blessed you after death with offspring?"

"I think that the god has fun inventing new ways to punish me." Kenjan's usually resonant voice turned dull and husky.

"Kenjan—" Gaia was cut off by the Kishocha waterway door flexing open. Gaia flipped the bus tub over the pog pods.

Seigata glided through the door, flanked by six guards. It saw Gaia and shuddered as if repressing a violent urge at seeing her exactly where she wasn't supposed to be.

"Gaia Jones." Seigata said her name as if it was an indictment.

"Noble Seigata," Gaia said. "I'll be right there."

"I was wondering did you forget our agreement?" Seigata asked.

"Not at all. I'll be right there." Gaia swam back. She wrung out her pant legs. Seigata ignored her, its attention fixed on Kenjan.

"You look ill, Ghost," Seigata called.

"I am dead. How do you expect me to look?" Kenjan leaned over the inverted bus tub and casually draped a hand over its own pit.

"For being so noisy, I did not expect you to look so frail," Seigata remarked.

Kenjan said, "My voice is fine. Never fear."

"Do you smell something?" Seigata snapped around to face Gaia.

"Chicken, I think," Gaia said. "Or cheese sticks. Have you ever had cheese sticks?"

"It is the smell of pogs." Seigata folded its hands. "What lowly creature has committed blasphemy with you, Ghost?"

"No one," Kenjan said. "I have only been, in the words of my guardian soldier, prodding my throat like an ugly."

"Liar."

"I do not lie, Most Holy Seigata. I have, indeed, become ugly. I am almost as ugly as you now."

"Are the pogs hidden under the gray shell, Guardian?" Seigata pointed to the inverted bus tub.

“What’s a pog?” Gaia said. If she was going to play dumb, she might as well play really dumb.

“What is under that gray shell?”

Gaia jammed her hand in her pocket. “I’ve got the necklace right here. I guess you can take it.” Gaia thrust the pit guard at Seigata. The alien swatted her hand away. The guard flew across the room.

Seigata clamped its hand around Gaia’s throat. “You will bring me the pogs. Do you understand?”

Gaia couldn’t breathe, she nodded. Seigata dropped her and she fell weakly to the floor. Wave darted out and grabbed the pit guard. It held the guard aloft.

“If you touch Gaia Jones one more time, I will take this to Oziru, telling the noble lord that you are the one who kills the most beautiful Kenjan with poison!” Wave shook all over. “You are the bad one!”

“What did you say, Wave?” Kenjan dived into the water.

Seigata turned to the Kishocha-side door. “Lock.” The door flexed decisively closed. From beneath its garment, the alien drew a slim vial. Then to its guards Seigata said, “Kill that one.” Seigata pointed to Wave.

The guards rushed forward. Wave darted back into Gaia’s room.

“Wave!” Gaia tried to lunge after Wave, but Seigata slammed its fist into her back. She hit the floor. Sounds of fighting erupted from Gaia’s room. Screaming and roaring curses. Gaia couldn’t pull her eyes away from the vial. The way Seigata held it—gingerly, yet purposefully—did not give her a good feeling about its contents.

Kenjan broke the surface of the water feet from them. It pulled itself up on the ledge and stood, steaming just inside the calligraphy line. “How could you do it? We are siblings.”

“I had a vision of the god. I acted according to the instructions I was given.”

“Murderer!” Kenjan bellowed. “Mate-stealing murderer.”

“I am a vessel of the god’s will. It was not the god’s will that Oziru should be burdened with a heretic for all time—no matter how lascivious the heretic should be."

Kenjan's muzzle curled up in a smirk. "You are just jealous. And frigid."

"And you are a faithless servant-fucker. Tell me who pierced you or I will blacken your waters with this poison."

"It was the god, giving me the gift of children in my death-exile," Kenjan said.

A last shout burst from Gaia's room. Sharkey stepped into the shrine. Blood streaked the soldier's body. Sharkey's spear dripped.

"Wave—" Gaia whispered.

"I am here." Wave stepped from behind Sharkey. Blood spattered Wave's white skin. Seigata looked irritated.

"Sharkey, you are meant to kill this orphan-servant." Seigata spoke as if repeating instructions to a moronic child.

"I apologize, but I cannot," Sharkey said. "I cannot kill Wave."

"For disobedience, I will skin you and feed you to the fish."

"I understand."

"Worthless animal," Seigata said. "Go await your fate in my chamber."

Sharkey started obediently toward the Kishocha-side door.

"No!" Wave clung to Sharkey's arm.

Kenjan said, "Do you really want to know who pierced me?"

"This worthless guard?" Seigata gestured toward Sharkey.

"Oziru. Even dead, I am better than you."

"Lying ghost!"

"Better than a murderer." Kenjan lunged forward.

Seigata raised up the vial of poison to smash against Kenjan's head. Gaia shoved all her weight against Seigata. Thick fluid spilled out over Gaia's forearms. Searing pain rushed through her. There was a flash. Metal sliced the air. Kenjan held Sharkey's spear to Seigata's throat.

"No wedding for you." Kenjan plunged the spear into Seigata's throat. Gaia choked on burning acidic air. She felt her throat closing. Grayness tinged the edges of her vision. She could no longer hear. Geometric patterns danced in front of her eyes. Was she dying?

It was okay. Wave had tried to save her. Sharkey had tried to save Wave. She had tried to save Kenjan. Kenjan tried to kill Seigata. As far as she could tell they'd mostly been successful.

She'd seen things no other human had seen.

She'd done her best.

Chapter Twenty-Seven: Struggling Free

Every night when Gaia fell asleep there was a blurry point when her rational thoughts flowed freely into the calming, timeless world of dreams. If, during this process, she noticed herself dreaming, she would wake up. Dreamtime was a state she could only enter without lucidity.

Not now.

She knew she hadn't been awake for a long time.

Her mind was less quiet than it had ever been. Visions of engulfing flames twisted through her. Hot, dank sheets twisted around her. She tried to scream and got doused in water. She floated along in Oziru's garden in the deep, red Kishocha sea. Wave beckoned her to unfurl her gills and she did, swimming alongside Wave as easily as a fish.

She woke up in the hospital. How much time had passed? Why could she hear Kenjan talking?

"My divine Lord Oziru would be displeased if Gaia Jones was not healthy by the time that our pogs struggle free."

Gaia pulled her eyes open. Kenjan stood in the hallway outside, talking to a medic. Kenjan was wearing the same golden couture it had worn in the informational video she'd seen. That had been so long ago. She felt like she'd been a different person then. She knew Kenjan had been a different person than the morose singing ghost it was now.

Why was Kenjan out of its shrine? Where was Wave? Where

were the guards? Maybe this was another dream.

"Yes, I understand that, Mr. Kenjan," the medic said. "We're doing our best."

Gaia's eyes rolled up into her head. She felt bleary and drugged.

"Do you know she is a demon slayer?" Kenjan asked.

"So you've told me," the medic said.

"With hands already scarred with acid from my own passage into the Sea of Death, she destroyed the demon who took my soul. She must be present for the birth."

"Be that as it may—" the medic began.

"Can you not use the shocking machine to wake her up?" Kenjan asked. "It is often done in the media. Before applying the paddles, you must yell, 'Clear!' That is all."

"Don't touch that." The medic moved to intercept the alien.

Fear lurched inside of Gaia. She tried to open up her mouth to tell Kenjan she was already awake, but she couldn't. She couldn't even keep her eyes open.

The next time she opened her eyes, the room was dim and quiet. Gaia felt better. Although her back was very stiff, she thought she might be able to sit up. Feebly, she tried to rise. She failed.

The third time Gaia woke, a chime sounded. A soothing digital voice intoned, "Gaia Jones, you are in the Medical Center of A-Ki Station. You've had an injury. Please don't try and get up without assistance. A medic has been alerted."

Two chimes sounded, then the recording continued, "Ms. Jones, due to heavy patient volume, all personnel are currently engaged. Please wait, and the first available medic will be with you shortly."

Gaia waited a couple of minutes then considered attempting to rise unaided. The recording seemed to know this. "We appreciate your patience and cooperation. It will only be a little while longer. If you—"

A medic arrived and deactivated the recording. "Hello, Ms. Jones. Do you know where you are?"

"The hospital on A-Ki Station." Gaia looked down. Tubes and wires exploded from her inner elbows, like the intestines of eviscerated machines. Her hands were bandaged again.

"Do you know why you're here?"

"I was poisoned, I think. How long have I been here?"

"You've been here for six weeks," the medic said.

"Six weeks?" Gaia tried to sit up again. Her stomach hurt like hell. "Who's taking care of the snack bar?"

"Please don't try to get up. The doctor is on her way." The medic busied himself checking the tubes and wires. "Mr. Kenjan has also been alerted, as per Oziru's instructions. If you don't want to see any visitors, we can keep the alien outside."

"It doesn't bother me." Gaia's arms looked pale and scrawny. Just above the bandages, she could see the tops of her guardian tattoos. She took a deep breath and tried to wiggle her fingers. She saw the bandages move and grinned. She could move her fingers. Her wrists didn't hurt at all. She could feel her fingers moving against each other.

She hadn't undergone another hand-replacement surgery. Gaia frowned. "Why are my hands bandaged?"

"There is some scarring from the poison that was used."

"Can I see them?"

"Certainly." The medic retrieved a pair of scissors. "The scars are pretty unusual."

"How?" Gaia asked. The medic pulled away a layer of bandage. Her palms looked like they'd been submerged in grape juice for six weeks. Purple streaks ran across the delicate skin atop her hands. She could see where the poison had dripped, carving tiny furrows. They looked almost like Kishocha letters. Gaia clenched her hands. She seemed to be able to feel things. Most of her fingers and fingertips were unmarked.

"So..." Gaia glanced at all the tubes again.

"Here's Dr. Black." The medic deferred to the short, dark-haired woman who'd just entered the room. Dr. Black explained that Gaia's kidneys had been replaced the previous week. It had taken more than a month to grow the organs. The doctor also told Gaia that she hadn't been unconscious for six entire weeks, but that the Kishocha toxin had been extremely painful and she'd been knocked out with painkillers most of the time. They had a brief chat about her recovery and treatment. She gathered that she'd be here for a while longer, but not forever.

The doctor suggested that she try to eat something very small and mostly liquid. Gaia asked for a Coke. Dr. Black left. A few minutes later Kenjan appeared in her room, carrying a plastic cup and a straw. Kenjan's gold headdress glittered. Its throat was encased in gold and diamonds. This was the Kenjan from long ago, bedecked with jewels, confident and graceful, and wearing silver eyeliner.

"Ah, my guardian, you are awake." Kenjan set the Coke down on Gaia's table. The Kishocha carefully placed a straw in Gaia's beverage. Kenjan seated itself on the bedside stool and leaned on the edge of her bed. Through the thick antiseptic hospital atmosphere, Gaia could smell that Kishocha scent: roses and battery acid. "I have come to feed you. Is it not so very ironic and reversed?"

Gaia narrowed her eyes. "Does this mean I'm a ghost?"

Kenjan made a smile-face. "Of course you are not dead, my guardian. You are moving around talking and drinking cola drinks. How can you be dead?" Kenjan's cranial tendrils coiled in unrestrained glee.

"Why aren't you in the shrine?" Gaia leaned forward and took a sip of Coke. Her mouth felt like it was trying to remember what to do in these circumstances. Gradually, she managed to swallow.

"I have been resurrected. After you beheaded my murderer, the traitorous Seigata—"

"But that was yo—" Gaia began, but was cut off by Kenjan's fingers lying gently across her lips.

"It was so confusing. I understand if you don't remember it correctly. When you seized the guard Sharkey's weapon and beheaded Seigata, I drank the steaming blood and was thus resurrected. The god showed me such favor that I was instantly blessed with pogs. One of them is a noble flyer. There is such joy now."

"I beheaded Seigata?" Gaia remembered it differently.

"Yes." Kenjan leaned close to her. "You are stronger than you look." She could see that this idea amused Kenjan immensely.

Gaia weakly scooted toward Kenjan. "No one is going to believe that."

Kenjan made the smile-face again. "Oh, my dear guardian, they already do. Sharkey has sworn it. Wave has told the story many times. My Oziru has made the report to our home world. It is the truth. Someday you will remember what happened correctly."

"Who's running the store?" Gaia asked.

"Do not trouble yourself. All is well. You should only think of becoming strong. I want you to be healthy enough to come to the ceremony to watch my beloved offspring struggling free of their pods. To ensure your health, I will take care of you every day."

She fell back into her pillows. "Seriously, what about Happy Snak?"

Kenjan cocked its head. "Is that all you and Wave can talk about? It is fine. Wave is a good servant and has cared for your belongings, including the hamster. Now please, drink your revolting cola beverage. I have brought the most recent and exciting magic-show film for us to watch together."

Gaia gradually drank the rest of her cola and watched two stage magicians saw a great white shark in half then put it back together again.

Chapter Twenty-Eight: High Heels

Gaia's fingers fluttered over the controls of the submersible. She traced a path through a three-dimensional model of the Kishocha waterways. She approached the huge siphon leading to Oziru's garden and glided through, smoothing her black dress with one hand. Her high heels sat beside her, next to her nice handbag and a wrapped gift. She'd left her Happy Snak smock and nametag behind. Roy and Cheryl slouched on the bench seat behind her.

As usual, Sudden Red Crush was happy to see Gaia's submersible. The shark nudged the vehicle. Cheryl squeaked.

"It's all right. He's friendly."

"Sure." Cheryl moved closer to Roy.

"Fitzpatrick, can you hear me? We've just come through the garden siphon. You should be able to see us soon."

"Excellent." Fitzpatrick's voice buzzed inside Gaia's earpiece.

Gaia took them up. The submersible bobbed to the surface, and the roof of the submersible peeled back like the roof of a convertible. They floated on the red waters of Oziru's garden in what looked like a very high-tech rowboat. Sudden Red Crush circled the small boat, his black dorsal fin cutting the water. Gaia reached out and petted it. The shark brought its anvil-shaped head up out of the water, mouth open.

"Do you want to feed him?" Gaia asked Cheryl. Cheryl

shook her head. Gaia dropped a honey-cured ham into Sudden Red Crush's mouth. The shark gnoshed noisily on the meat. "Good boy."

Roy stared up at the twisting pillars of Oziru's garden. Cheryl kept her eye on the shark.

"I see you now," Fitzpatrick said. "That is such a nice vehicle."

"Thanks. How did you get here?" Gaia reseated herself.

"Tandem scuba. A guard called Stinger brought me."

"Isn't that hard on your hairstyle?" Gaia strained ahead, trying to see Fitzpatrick. Oziru's pillar swarmed with Kishocha, and Fitzpatrick was hard to pick out amid so many bodies.

"Didn't you say you like it when I look a little scruffy?"

"I do, but I don't think Blum will."

Gaia looked back at Roy. The man's jaw actually hung slack. Cheryl managed to keep her mouth closed, but her eyes widened superhumanly, as if to make up for the mouth.

"Will Wave be joining us?" Fitzpatrick asked.

"Of course," Gaia said. "Wave decided to swim in early."

"Well, this is totally unofficial, but Oziru told Blum that it will be awarding you two soldier-servants for your service."

"And one of the soldiers will be Sharkey?"

"Without question," Fitzpatrick said. "Incidentally, have you eaten?"

"No."

"You really should have."

"You're nagging again," Gaia said.

"So I am."

She saw Fitzpatrick standing near the bottom edge of Oziru's spiral, towel-drying his hair. A blue-spotted octopus sidled up beside him and made a grab for his briefcase. Fitzpatrick retaliated with a quick punt. The octopus plopped into the water.

Fitzpatrick unzipped his drysuit. He peeled the top back to reveal a perfectly pressed tuxedo jacket. His shirt blazed white. He straightened his cuffs.

After he stripped off the rest of his drysuit, Fitzpatrick opened his briefcase and removed a pair of immaculately polished black dress shoes. His suit was perfect, some kind of new fabric developed for the jet-setting black-tie guy. Wave pulled itself out of the water near Fitzpatrick.

Gaia turned back to Roy and Cheryl.

"Look! You can see Wave up ahead."

Roy lurched forward, waving. Wave's response was equally enthusiastic. The alien wore its gold Happy Snak pit guard and a short shell-vest. Wave also carried a small red box. Gaia wondered what gift Wave had brought for Kenjan. Probably a gift certificate.

Sudden Red Crush trailed them up to the spire, and Wave tied off the submersible while she, Roy and Cheryl waded up to the dry area.

"Look at these." Roy pointed at the bed of anemones, which covered the spire's surface. "Where do I walk?"

"On them, of course!" Wave said. "What else are carpet anemones for?"

"Right..." Roy didn't move.

Cheryl said, "Roy, come on, the Kishocha are staring. We look like tourists." She pulled him along. Gaia paused long enough to get her shoes on, though her feet were still unpleasantly damp. Wave shook its head.

"Those make your feet look so small and ugly, Gaia," the Kishocha said. "You should wear those nice black flippers."

Gaia's heel sank into the soft body of an anemone.

"I concur," Fitzpatrick said. "I love a woman in flippers. By the way, Wave, is there anything we should be expecting from this ceremony?"

"Great joy at the birth of a new flyer, and at the miraculous resurrection of Kenjan. And there is a chance that some among us may receive huge presents." Wave's cranial tendrils quivered with restrained excitement. "Good presents. And we shall see the pogs as they struggle free of their sacs and begin to swim. So much joy, we may all die of it." Wave burst into spontaneous dance.

"Let's hope we manage to survive," Fitzpatrick said, dryly.

Gaia took a step. A terrible squealing sound erupted from under her foot. She sat back down and unbuckled her shoes.

"We're going to be late," Fitzpatrick said.

"Go ahead without me," Gaia said. "Take Roy and Cheryl with you."

Fitzpatrick ushered Roy and Cheryl up the ascending spiral.

"Gaia." Wave put its hands on its hips, and shook its head despairingly. "You have forgotten your name badge."

Wave wore its own engraved name badge pinned to its vest. It said:

Wave Walker

Mini-Snak Manager

Certified Frymaster Repair Technician

"Oh yeah." She hadn't really forgotten so much as refused to wear her name tag to this event. Hardly anyone could read English here anyway. "Too late now, huh?"

"Surely it is not." Wave handed her the small, square package. "This is for you."

"What about Kenjan?"

"Kenjan can get its own present. Kenjan is very rich, you know."

Gaia opened up the box and saw a rectangular gold nametag, etched with black letters.

It read:

Gaia Jones

Happy Snak Owner

Holy Oziru Designated Special Human

Best Friend

About the Author

Nicole Kimberling lives in Bellingham, Washington with her partner, Dawn Kimberling, two bad cats and approximately 100,000 bees. Her novel, Turnskin, won the Lambda Literary Award for Science Fiction, Fantasy & Horror.

LaVergne, TN USA
29 August 2010
195058LV00006B/1/P